SALTWATER

SALTWATER

JESSICA ANDREWS

FARRAR, STRAUS AND GIROUX
NEW YORK

Farrar, Straus and Giroux
120 Broadway, New York 10271

Library of Congress Cataloging-in-Publication Data
Names: Andrews, Jessica, 1992– author.
Title: Saltwater / Jessica Andrews.
Description: First American edition. | New York : Farrar, Straus and Giroux,
2020. | Originally published in 2019 by Sceptre, an imprint of Hodder &
Stoughton, Great Britain.
Identifiers: LCCN 2019037893 | ISBN 9780374253806 (hardcover)
Subjects: GSAFD: Bildungsromans.
Classification: LCC PR6101.N349784 S25 2020 | DDC 823/.92—dc23
LC record available at https://lccn.loc.gov/2019037893

Our books may be purchased in bulk for promotional, educational, or business
use. Please contact your local bookseller or the Macmillan Corporate and
Premium Sales Department at 1-800-221-7945, extension 5442, or by
e-mail at MacmillanSpecialMarkets@macmillan.com.

www.fsgbooks.com
www.twitter.com/fsgbooks • www.facebook.com/fsgbooks

1 3 5 7 9 10 8 6 4 2

For my mam;
a glimpse.

Prologue

It begins with our bodies. Skin on skin. My body burst from yours. Safe together in the violet dark and yet already there are spaces beginning to open between us. I am wet and glistening like a beetroot pulsing in soil. Gasping and gulping. There are wounds in your belly and welts around your nipples, puffy and purpling. They came from me, just like I came from you. We are connected through molten rivers like the lava that runs beneath the earth's crust. Shifting. Oil trapped beneath the sea. Precious liquid seeping through cracks. This love is heavy; salty and viscous, stinking of seaweed and yeast. Sweat is nourishing and so is that tangy vagina smell that later men will tell me tastes like battery acid. But there are not any men, not yet. For now our secrets are only ours. You press me to your chest and I am you and I am not you and we will not always belong to each other but for now it is us and here it is quiet. I rise and fall with your breath in this bed. We are safe in the pink together.

Part One

I

My first dead body was my grandfather's. My mother and I sat in the funeral home at his wake in Ireland for two days while people I had never met came to pay their respects. I moved to the back of the room because I thought the blue in his eyelids might pierce my skin if I sat too close for too long.

The last time I saw him alive, he was in hospital. I kissed him goodbye and left the imprint of my lips lingering on his cheek. I wore bright red lipstick and it made his skin look grey. I tried to rub it away with my sleeve and he said, 'Oh, leave it. I'll keep it there, 'til you come back.' I reached for his cold hand, fluttering on top of smooth sheets.

2

Before I came to Ireland, I was living in London. I was seduced by coloured lights hitting the river in the middle of the night and throngs of cool girls in chunky sandals who promised a future of tote bags and house plants. I thought that was the kind of life I was supposed to want.

I worked in a bar every night while I figured out how to get there.

3

I never did go back to the hospital.

During my grandfather's wake, I looked for the trace of my kiss on his skin.

I could not find it.

4

London is built on money and ambition and I didn't have enough of either of those things. I felt as though the tangle of wires and telephone lines strung through the city were strings in a fishing net filled with bankers and nondescript creatives, shimmering in banknotes and holographic back-packs. I was something small and weak and undesirable. I was slipping through the holes and down into the deep underbelly of the ocean. I watched these people from my vantage point behind the bar. I noted the colour of their fingernails and the smell of their perfume and how many times they went to the toilet in one night. They did not notice me.

5

I am just another impossibility. Colourless. Unformed. You cannot imagine anything as fiercely small, as fiercely hungry as me. There is a splitting that has not happened yet. This is you before me. You are a daughter and not a mother. Not yet. And yet; there are invisible things drawing us close, even here. Fall into those molten afternoons, his hands all over your body. Spill towards me.

6

My grandfather was born in Glasgow. He and his brothers and sisters were small and soft beneath the tenement buildings. Their father went to the pub one day and never came back. Their mother died soon afterwards, 'Of a broken heart,' people tutted, shaking their heads and supping the tragedy from fingerprinted pint glasses. The children were shipped this way and that by strangers and well-meaning relatives. They ended up in an orphanage, where priests cupped and kissed them in terrible places.

They had an Auntie Kitty who lived in a small fishing port on the west coast of Ireland. She sent for them and they stayed with her and slept in the hay with her animals, warm dung sticking sweetly to their clothes and matting their hair. They walked along the dirt roads to school with bare feet and broke in wild horses while they were light enough to cling to their backs without being thrown off. They raced through long grasses and swam in the rough sea and learned to light fires by rolling oily twists of news-paper and drying out kindling in the sun.

Auntie Kitty rationed the hot water and made anyone who entered the house throw holy sand over their left shoulder, To Keep Away The Devil. Her husband was involved in the IRA and they housed members in their attic. In the springtime she marched around the garden with a pair of scissors, snipping the heads from any flowers that dared to bloom orange.

'Just off out on me horse!' she called as she wheeled her rusty bicycle down the hallway. She was a self-educated woman, and she taught my grandfather how to write and to read constellations in the salty night sky.

As my grandfather grew he worked as a gardener, pruning rhubarb and thatching roofs and occasionally mending leaky plumbing. When he was old enough, he travelled to England on the boat with the rest of the boys, looking for labouring work. He helped to build the Tyne Tunnel, spending his days deep beneath the ocean, installing lights so that strangers could see in the dark.

He found himself in Sunderland, among the crashing and clanking of the shipyards. He lived in a boarding house run by a gentle woman and her sharp and gorgeous daughter. He befriended Toni from Italy, who ate cocaine for breakfast and dreamed of running a café, and he shared a room with Harry from Derry, who played the spoons and had a crucifix tattooed across his chest.

He liked Johnny Cash, horse racing and Jameson's whiskey. He always wore a suit and carried a packet of Fruit Polos in his inside pocket. He was at home by the water with the rust and the metal.

7

I am living in Burtonport, a tiny fishing port in County Donegal, on the north-west coast of Ireland. In order to get here, you have to travel through the Blue Stack Mountains. Time alters as you drive into them. They are brown and reassuring but appear blue in the shifting light, dripping navy and indigo into the valleys.

When I was a child, my mother, brother, and I spent dusky Augusts in Donegal. We felt safe when we had passed the mountains, cut off from the tumult of our lives at home. As soon as we arrived, my mother turned off her Nokia and put it in the glove compartment of her car. She didn't switch it on until summer was over and we were back on the motorway.

As a teenager I ran from solidity and stasis and shades of brown. I wanted things that flashed and fizzled. Now that I am here, beneath the peat smoke and the penny-coloured skies, brown seems like a safe place. I can crawl into it and swallow fistfuls of soil.

8

When my grandfather died, I called the pub.
    'I'm really sorry, Deborah, but I can't come in today.'
    'You what, babe?'
    'I think I need to go away for a bit.'

'Speak up, will you? Line's breaking up.'

'I have to go to Ireland for a funeral. I don't know when I'll be back.'

'Who is this?'

'I'll come in and see you when I'm back in town.'

I saw a chance and I grasped it. I texted my landlord and told him to keep my deposit. I put my books into boxes and gave all of my clothes away. I took the train north to my mother's house, then we boarded an aeroplane and hired a car and now here I am.

9

I am creeping. The future unspooling. I am forming slowly inside you. Barely even an idea. There are so many ways in which you do not know yourself yet, blue-black and heavy like reams of crushed velvet. All the broken objects of our lives are stretched in front of us, gorgeous and unknowable.

10

My mother and I have inherited my grandfather's small stone cottage, through the Blue Stack Mountains by the sea. It is tucked into a nook crammed with giant rhubarb and purple hydrangeas. There are wild potatoes and mangy kittens and clumps of shamrock clustered in the corners.

The garden is very overgrown but if I climb onto the kitchen roof I can see the sea.

We arrived to find that colonies of mould and specks of damp thrived in my grandfather's absence. They were splattered across the walls and ceilings like a sludgy Pollock painting. Tiny worms and mites had burrowed holes in the wooden furniture. The drawers and cupboards were crusty with rust and the fridge stank of sour milk. The mattresses were crawling with bugs.

In the months before my grandfather's death, something between my mother and me was fractured. Her presence in my life had been solid and gold, then suddenly she was not there any more. I felt her pulling away from me. It hurt inside of my body, my intestines stretched and sore. I felt confused by love; the way it could simultaneously trap you and set you free. How it could bring people impossibly close and then push them far away. How people who loved you could leave you when you needed them most.

We talked about practical things when she called me in London; when the funeral would be and how I would get there. We listened to the radio during the drive from the airport and at the wake we chatted to my grandfather's neighbours and friends. It wasn't until he had been buried and everyone had gone home to their brandies that we were alone together in the silent cottage. The distance glinted between us, sharp and dangerous. We sat on a sheet of newspaper on the floor and looked around.

'What are we going to do?' I asked her.

'Burn it,' she said, blowing on a cup of tea.

'You what?'

'We're going to have to burn everything.'

'Burn it where?' She paused.

'In the garden.'

'Everything?'

'It's the only way.'

She gave me a look. I knew she was trying to teach me something, but I didn't know if I wanted to learn it. I knew she wanted me to let go of things that did not belong to me, but I could not work out which things were mine. I did not know how much of my story I was entitled to take, and how much of the past I was allowed to leave behind.

We lit a bonfire and it burned for three days. We fed it everything: the mattresses, the bed frames, the chairs, the rugs, the chest of drawers, the dishcloths, the wardrobe. Scraps of paper scribbled with his handwriting, pink betting slips, old photographs, boxes of tablets and thick-rimmed glasses, his spare set of teeth. I reread musty letters I had sent him and found forgotten Christmas cards lodged between radiators and walls.

We shuddered as the duvet went up in a flash and took hammers to the dining room table. We emptied bin liners filled with socks and underpants into the flames. I liked watching the sofa best. The upholstery burned in jagged shapes, leaving the wooden skeleton standing on its own for a moment, naked and shy.

Plasticky smoke gathered in the trees.

'Are we allowed to do this?' I asked my mother.

'Probably not,' she replied. 'It feels good though, doesn't it?' She squeezed my hand. Our faces were hot from the flames.

We cleaned the house as the fire razed the garden, clearing the cupboards and scrubbing the sinks. We sang along to the Shangri-Las and the Ronettes, bleaching the kitchen counters until they were bright white and dazzling. I covered my mouth with a scarf, trying not to breathe in black smoke. I didn't want tiny pieces of my granddad's clothes and furniture to settle in the back of my throat.

'Let's get some taties on this fire, eh, Luce?' she joked, stoking the embers with my grandfather's walking stick. I looked at her. She had mud streaked across her forehead. I felt the sharpness between us soften a little, as though the edges had been rubbed smooth. She laughed.

'Don't look at me like that. It's only stuff, you know.'

11

The debris of my grandfather's life landed on our clothes and in our hair. It coated our skin. I learned that the drifting bits of ash are called 'fire angels.' After a house fire, they are considered to be very dangerous because they can re-ignite the blaze. They are small and fragile, but they are still smouldering.

12

When I was a toddler, my mother, my father, and I went on holiday to Tenerife. We stayed in a hotel for non-Spanish-speaking tourists, whose name translated to 'Hotel Dead Donkey.' There was a cockroach infestation and they climbed up the walls as we slept, their hard bodies glittering in the moonlight.

Days passed in a haze of hair braids and Mini Milk ice

lollies, cold and smooth against my sunburned lips. I loved the rubbery smell of my inflatable crocodile and the bitter taste of sun on my skin. We went to the beach one day and I paddled in the sea in my white T-shirt, while my mother and father watched from gritty beach towels on the shore. I waded in up to my waist and squinted in the sunlight. I watched the waves dapple my arms and legs and shrieked as the droplets caught the light. I heard an angry noise and turned towards a small motorboat filled with strong, tanned men in fisherman's caps moving steadily towards me. I froze in fear and turned to see my father's arms making big white arcs in the water. He scooped me up.

'My kid!' he shouted at the men. They laughed and waved their arms nonchalantly.

'No problem.' They smiled. 'No problem.' Their teeth were so white against the blue sky. I lay wrapped in the beach towel for the rest of the day, savouring my escape.

13

My mother left Ireland after the burning. Things were still not right between us. I knew she was trying to teach me something important, about how to be in my life, but I was too angry with her to listen.

I am not going back to London. Once I craved the speed and proximity to a centre, the sense that something was always about to happen, just out of reach. The city was a shape that could not be classified, shifting and moving, infinite possibilities hanging from the streets like fruit.

Now, when I think of the city, it is in rectangles and squares; impenetrable shapes with fierce elbows, shutting me out.

I have been dreaming of tube tunnels, smoky and choking. I am feeling my way through them, touching the walls. I am straining my eyes for a glimpse of my father, who is lost somewhere in the darkness, always just out of reach. I am calling for my mother and my voice echoes along the tracks.

14

Redness cracking. Fissures forming. You are falling towards us, rich and syrup-soft. Flesh roiling. Bones shifting. Tongues over bellies and fingers in wet places. Salt stains the mattress; seeps into places where hands cannot reach. Tissues twisting and saline dripping into something new. Sink into the thick of us. The peach pit slick of us.

15

My mother is beautiful. At twenty years old she had long, dark hair and something untamed about her. She wore floral jeans with leather belts and men's shirts knotted at the waist. She played her Marc Bolan record with the leopard-print label over and over as she hairsprayed her perm to go out at the weekends. She drank lager and lime and sat with her elbows on pub tables, dimpling her cheeks at the local boys and smuggling secrets in her eyes through the smoke.

16

There were moments when London felt like it belonged to me. Lying in the dew on the top of Telegraph Hill after a party, apricot leaking across the skyline. Cycling through traffic in the summer wearing a thin dress, one hand on my handlebars and the other trailing through the air, clutching invisible threads. Dancing in a dirty warehouse with sweat dripping between my breasts like syrup and my friends twirling shapes around me.

I think perhaps that is the allure. London pushes you further and further to the edges and when you feel like you are about to fall, it lets you know, just for a moment, that you have found a place where you belong.

It is a city of constant renewal and in the clamour of pop-ups and shut-downs I began to lose sight of who I wanted to be. I lay in bed watching the sun melt into streetlights and back again, tracing my fingers through the patterns the shade made on my skin.

17

When she was sixteen, my grandmother found a job on the fish stall in Jacky White's Indoor Market. She spent the next thirty years gutting mackerel and slicing salmon, scrubbing surfaces with bitter chemicals until she could see the pale shape of her face in the counter. There was a record stall opposite and she twisted her hips to the music, sliding around on the slimy lino and laughing.

'It's tearin' apart my blue, blue heart,' she sang along with Neil Diamond as she set up the stall, her gold rings skittering across surfaces and an Embassy Regal cigarette dangling from her fingers. In the evenings she delivered fresh fish to the boarding house, wrapped up in newspaper and carried in red and white striped plastic bags.

Everything about her was silver; her voice as she sang along to the radio in the mornings, the shiny fish scales caught on her tabard at the end of the day, and the hole that she left in our lives when she died, edged like a fifty-pence piece.

18

I spent invisible days watching strands of sky get trapped in the windows of office blocks. I walked past the mobile phone men playing music from plastic booths and ran my fingers over fruit and vegetables rotting in the daylight, filmy with dirt from passing buses. I wandered hungry through markets bristling with raw meat and vinegar, the smell of hops bulging from pubs. I craved grimy light on sun-starved shoulders and the thrill of that hot Hackney jerk chicken tang in the summer months.

My auntie trained to be a beauty therapist and went to work in a salon in Yorkshire. From Monday to Friday she waxed eyebrows and plucked ingrown hairs from the creases between ladies' thighs in an attempt to make them feel like they were in control of something.

My mother went to nursing school and lived at home. She kept my auntie's gold slingbacks under the radiator in the hallway because it made her feel safe, as though my auntie had just come in and kicked them off by the front door.

On Friday afternoons, my grandmother wandered around Jacky White's on her lunch break. It was the eighties and the clothes in the market crackled with static. She sighed over Madonna blouses with bloated shoulder pads and fingered pastel legwarmers wrapped in plastic. She didn't have much money, but everyone knew her so they gave her special discounts.

As soon as my grandmother came home, my mother laid the treasure out on my auntie's bed. She positioned blouses or dresses over jeans and tights and picked out colour-coordinated bras and knickers with lipstick to match, a pair of high heels propped on the pillow. She called her sister from the phone box at the end of their road.

'What time will you be back?' She twirled the cord around her fingers. My auntie raised her voice above hairdryers.

'I'm on the six o'clock train.'

After she had swept up the dead hair and turned off

the sunbeds, my auntie rushed home, drank a vodka tonic, and put on whatever clothes were waiting for her. They watched bands play at the Borough and danced to Orange Juice and Depeche Mode. They woke in the mornings with curry sauce and chip grease smeared across their bedsheets.

'Get up, you lazy beggars!' The stench of my grandfather's kippers wafted up the stairs and sneaked under their blankets.

20

When I was a child, there was a council estate behind our house that was evicted and demolished in order to make way for a new development of identical Wimpey show homes for different kinds of people. The clapped-out cars and broken bicycles disappeared to make way for diggers and breeze blocks. There was a couple who refused to move and their house stood alone in the rubble, their windows boarded up and a St. George's flag floating resolutely from their front door.

My dad took me out riding on his motorbike, flying over football fields and turning circles around the abandoned estate. I slotted onto the leather seat and wrapped my arms around him, breathing in smoke and oil laced with Midget Gems.

'Hold on tight,' he warned as he started the engine. 'Whatever you do, don't let go.'

I loved the way the wind tore my hair from my skull and it bobbed out around us like dandelion fluff. We got home full of the sting of it, dirt-piles and goalposts rippling under our skin. My mother breathed through her nose as she dished up potato smiley faces and beans for tea.

'I don't want to know about it,' she said, soaking her cracked hands in the kitchen sink.

21

I am trying to work out why my mother did not stay with me in London when the sky was cracking. Why she boarded a train and left me to look for my father alone. I think it is about taking the things that are yours and not holding back for the sake of other people. I think it is to do with letting things go.

22

Burtonport is full of multitudes. There are traces of my past here, in the damp that permeates my grandfather's house and the flashes of places that hold the secrets of my childhood. The curly ferns and the rough, mottled rocks stretch backwards through the years, away from my adult life here now, towards a smaller version of myself.

I hated it sometimes as a child, when rain fell relentlessly and the beaches seemed to stretch on forever, vast and unchanging. I sat in the corners of pubs while the adults sipped away the days and I sucked the salt from soggy crisps and slurped Cavan Cola, feeling the weight of the afternoons, heavy in the back of my skull.

Summer is ending and autumn is creeping in. I have a different sense of this place, one I could not detect before. There is something fast beneath the earth, brown and dirty. It is charred and dangerous, like whiskey and bonfires. I can sense a dark shape just outside of my grasp, calling to the reckless parts of me.

23

When my mother was twenty-one, her boyfriend took her on a trip to Paris. They spent twelve hours on a coach to walk along the Seine in trench coats. She has a Polaroid picture taken under the Eiffel Tower. She stood at the top of the steps by the Sacré-Coeur, looking out across the rooftops, and wished that her sister was there.

On the last night of their trip, they went for a meal in a tiny French restaurant. They both chose pasta because they didn't know how to pronounce anything else on the menu. Over complimentary crème brûlée, her boyfriend took a ring out of his pocket and pushed it across the table. He looked at her for a long time.

'Will you?'

'Oh, God. Yes?' She shuddered as she picked up her spoon to crack the sugar crystals.

When she arrived home, she told the story to my grandmother with salt-speckled cheeks.

'I don't want to marry him, Mam,' she choked. 'I didn't know what else to say.'

'For God's sake, Susie. We'd better call your Auntie Doris. She'll know what to do.' Doris was believed to be an expert on matters of the heart, having been married and divorced three times. She came round reeking of tobacco and cheap perfume. She heaped three sugars into her tea and fixed her niece with a lipsticked smile.

'You're just gonna have to tell him it's off, Susie pet. Why on earth did you say yes in the first place?' My mother shrugged and fiddled with her hair. Doris's big gold earrings glittered through the cigarette smoke.

'Shame, like.' She picked up the ring and attempted to jam it onto her swollen finger. 'Proper pretty piece of metal. Must've cost him a bloody fortune.'

When my mother told her boyfriend that she didn't want to marry him, he threw the ring over a cemetery wall in a fit of rage.

24

A few years later, an Asda superstore was built backing onto the cemetery. My mother liked to imagine that the ring was mixed into the cement and those tiny French sapphires were buried under stacks of Kellogg's Cornflakes and jumbo bottles of Fairy Liquid.

My grandparents went dancing, drinking, and to the cinema. He wandered around the market when she was at work, pretending that he didn't know her.

'I'll have ten prawns, six mussels, four crab claws, and a kiss later.' He winked, adding and subtracting whelks while she rolled her eyes and a queue built up behind him, snaking past jars of strawberry bonbons and piles of lacy underwear.

'We haven't got all day, pet,' someone wheezed in the background.

One day as he passed her some coins to pay for a cod, he slipped a shy diamond ring into her palm. She gasped and dropped it under the counter, where it sank into the shaved ice. She had to wait until the end of her shift to retrieve it, when they packed up the fish and drained the day away. She boiled it to get rid of the smell of seawater.

They moved into a council house in Pennywell. They steamed the dirty carpets and repapered the walls with delicate roses. Her mother gave them the mismatched crockery from the boarding house and my grandfather bought a knock-off electric blanket, 'To keep us warm in the winter, doll.'

Their next-door neighbours fought and swore and screamed sex through the walls but my grandparents just turned their radio up, giggling and smoking their way through the dark nights.

On Wednesdays she finished work early and went to meet him by the docks. Oily men in overalls with thoughts of home smeared across their faces shouted to each other above the wind.

'Alright, Linnie?' They nodded to her, small beneath the cranes in her long coat.

His face always softened when he saw her. Sometimes he welded bits of metal together to make birds and flowers that fit into the palm of his hand.

'Got something for you.' He kissed her gently and pressed his latest masterpiece onto her. They walked along the seafront and had fish and chips for tea. He licked the salt and vinegar from her fingers.

'Gerroff!' she squealed, pretending to bat him away with her handbag.

My grandmother gave birth to twins on the bathroom floor. One of the babies died instantly and my grandfather wrapped it up in a bedsheet and took it to the hospital, blood seeping through cotton as he hurried through the quiet streets.

A year later she had another daughter, fracturing her narrow pelvis with the effort. The baby turned blue and had to be resuscitated in front of the fire. My grandmother went to bed with two tiny people tucked up beside her.

'Brought you a tea, Linnie.' My grandfather crept into the room and kissed his daughters on the soft tops of their heads. Their scalps smelled of milk and something deep and rich and dangerous he couldn't understand.

My parents bought a bungalow in a cul-de-sac in a Sunderland suburb with an enormous hole in the sitting room
floor. All the neighbours were old people, tottering to and
from bus stops with their blue rinses, passing the days
before it was their turn to die. My dad paced from room
to room, knocking on the walls.

'I'll just do it up, and then we can sell it, like. We'll get
somewhere better in a few months.'

They went to work painting and stripping and knocked
down the rotten porch with a rusty hammer. They papered
the kitchen in fat brown hens and found a second-hand
sofa in a mossy velour. My mother made her own curtains
from Laura Ashley fabric, spending her evenings hand-
sewing the hems because they didn't have a sewing machine.
She squinted to see in the dark because the electricity hadn't
been turned on yet.

'You'll look at them stitches and remember me when I'm
dead,' she joked.

They had friends round and showed them before and
after pictures of the giant hole.

'You've done a lovely job.' They clicked and tutted as
they walked around the house, touching surfaces and
sniffing potpourri.

'It's just for now, like. We'll do it up and sell it, then
we'll get somewhere better. Somewhere in Durham, maybe.
Isn't that right, Tom?' My father smiled vaguely from the
doorway with his cigarette.

27

Years later my mother looked out of the window at the squat stone houses across the street and felt her youth had drained out of her. She rearranged her hand-stitched curtains with a panic-stricken look in her eyes.

'I feel like I'm going to be here forever,' she said to me. I pulled cushions from the sofa to make icebergs for my teddy bears to float on.

'I want to live here forever,' I told her. 'It's our home.'

28

In Donegal, people are identified by the names of prominent members of their family. Auntie Kitty brought my grand-father up, so he was known as 'Micky-Kitty.' When my mother is here, she is known as 'Susie-Micky-Kitty.' When I was younger I found this stifling, whereas now the trans-parency is comforting. I have been floating, without edges, waiting to be snagged on the next jagged thing. The names of my ancestors anchor the cottage to the ground like rope.

29

When I first moved to London, I didn't have a smartphone. Every day before I unlocked my bike and set off, I tore a page from my notebook and copied a wobbly line map of my route from my laptop screen. My pockets were stuffed full of inky squiggles linking parks and libraries with land-marks that meant nothing to anyone but me. I Blu-tacked them to my wall so the lines matched up. They wriggled around my room like a heart monitor, mapping my pulse across the city.

30

Now that I am in Ireland, I am screaming on vast beaches when there is no one else around. I am swimming in the sea, spreading my body wide in the water, feeling my limbs and my lungs stretching as far as they can. I am lying in the grass in the cottage garden and watching the stars at night, letting my thoughts wander, limitless, without cut-ting them short, or backing them up, or squeezing them into too-small spaces.

31

There are traces of my grandfather in this house. A bottle of holy water. A plate with a painting of a pope on it. A china dish patterned with tulips. I walk from room to room touching objects. I like the way they are solid in my hands. They are my things now, and yet they do not seem like my things. This house is part of my history, yet it is so unconnected to my life in London. This is my story, and yet it is not my story. I water my peace lily with his holy water, just to see what will happen.

32

When my mother and her sister grew older, they started ice-skating. Their drainpipe jeans were so skintight they had to lie on their beds and pull them up with coat hangers. They bundled up in scarves and hats under my grandmother's watchful eye, then stuffed them in the bush behind the bus stop, so they could pick them up and put them on again on their way home.

They skated forwards and backwards and spun in circles on one foot, moving so fast they left ice gathered on the surface of the rink like snow. They drank Coke from glass bottles through candy-striped straws, silver blades flashing as they swung their feet from fold-up seats.

33

The council eventually knocked the ice rink down. They got rid of the leisure centre with the slide and the wave machine to create a cultural quarter that would regenerate the town. My mother and I walked through the empty space and she started to cry.

'That ice rink saved us,' she said.

'From what?' I asked her.

'Other things.' She looked at the ground around her feet as though that time were a stray coin she could pick up and put back in her pocket, if only she could find it.

34

By the endless sea, beneath the infinite sky, I am craving fat tower blocks. I want gutters filled with rubbish and streets lined with cigarette butts and broken shoes; neon lights and violent, man-made things. The canal filled with sludge and smog settling over the river and the stench from the back of the bus getting into my lungs and staying there. When you breathe in dust you can never expel it. Everything important contains its opposite.

35

When my grandfather came home in a rage, my grand-mother locked herself in the bathroom with her daughters. She ran a bath so the rumble of the back boiler and the gurgle of the water blocked out the shouting from down-stairs. She sank into the hot suds and the girls rubbed Lifebuoy soap into her back, tracing their small fingers over the ridges of her spine. They stayed in the bathroom until their skin whorled and pruned.

36

My father is tall and gentle. When he was young, he bleached his curls with lemon juice and a bottle of Sun-In. He wore a gold hoop earring and wrinkled shirts rolled up at the cuffs. He had a home-made tattoo at the base of his left thumb and he liked David Bowie, walking on the beach, and drinking lager. He wrote funny poems in capital letters with all of the words misspelled. He smoked Lambert & Butler cigarettes leaning against sticky night-club walls in dank Sunderland basements, rolling his eyes in a midnight haze and smirking shyly through the dark, disco lights snagging the silver bangles he wore lightly around his wrists.

He lived with his parents in a house in Tunstall that had ivy blooming across the porch. He and his brother made their own surfboards from pieces of wood and went on holiday to Scotland to try them out, playing the Beach Boys in the car at top volume. They rescued an injured barn owl and it lived in their garage. There's a newspaper cutting of them somewhere; my uncle with his dark, naughty eyes and my father so small under white-blond curls, curved talons digging into his arm.

He had a knack for fixing things. He could take anything broken and within minutes he would have pulled it apart and worked out what the problem was. He fused wires and fiddled switchboards and wound the electricity meter back so that we could sit in front of the electric fire for as long as we wanted without having to worry about the bills.

37

I have noticed that many of the young men in Donegal have shaking hands. When they pass over change in the supermarket, or put salt and pepper on their food, or hold out their keys to unlock their cars, they are all trembling. In the pub after my grandfather's funeral, I ask my mother what it is that makes them shake.

'It'll be the drink,' she says, sagely.

38

My parents blew all their wages on holidays in hot places and supped cold beers wearing imitation Ray-Bans. They slathered their skin in baby oil and played Talking Heads from a portable radio, collecting iridescent shells and leaving streaks of sand between their bedsheets.

They went to Florida and posed for pictures in front of the fairy-tale Disney World castle. When I was born they bought me a plastic version. It had a button that made gold lights flicker above the turrets like fireworks. They drove through Miami with the car windows down and hired a motorbike to explore the beaches. They both wore denim shorts and big white T-shirts. My father got drunk one night and went to kiss my mother, but threw up in her mouth instead.

They always spent Christmas at my uncle's house. He had a dodgy car business and a fancy cottage panelled in dark wood with a Jacuzzi and a walk-in wardrobe. Everyone pulled crackers at the table, tingly with the promise of the future.

'Happy Christmas, pet.' My nan kissed my mother on the cheek, her paper hat falling down over her eyes. 'Tom thinks the world of you, I hope you know. We all do.'

They danced around the living room to 'Fairytale of New York,' screaming, 'You scumbag! You maggot!' and clinking glasses of Asti. My father passed out on the faux sheepskin rug in the living room while everyone frolicked around him.

39

How to make sense of soft shapes in the dark? The shiver of milk. Cold hands on my face. Hankering after softness. A pink jumper. The swell of a breast. I am fluent in the language of your body. Brown freckles in the raw of you. My dimpled knees. My fat, strange elbows. A dark, secret space of warm things and good things but he is a hard thing. Lurking around my edges. Fingers rough and smoky delicious. Cradling me like he doesn't know how. My skin is not tough enough. My unlearned fingers cannot hold. So quick there is a space in me, where other things should be.

40

I was blonde and shiny and ate pears and ice cream. I liked stories and magic and roller-skating in the street. I shuffle-ball-changed around the kitchen in my silver tap shoes, pattering out the rhythms that grew under my pillow at night. My mother dressed me in frilly socks and floral dresses with matching hairbands. She ruffled the tops of my puffball sleeves.

'There! Just like a princess.'

'I don't want to be a princess.' I pouted. I dug worms from the garden and took them to school in my pockets, kissing their slippery heads under the desk when no one was looking. I was worried they had no one to love them.

41

My parents met in the Queen Alexandra pub in Grangetown, just before Christmas. 'The Whole of the Moon' by the Waterboys had just come out and it played on repeat. My mother had been shopping and carried a blue silk dressing gown painted with flowers in a paper bag. My father put it on and slithered off his jeans, flouncing around the pubs in his bare legs and big work boots. He wore it to walk home in the cold and my mother had to go and collect it from his house the next day. She sponged off the wine stains and wrapped it up and gave it to her mother on Christmas morning.

'It's lovely, pet.' My grandmother put it on over her dress, holding her cigarette like a French film star. 'Dead glamorous.' My mother never told her the story.

My mother and father went out one night and walked home along the Wear as morning seeped through the clouds.

There was a sour sort of stillness in the air, the kind that comes before the brightness of the dawn, when it feels like the world belongs to someone else.

They wandered hand in hand, not wanting to go home and let the magic pass. They crossed Alexandra Bridge and paused in the middle to eat ketchupy chips from a warm carton. My father swung himself nimbly onto the big iron girders and sat with his legs dangling over the edge.

'Tom?' My mother was nervous.

'Come on, man.' His eyes crinkled. 'Give us your hand. We won't fall.' She giggled in spite of herself and offered her hand to him, leaving the chips by the side of the road. She stuck her legs over the edge and exhaled quickly.

'Proper good, isn't it?' He put his hand on her thigh. They watched the grey river swelling underneath them and heard the beginnings of the traffic sputtering into life. They sat in silence for a long time, watching the sun glint off the bits of metal in the old shipyard and noticing the way the empty water towers were like giant trees that had shed their leaves. They tried to read the graffiti scrawled on the walls along the river banks in dismal neon.

'Do you do this a lot?' She watched the sun work its way through his curls.

'Sometimes. Helps me to think about things.'

'What kind of things?'

'Just stuff. You know.' A car tooted on the bridge and they both shuddered, wavering on the edge of the girder. A man wound down his window.

'Fucking jump then, you pussies!' My father turned around and blew him a kiss.

'Come on.' He swung his legs back over the bridge and into the day. 'Let's go home, eh? I'm bloody freezing.' My mother jumped down after him. She picked up the box of chips and threw them into the water where they sank, making lazy ripples that barely disturbed the surface.

They went to see Lloyd Cole and the Commotions at the Telewest Arena in Newcastle. My mother changed in the toilets on the hospital ward when she finished work. She wore a Princess Diana dress with a lace collar and her Elnett threatened to set off the fire alarms. They drank warm lager and twisted and spun together. My father fell asleep on the train home and she let him rest his head on her shoulder, watching the lights drip across his face as they passed over the Tyne.

There was a strange sprig of madness that grew inside of both of them.

'Made for each other, you two are.' Their friends pulled faces behind their backs, itching to drag them away from each other so that they could head to the next bar or club. They slid winkle-pickers across slippery dance floors, tottering in kitten heels and writhing in the stretchy quality of the night. Cameras flashed in the darkness trapping moments in bright whiteness, developed later and shoved into an album somewhere, my mam hanging off my dad's arm, all pearly teeth and crinkled eyes, and my dad shy and lost, gazing off into the distance as though he couldn't quite believe his luck.

42

I didn't see a picture of their wedding until I started university. I asked about it over Christmas and my mother dug her album out of the loft. The plastic figures from their cake were tucked inside the cover, wrapped up in cream tissue paper, icing sugar clogging their feet.

43

There is a home video of my christening. The house is filled with light and unwrinkled versions of the people I grew to love, toasting fizzy wine and smoking in the garden. My father is passed out in a chair and I am dozing on his lap in a mushroom of white lace. He has blue eyeshadow smudged across his eyelids.

44

There was an unpredictability about him that appealed to her. She couldn't bear the feeling of all of the years of her life stretching out before her in a series of jobs and cars and weddings and grey Tuesday afternoons with freshly Hoovered carpets. He was inconsiderate and unreliable but he was a nicotine sort of electric that kept her on her toes. He rejected the smallness and the staleness of things and so did she. There was something beyond the factory car parks that they could both sense, in the crumpled lyric sheets slotted inside of their Oasis albums.

45

My sweat has begun to smell like the Atlantic sea. My clothes are coated in rusty dirt from the ash pile and I can taste wet grass and cool stars and satsuma-scented kitchen cleaner. There are small stones inside of my socks and I rub out my lacy knickers in the sink. The sunsets are crisp and smell of cardigans. My nights are filled with candlelight and sleepless hours twisting under icy bedsheets. The soles of my feet are black with dirt and there are bits of firelighter smushed into my fingertips. I drink red wine and I eat apples and spinach and chickpeas, bananas and raisins and porridge with honey. I scrub my skin with minty shower gel and spill candle wax on the floor, where it hardens into a long white scar. The very atoms of this place are burrowing their way under my skin, mingling with my neutrons and electrons and all of those other tiny, complicated things.

46

My parents were married the year before I was born. Her dress was white satin with stitched peonies. She wore pink roses in her hair and silky slippers on her feet. My father went out the night before the ceremony and got so drunk that he lost his shoes. He turned up late to the church with red-rimmed eyes, wearing his brother's brown brogues, two sizes too big. He shuffled up the aisle with trailing laces and spent the rest of the day in his socks. He sat at the bar, so nobody noticed. My mother ordered a cream basque from the Freemans catalogue, tied up with a tiny blue ribbon. She looked at his unconscious form on her wedding night and quietly changed into her nightie, folding up the basque and wrapping it in plastic. She sent it back the next day for a refund.

'I should have known then, shouldn't I?' she sighed, every time she told the story.

47

When my mother was a child, my grandfather started spending every night after work in the Irish Club down the road. He nipped out to the betting shop between pints to put his wages on the horses. He liked the ones with religious names like Holy Trinity or Mary Magdalene. He stumbled down the aisle of the last bus home.

'English Trash!' he spat at the other passengers when he reached his stop.

There was a billboard opposite their house that advertised Pretty Polly stockings and tights. The girls tucked their skirts into their knickers and can-canned around the sitting room, crossing and uncrossing their legs like the long, tanned pair in the advert.

One afternoon while my grandfather was at work, a man turned up with a ladder and a bucket of paste. The girls watched him from the window as he papered over the peeling legs with fresh strips of paper. They felt sad, as though something had been lost. The man stepped back to admire his work.

'The British Army Needs You!' A soldier smiled from

beneath a salute. My grandmother made the sign of the cross.

'What the bloody fuck is this?' my grandfather cursed when he got home, throwing the gravy boat at the wall. It bled down the faded roses. 'Bloody British bastards!'

My grandmother ushered the girls out of bed and toggled their duffle coats over their nighties.

'Come on.' She shook them out of their dreams. 'Let's go on an adventure.' They walked around the streets in the cold, trying to stay wrapped up in the orange fur that pulsed from the streetlights. When enough time had passed, my grandmother took them home and they crept up the stairs, being careful not to wake him as he snored on the settee with his mouth open.

48

Soon after my parents met, they went for long walks on Seaburn Beach in the cold, standing on the edge of the pier and looking up at the lighthouse.

'Me and our Pete got stuck out here one night, when we were kids,' my dad said. 'It was dead stormy and the waves came up over the pier. We would have got pulled under if we tried to go back.' My mother ran her thumb along a smooth pebble in the palm of her hand.

'What did you do?'

'We called the coastguard and he told us about a trap-door in the floor around here somewhere. We climbed down it and there's a tunnel that leads all the way down the inside of the pier and back to the shore.'

She looked at him. 'No there's not, man.'

'There is, I promise. It was pitch black and stank of rotten fish. Brought us all the way back to land.'

'Show us now, then.'

'I can't remember where it is.'

She rolled her eyes.

'Honest. It was dark. It's something to do with the war.'

He was always telling stories like that. He had a big white scar that puckered the length of his thigh. He told me he'd been chased by a lion that escaped from the circus. I pressed horrified fingers to his skin. It was smooth and cold like marble.

'Really?' I fiddled with the hem of my Tinker Bell nightie.

'Really, Lucy Lou. It was in the *Echo*. Your nan's got a clipping of it somewhere in the loft. Ask her to get it out next time you're round.'

My mother told me he lit a bonfire and was caught up in the blaze.

49

And then, growing. Moving and changing and sprouting and bulging. New things coming and old disappearing. Teeth under pillows and locks of hair on barbershop floors, rescued and taped into baby books. You rub suncream under my T-shirt and I touch your freckles with my fingertips. I can smell the sun in your skin. It is lemony strange and not the way it smells in mine. I have fewer layers for the light to penetrate.

50

During my bike rides into town to pick up lentils and cans of tinned tomatoes, I listen to podcasts. I do not speak to many people over the course of a day but I listen to radio hosts and writers and musicians and news reporters as I push myself up the hills. I have been thinking about voices a lot; the way that some are louder than others. I often speak aloud to myself while I'm cooking or brushing the ashes from the fire. I imagine telling people difficult things I have not had the words to speak aloud until now, rolling the hurt across my tongue to see how it sounds. My own voice is much louder here in the silence, away from the city that was drowning me out.

I have been thinking about language as a place to put your feelings. Before language, everything is mixed up and curdled inside. Babies cry all of the time; they are full up with feelings and don't know where to put them. Children bury their feelings in objects to keep them safe. They grab handfuls of their hurt and smush it into the middle of sandpits and swimming pools and old stuffed toys like buried treasure. Occasionally in adult life we find objects with our old feelings locked deep inside. A packet of Fruit Polos. A face caught in the folds of a curtain. A scratched Oasis CD.

My grandmother died when I was one year old. She had oesophageal cancer and the doctors cut out her voice to save her life. She wrote down the words she couldn't say on a little yellow notepad. My mother went to visit her and found her slowly knitting woollen squares.

'It's a blanket,' she wrote, her thin hands quivering with the effort of pressing down the biro. 'For the baby.' She died before she had a chance to finish it, and years later I found an old carrier bag stuffed in our loft with the knitted squares and the notepad inside of it. I followed her handwriting with my fingertips; traces of a person I could not remember existing.

My grandmother was born in a poppy field embroidered on a carpet in a boarding house in Sunderland. She had a twin sister who didn't survive. Her parents buried the broken foetus in the garden and planted a geranium over the spot. They didn't say a word about it until ten years later, when next door's dog dragged up a tiny femur.

Her father was a shoemaker. He spent his days stitching and sticking and pressing and hammering. He made tools and stools and bicycles. He built her a doll's house and painted it yellow. He smelled of leather, superglue, and love.

Her mother looked after a boarding house for foreign workers, and women and children on the run from mad husbands. They were sometimes Polish and often Italian but mostly Irish. A lot of drinking and swearing and sweating and fucking went on behind her thin lace curtains. They all missed their mothers, and treated her like she was their own.

*

My mother said she lost a part of herself when her mother died.

'I was never really the same again,' she told me. 'A loss like that.' She shook her head, sadly. 'She was so young.' I wrapped my arms around my knees and squinted at her, trying to see what had changed. 'I used to be different,' she said, turning up the electric fire.

'What kind of different?'

'Just different. Ask your dad.'

52

We lived in Houghton-le-Spring, an old colliery town comprised of a Kwik Save, a Greggs, and a library full of gory crime novels. There were a few pubs struggling under soggy St. George's flags and a park where gay couples and teenage goths got stabbed on Saturday nights. I slid my feet around Woolworths after school, begging my mother for stale pieces of fudge from the pick and mix section and twisting for bottles of pirate-shaped bubble bath from Savers.

My dad worked away a lot. When I phoned him he told me his hotel room was so small he had to sleep with his feet hanging out of the window. I stretched my bare toes over the edge of the sofa and pointed and flexed them, the way I learned in ballet class.

'Do the birds not peck your toes?' I asked him.

'Sometimes.'

On the odd weekend he was home, we used to get up early on a Saturday and go to car boot sales. We traipsed through discarded bits of people's lives in the white of the morning, plunging our fists into plastic buckets filled with mismatched wires and fingering bits of fabric and broken gadgets. My dad always bought a cup of tea from the van that sat in the corner of the field and he let me cradle it between my cold fingers as he smoked his cigarette, nodding, 'Alright, mate?' to the men toting cyberpets and jigsaws with important pieces missing. I dragged home dolls with scribbled faces and teddy bears smelling of other people's dinners. My mother wrinkled her nose and shoved them in the washing machine.

My father built a garage in the bottom of the garden for his tools. It smelled of damp and dirt and I loved it. He nailed together cabinets with tiny drawers and filled them with washers and screws in different sizes. I spent hours pressing his yellow spirit level against surfaces with my tongue between my teeth, eager to see the magic bubble resting perfectly in its case, indicating that everything was in the right place.

He poured wet cement around the garden and pressed his fists into it to make paw prints.

'Luce, come see! There's a family of bears living behind the garage.' He showed me the claw marks. 'See?' I was saucer-eyed in my flowery wellies. My hair bobbles bounced.

'I'd stay away from there if I was you. They eat little girls for tea.' He poked me gently in my stomach to emphasise his point.

I squirmed. 'Bears do not eat little girls.'

As soon as my parents' backs were turned, I scraped my knees over branches and breeze blocks and crawled behind the garage. I saw plenty of paw prints but there were never any bears. There were rows of empty Foster's cans lined up among the detritus.

'Do bears drink beer?' I asked my mother.

53

When my brother and I were children, my mother blew a bubblegum-pink bubble and kept us safe inside of it, where sharp reality could not pierce. I never once heard her say the words *alcoholic* or *depression*.

As an adult, it feels liberating to name things; to push them out of my body like long, sharp splinters and mould them into words. Naming things gives them shape and form, which means they can be picked up and taken away.

54

You wipe a ketchupy smile from my mouth and tease mashed potato from my hair. I breathe you in. White musk and face cream. I like you best in the mornings when you are naked, your face lightly lined and your skin red and blotchy, belonging to me before the mask of your day. Freckles tucked into soft dressing gown, pink and hot from the shower.

55

Our house was in the corner of the cul-de-sac, so we had a proper garden. All of the other kids from around the block used to come and play in it. Summer passed in a trickle of paddling pools filled with water from the kettle, bits of grass worming their way inside our Little Mermaid swimming costumes. We had a Crazy Daisy that spun in drunken circles, soaking our hair as the sunlight dripped through our jelly shoes. We ate sausage sandwiches outside, slurping butter from puckered arms and sitting on old bedsheets in the grass like magic carpets. I woke up first and climbed to the top of the slide in my strawberry-print shorts, learning the quiet shape of morning.

One afternoon, a couple of women from the local church came to our front door, rustling leaflets and rattling donation buckets. My mother invited them into the garden and they drank cups of tea with delicate sips, sliding around on sun-stained cushions that were too small for our plastic patio furniture.

'Are these all your children?' they marvelled as we squealed and threw water balloons through the sky.

'Oh, no.' She smiled. 'Just the one. The rest belong to the neighbours. I end up with them all in the summer 'cos we've got a big garden. The rest of them have only got backyards.' The women nodded approvingly and daintily nibbled the edges of digestive biscuits.

'And your husband?' They presumed. 'Is he at home, too?'

'He's at work,' she lied. He had been missing for days. The women smiled and wobbled their heads and thanked her for the tea.

'Best be on our way, then. God bless.'

They appeared again a couple of hours later and found us in ball gowns, spinning in circles through the flower beds and transubstantiating beetles into ducklings with tinfoil wands.

'Everything alright?' My mother frowned as they squelched their way across the grass towards her.

'Oh, yes.' They beamed. 'We're on our way back to the church but just wanted to call in again. There is such a feeling of love here.' My mother bit her lip and blinked back tears because they were right. There was so much love.

56

The cottage has a real turf fire. I spent a few evenings watching it splutter pitifully and feeling pathetic for being unable to do something so basic and elemental, but after a few days I had the hang of it and the flames crackled into life.

I ordered some bags of turf from a local farmer. He turned up on a tractor with fifty full sacks and a wild mountain look in his eyes. I came to Ireland with just two weeks' worth of pub wages, and the turf cost almost all of them. The exchange happened quickly, before I had a chance to protest.

After the farmer left I climbed up onto the top of the turf pile and cried with my face in the dirt. I felt angry at myself for wasting the only money I had left. The fat mounds of turf sulking in their white plastic coats seemed like impossibly heavy symbols of all the cold nights I will be spending here alone. I called my mother and she laughed at me.

'It's a good thing, Lucy!' she said. 'At least now you don't have to worry about being cold.' I am so afraid of having too much.

57

Now bigger. Growing taller, wanting rollerblades and bicycles, toes turning blue beneath swimming costumes. Goosepimpled flesh and socks pulled down to catch the thrill of the street at night. Fizzy cola bottles, strawberry bonbons hard and powdery, breadcrumbed dinosaurs, alphabet spaghetti. There are never enough letters to spell both our names. Your hands washing and scrubbing. There are burn marks on your arms from the oven. I can see your scars now. Stubble on your legs all black and prickly and you tell me that's what ladies do. I touch my own, downy white with summer. I am light and you are dark. You are freckles and sunspots where I am tracing-paper thin. I want to be full and alive like you. Flip over handlebars all cuts and bruises. Wrapped up in arnica, bitter and sweet. Calpol kisses with a biscuit and a glass of milk. I can't sleep at night in my vest and knickers, blanket pulled off and cheeks all red. You come straight to me. I breathe in your jumper, perfume and cups of tea and the smoke from his cigarettes, lovely and horrible all at once.

58

My mother posts me the Laura Ashley curtains with a handwritten note. 'Found these in the back of the wardrobe. Thought they'd be nice in the cottage.' I hang them up at my bedroom window. As a child I spent hours lying upside down on my mother's bed, coaxing ladies with long hair from the wisteria pattern. I wake every morning as the light falls through them but I cannot find the faces any more.

59

I spend days wondering what exactly I am doing in Donegal. I am so drawn to difficult things. I am always travelling far away from the people I love. I am constantly searching for something that I cannot articulate, uprooting and disappearing based on an abstract feeling in the pit of my belly. What if it was not the right thing to leave London? What if this is not the right way to live? Perhaps it is better to want tangible things, like bodies and objects. Everything I want is invisible. Do invisible things have worth?

60

My mother and auntie spent their childhood sitting on other people's walls in off-white knee socks, picking pink pieces of Wham Bar from between their teeth. They made up dance routines in the middle of the estate and pulled the wings off insects with dirty fingers. They ate boiled potatoes for tea out of a china dish painted with tulips and played Kissy-Catchy with the boys across the street.

'Your dad's a fucking paddy,' hissed a boy with a runny nose, poking them in the ribs until they shared their rhubarb and custards.

'At least he's not a mackem like yours,' they said, pointing their pink tongues at him.

They shared ice cream floats in Toni's Caff, sliding down glittery seats in plastic booths as he gushed, 'My sugar plums!' across the counter. There was a jukebox and they pushed hot pennies into the slot, coolly choosing Elvis and swirling their ice cream with faraway faces.

They went to a Catholic girls' school run by nuns. On Fridays as they skipped out of the classroom, crumpling paintings and trailing daisy chains, their teacher handed them each a peach-coloured raffle ticket, folded like a pursed pair of lips.

'Now, I'll be collecting these at mass on Sunday. I hope you're all going to be there.' Those who still had their tickets on Monday mornings got a wooden ruler whacked across their knees as they trembled in front of the black-board. My mother held séances in the stationery cupboard.

61

Hot wet on your pillow and new pencils for my homework. Fresh and polished patent leather. You crease everything clean and I soap-powder scuff along schoolyards in T-bars. Smack as my knees hit the ground but I don't cry. I'm a tough girl now. Poster paint on my elbows and rice pudding down my pinafore. You wipe me clean and rinse out our suds. Creamy Cussons soap caught in my cuticles. There is something new in your eyes, dark and lurking.

My best friend Rosie and I squeezed into pastel leggings on Saturday mornings and pirouetted around a cold dance studio, desperate for the lesson to end so we could swipe sticky Drumstick lollies from the plastic jar at reception. We took part in competitions and my mother stayed up for nights sewing constellations of sequins onto my leotards. Her fingers were bloody from the needles.

When we arrived at the venue she tied my hair up in shiny ribbons and smudged glitter carefully across my eyelids. I watched the older girls flit across the wooden floor in their iridescent ballroom shoes and flesh-coloured fishnets. Opulent feathers bloomed from their shoulders and their breasts were encrusted with cubic zirconia diamante. They moved like tropical birds.

'Mam,' I breathed. 'I want a costume like *that*.' She pulled a grip from between her teeth, hairsprayed me into a silver cloud.

'Have you seen how much they cost? They're too expensive, sweetheart.' I slid off the staticky chair and sulked my way through the warm-ups. My mother's patient knots were itchy on the wrong side of my leotard. With every twist I was prickled with the image of her small hands stitching through the dawn.

Each October, the local council put on a festival. We could see the lights being strung between lampposts from our school desks and a ripple of something cold and fresh sneaked under our cardigans. We rushed home to wolf down our tea, then my dad took us to the fairground. On the first night everything was half price and we clamoured for two-pound coins, enjoying the smug weight of them in our Puffa jacket pockets. My favourite was the hook-a-duck. I was seduced by the goldfish quivering in pools of neon and the glittery promise of 'Win a prize, every time!'

The most white-knuckle ride was the sticky wall. We stood with our backs against the wall until the cylinder began to spin. The floor dropped as we gathered speed and gravity took hold. People were sick and it stuck in their hair. My father laughed at our queasy faces.

'What did you think, girls?' Lights from the waltzers flashed across our bodies in bursts.

'Brilliant, Dad.' Rosie and I held hands as we walked home through the park, faces looming in the dark. Girls with orange cheeks in push-up bras brushed past us, smelling of the future.

63

Look at me dance. Look at me twist. Look at these things I can do with my body. I put on my leotard and ripple like silver. I have a best friend now. We cut open our wrists and smush blood together. We want to be joined forever. We dance intricate steps and feel we are made from air but then there are tap shoes, glitter and stamp. Cartwheels in the grass. Handstand elastic band, who can stay up the longest? You do my make-up for the dance competition. I love the thrill of your hand on my cheek. Our hair pulled back in buns so tight they stretch our faces. Aren't they little angels? Aren't they gorgeous?

64

I thought that perhaps here, away from everything that is familiar, I might become the most absolute version of myself. I watch cold days bleed into dark nights as lights flicker across the sea on Arranmore Island. Every twilight has a different texture. I am beginning to suspect there are no absolutes at all.

It gets dark very early and there is nothing for me to do in the evenings but light a fire and read. I have read so many books and articles that they have all begun to blur into one. I can't remember who said what, which is a problem.

I read somewhere that art, science, and politics are all shades of grey, that nothing is concrete and we will never reach the glistering thing at the centre. The article said that all we can do is blindly feel our way around things with visuals and signifiers, occasionally skirting the edges.

Here, at the edge of the country, things aren't grey at all. They are brown and gold and shocking, violent red. I used to think that cities were the centres of the world, but here there is a power, a kind of ancient I have never felt before, deep in the dirty ground.

65

When my father would go missing, my mother made up stories as she squirted Johnson's shampoo onto my scalp and it ran down my back like honey.

'He's working on a desert island,' she told me, rinsing clouds from my shoulders with a plastic jug.

'Where is it?'

'Very far away. He has to get a boat and it takes a long time.'

'Is he a pirate?'

'Sort of.'

'Is he a bad pirate?'

'Sometimes.'

'Can I be a pirate?'

'If you're very good at school then maybe, one day.'

He took plastic bags filled with cans of beer and slept under trees in parks for weeks, allowing the wife and mortgage of his life to evaporate with the dew. My mother fretted around the telephone, wondering how many more days would pass before she should call someone.

He always came back eventually with red-rimmed eyes, his skin sallow and his fingernails rimmed with dirt. He crawled under the duvet and stayed there for days. I mooned around the doorway, creeping into the dark when I dared, to marvel at his drool on the pillow.

'He smells like the sea,' I whispered, tasting his sweat as it caught the back of my throat. I burrowed my face into the duvet, dreaming of shipwrecks and electric eels.

'Go away,' he groaned from the deep.

Often he would have eaten so little and drunk so much that he would have to go to hospital to be put on a drip and be rehydrated. His whole body shook and blood dribbled down his arms as my mother ironed her heart into the creases of my school shirts.

One night, my mother and my auntie woke to smashing and clattering pounding up the stairs. They held their breath as the bed shook and shouts leaked between the floorboards. The next morning there was a strange metallic smell in the kitchen.

'Your bloody father!' My grandmother strained a smile over toast and jam. 'Lost it and started flinging a tin of beans around. Thought he was going to put a hole in the flipping ceiling. Had visions of you two coming down on top of us in that bed!' The girls looked at each other. They imagined a pair of ruby slippers sticking out from underneath their house and clicked their heels together under the table.

Their friend Frances broke her leg roller-skating and stayed off school for a whole month. The girls went to visit her and eyeballed the stacks of magazines and the purple smirk of chocolate bars shimmering on her bedside table. They watched her dad kiss her mam on the top of the head, and overheard her mother in the street saying, 'You know, it's funny, like. Having our Frances at home has changed him. He's so fucking *gentle*.'

My mother went into her parents' bedroom one afternoon and climbed onto a chair to reach the box of razor blades my grandfather kept on the top of the wardrobe. She carried them reverently into the kitchen where my auntie chipped ice cubes from their plastic holders. They wrapped the ice in a tea towel and held it on their arms until their skin goosepimpled. When the ice pooled they each picked up a blade.

'I'm scared, Suze. What if we get in trouble?'

'It'll be fine, man.'

My auntie furrowed her brow.

My mother rattled the box. 'Don't you trust me?' They pressed the razors down into each other's arms. They gasped at how easily their flesh sliced open, as though they were made from margarine. My grandmother found them ashen on the kitchen floor, their pink dresses smeared in wet red blood.

'What were you thinking?' she asked them later, bathed and bandaged in front of the fire.

'We wanted to stay off school like Frances,' my mother said sweetly, as she dipped a bourbon biscuit into a glass of milk.

67

I find it difficult to sleep in the cottage. I think it is because I don't have many people to talk to, so my thoughts get trapped under my skin like blisters. There is nowhere else for them to go and they drift around my body as I lie in bed, rubbing against my edges.

68

My mother started wearing a terracotta turtleneck that bloomed over her stomach. People turned up their eyes when they saw her in the street and cooed and whispered over my head. She pursed her lips together and forced a smile.

We were leaving Asda one day with a trolleyful of heavy shopping bags when she paled and clawed at her stomach through her coat.

'Did you hear that?' I looked at her from behind my *Mizz* magazine, fresh from the plastic wrapper.

'Hear what?'

'A cry. There was a baby crying.' I pressed my cheek to her stomach.

'Your baby?' I looked up at her. She was pale and confused.

'I. No. No, of course not. Must have been someone in the car park. Be a sweetheart and put the trolley back for me. You can keep the pound.' I wheeled the trolley through the afternoon, resting my weight on the handle and slotting my feet on top of the wheels, flying over concrete without touching the ground.

Her colleagues at the hospital gave her a hamper full of blue baby clothes and blankets. She sneaked them in from the car and we buried them in the back of her wardrobe under shoeboxes and suitcases. My father refused to acknowledge her straining stomach and she didn't want to do anything that might provoke a disappearance. Another baby was further evidence that time was moving forward and life was happening.

One night they sat at the kitchen table. She had her arms folded over her body, trying to suppress the eager bulge of her stomach.

'So.' He scraped his knife across the plate. 'Where are you going to put it?'

My mother unearthed the Moses basket from under the

bed. I lined up my Barbies and narrowed my eyes, choosing who to sacrifice to the baby. I never liked Sindy in her tacky yellow dress. I wrapped her up in a piece of kitchen roll like a shroud and gave her to my mother to take to the hospital.

69

You are somewhere else and I am with him. His body does not hold mine the way yours does. He is cold to the touch but smells grimy delicious. All your rules are broken and there are no cloudy bathtimes or reading books in bed. He tastes of earth and sky: a good kind of dangerous.

70

My brother was born by Caesarean. It was a traumatic procedure and he arrived in the world swollen and covered in bruises, screaming down the hospital. There was an advert for Tefal electrical products on the telly. The micro-waves and blenders were operated by scientists in white coats, their foreheads huge and domed to fit their massive brains. My dad nicknamed the baby Tefal for six weeks, until we all agreed on Josh.

'Funny name,' said my Uncle Pete as he peered into my brother's yellow face. 'Sounds a bit soft, like. Might turn out to be a puff, with a name like that.' He had a coloboma in his right eye and three holes in his heart.

71

Medicine sting at the back of my throat. Blood and crusty stitches. I press my fingers to the marks the doctors made. How did that tiny body do that to you? He is bruised and screaming. Did I do that to you? Parma Violets give me headaches. I hate the green Opal Fruits but I must suck them while the adults talk. Your stomach is puffy and pink but there he is, swaddled safe in soft blanket. Shush, the baby is sleeping but I don't want a baby. I want to run up and down in my tap shoes. I want you to hear me.

72

Our house contracted jaundice. Everything existed as normal but all of the colours were sickly. My mother could see the imprints of hospital walls on the backs of her eyelids. My father hovered around making cups of tea and putting things away, not knowing where to keep the dread that loomed in the doorways.

I took advantage of the distraction to wear my hair down for school. I skipped through the corridors with it streaming behind me. My mother sat for hours with the nit comb, dragging tiny eggs from my head while my new brother grizzled on her knee. The tea-tree oil smelled sharp and clean, mingling with the disinfectant in hospital waiting rooms.

Our parish priest turned up at the front door wielding rich, heavy incense and anointing oils and a bag full of candles and laminated prayer cards emblazoned with pictures of patron saints.

'Please.' He drew the curtains slowly. 'Turn off the lights.' My baby brother lay in the furry brown pile of our living room rug. I imagined that to him it must seem like a forest in winter, the leaves fallen from the trees.

'Our Father who art in heaven.' The priest closed his eyes and began to murmur, rubbing oil between his fingers, placing his hands on Josh's head and over his heart. My mother kneeled reverently in the corner while I clattered up and down the hallway in my tap shoes singing, 'Everybody needs a bosom for a pillow' along with the radio.

'This is bullshit you know, Suze,' said my father later, from his perch in front of the fire.

'What is?'

'All this God stuff.'

She gave him an exhausted look.

'What else do you suggest?' she asked him.

His cup of tea shook in his hands. They watched it slop onto the carpet and they cried together in fat wet drops, tears mingling with the biscuit crumbs and bits of fluff.

73

I am spreading out my life across my grandfather's cottage. I try to make space for my things in the kitchen cupboard and the pope plate falls out and smashes on the tiles. I look at the shards for a moment and wonder whether I should feel guilty. I consider collecting the pieces and gluing it back together. I decide that sometimes things are just broken, and it is better to leave them that way.

74

His body is fragile. We have to be gentle. How can anybody be so small? Look at those tiny fingernails. He is yours now too and there is less of you for me to hold. I run my own bath and brush my own hair and wear my tartan skirt that I am not usually allowed to wear. I am loud and wild in the schoolyard. I have to clatter shriek and get it all out until back home to shush now, the baby is sleeping.

75

Burtonport is a remote place. There are fields and beaches and a smattering of houses. The fishing port is almost defunct due to laws passed to save the seabed and the pubs and shops and restaurants that lined the street when I was a child have closed down. There is a small town a few miles away with a SuperValu, a betting shop, and a library in a disused church. Old men in waterproof coats shuffle up and down Main Street and young boys in fast cars come out at night, revving their engines in the supermarket car park. I cannot drive so I cycle there and back a couple of times a week, my backpack bursting with vegetables and bottles of whiskey to get me through the nights.

My little brother passed his driving test a few months before I left and took me out for a spin in his new car, delighting in having passed a milestone before me. I looked at his hands on the steering wheel and noticed that his long, clever fingers are exactly like mine.

'Look,' I said, spreading my palm like a star and resting it next to his. 'Our hands are exactly the same. Isn't that weird?' He moved his hand to change gear and rolled his eyes.

'Not really,' he said, as though it was obvious. 'You're my sister.'

76

My mother and my auntie tucked Josh into his baby carrier in the back of her red Panda and drove up to Holyhead in the middle of the night, where they caught a ferry across the dark ocean to Belfast. They took a flask of hot tea and a batch of egg mayonnaise sandwiches wrapped up in tin-foil. They stopped at the services to switch drivers.

'Have a sarnie, Susie love.'

My mother zipped up her baby inside of her coat and held him close to her heart, guilty that it was beating so loudly against his small, broken one.

'I wish I could feel the pain for him,' she said, pressing her fingers into stray grains of salt on the sticky table. 'Why can't you do that? Take someone's pain out of them and carry it?'

'Oh, Suze.' My auntie put her gloved hand over my mother's bare one.

It was winter and they drove all the way to the west coast through the fog-smothered mountains. The roads were cling-wrapped in ice and lights trembled in the hills like beads from a broken necklace. They followed directions scrawled in blue biro on the back of a hospital appointment card to a house on the edge of a village.

'Hello. Hello. Welcome.' A small woman in a woollen jumper kissed cold cheeks and foreheads, her brow knitted with the night. 'Come on in. Come on in. We've been waiting for you.'

They followed her into a sitting room smelling of candle wax and peat smoke. A table had been pushed against the back wall to form an altar. It overflowed with wooden rosary beads and tarnished silver crucifixes and plastic flowers and prayer cards and images of the Virgin Mary in gold gilded frames. People wrapped in coats perched on chairs or cushions on the floor with their shoulders hunched and their eyes closed, noiseless words dribbling from their lips. Ill and elderly people formed a line by the fire, wheel-chairs and breathing apparatus glinting in the firelight. The air was heavy with incense. Josh was the only baby. Father Sweeney was a healer. He walked into the room with his eyes lowered and a ripple of hope flickered across the carpet.

'Welcome, everyone,' he began in a soft voice. 'We are gathered here tonight to ask the Lord our God to have mercy on the people we love.' He looked around the room slowly, meeting the eyes of every person and smiling gently into their wan faces. 'Let us pray not only for the sick and elderly among us, but also for the friends, fami-lies, and carers who have brought them here today. Let us lift up our hearts to the Lord and ask him to fill us with strength during this difficult time.' People lowered their heads and murmured 'Amen' to the carpet.

'We will begin with a decade of the rosary and then I will spend some time with each of you individually. Please feel free to move around the room but do respect the needs of others. It's a small space.' He closed his eyes as people rattled rosary beads on bony wrists.

Father Sweeney walked around the room reciting prayers in a low voice and laying his hands on the people who had come to him for healing. He spent a long time bent over Josh in his carrycot with his eyes tightly shut, resting his hands over my brother's tiny body without ever making contact with his flushed skin. When it was time to leave, the housekeeper took my mother gently by the arm.

'I have never seen Father spend that long with anyone. Something special is going to happen for your son.' My mother crossed herself with holy water and they bundled back out into the night.

They brought me back an illustrated children's book of the story of St. Bernadette and a string of heart-shaped rosary beads made from pink faux pearls. I wore it under my school blouse like a necklace.

77

My mother went back to the heart doctor. He was a doctor of physical hearts, the type that pulse beneath ribs and lungs, but not the other type, the raw kind we couldn't see. He smeared jelly over my brother's shallow chest and put the cold instrument on his skin. He frowned and looked at the monitor, speckled with snow like a television lost between channels. It was indecipherable to us, the uninitiated. My mother jumped involuntarily, her muscles warped and tangled through months of pregnancy and fear.

'Very strange,' murmured the consultant to no one in particular.

'What is it?' she choked. She thought about walking out of the room and leaving us there. The doctor with his cool hands, the sad baby on the table, me, my father, the dark knot of the future. She could start a new life in a different place and pretend that none of it had ever happened.

The consultant switched off the machine and gently wiped the jelly from Josh's chest. He took her hands in his.

'Mrs Bailey,' he said. 'The atrial septal defect does not appear to be showing up.' My mother bit her lip. 'That is to say, the holes in your baby's heart have closed of their own accord.'

She looked into his face. 'Closed?'

'Yes. Closed. This is very unusual. The heart is a very powerful muscle, Mrs Bailey, but I cannot provide you with a detailed explanation of how this has taken place. It is something of a miracle.' The consultant smiled at her very gently and pressed his gloved hands onto her baby's head.

'This child,' he said, 'wants very much to live.'

78

The seasons are beginning to change. There is a chill in the air and it is tangy and sweet. It is the feeling of cold air on bare legs; playing out in the street as a child as the night closes in. Breathing in the dusk like smoke. Knowing that at any moment my mother will shout my name from the doorway, calling me home for the night. Secretly wanting her to; that safe, yellow space of bedtimes and steamy kitchens.

When the sun sets here, the clouds are edged in brown, as though they are fruit that has been left out for too long. I think that if love was a colour then it would be brown. It is the colour of rust and rot and decay, of avocados spoiled by the passing of time, and of dirt and age and things that have been forgotten. It is the colour of tobacco and coffee, of soil and chocolate and whiskey; things that are delicious in a heavy, cloying way.

When the tide is out and all the rocks are exposed, everything is brown. The seaweed rotting in the air, the mulchy seabed, the sky and the sea and the sand. It is a bruised, violent kind of beauty and it seems to me that maybe that's what love is like, in its purest form. Maybe it is no coincidence that bloodstains are brown. That dried-up, flaky residue that leaks from the heart.

79

Josh usually sat in front of the television watching cartoons, or crawled around the sitting room smashing Lego bricks together and screaming.

'Something is wrong,' said my mother. She vacuumed around his cot while he was asleep but he didn't stir. My father slammed doors and sang songs at the top of his voice but my brother didn't turn around. He lay on his back staring at the ceiling, unresponsive to the cooing and trilling around him.

'It's alright, man,' said my father, trying his best to be tender. 'You've just had a bit of a shock and now you're expecting the worst. Everything is going to be alright.'

My brother was diagnosed with deafness a few weeks later.

'Your child is profoundly deaf,' said the nurse, her finger-nails catching on sheets of paper as she pulled them briskly from a plastic wallet. 'He was unreceptive to sounds of up to one hundred decibels. He certainly cannot hear the frequency of human speech. We will provide him with hearing aids but his hearing loss is so severe that it is very unlikely they will make a difference.'

My mother felt the walls of the consultation room pressing into her, crushing her bones and making her smaller.

'You will be eligible to claim disability living allowance from the government,' continued the nurse. 'Here are the forms.' She handed them to my dad.

My parents walked dizzily into the daylight. They looked at each other. My brother started to cry. My father passed baby Josh to my mother and then he turned and left her alone in the middle of the car park. The sun bounced on car windscreens, mocking her with its vitality. She envied the cars their neat, ordered boxes, logically planned and painted carefully onto the ground.

When she was home, my mother sat alone in the silence of the sitting room and wrote her feelings into letters she would never send. She stroked my brother's skin over and over. It was soft and kept her tethered to the tangible world. She couldn't bear that he had no idea what sort of life the world had in store for him. It was such a terrible kind of innocence.

My father walked through parks and fields and forests, sleeping rough and trying to shake off his own shadow. My mother was sick with worry, but she knew from experience that he would come back eventually. He was gone for three days.

80

How to know this baby? This person who is us and yet not us. We press our hands to the small of him. His talcum powder sick. I want to lose my face in his peachy soft but I cannot. There are always walls between us. Beds and blankets and doctors. We are the only ones ever to be shaped from the same kind of strange and yet there are words making spaces. Sounds he will never know. A kettle boiling. A car door slamming. Frantic whispers in the night. Your hands can be his words but I am only small and I need something to hold on to. How can we crack open the silence? How do we break invisible things?

81

I have felt desperately lonely before, in the middle of a city holding hands with a lover. The kind of loneliness that grips your heart in its fist and squeezes until there is nothing left. I am very alone here in Ireland, but I am not particularly lonely. There is a gentle isolation in remote places. I think of my ex-boyfriend in London, but I do not feel sad. From time to time I think it would be nice to feel the touch of someone else's hand on my back, just for a moment.

82

'It must be my fault,' my mother cried to Auntie Marie over cups of tea in scornful orange mugs. 'I must have caught something when I was pregnant without realising.'

'Oh, Suze.' My auntie cradled Josh in his blue knitted blanket. It was edged with a silky ribbon and he liked to rub it between his thumb and forefinger, soothed by the softness. 'Don't be like this. He's perfect as he is. He'll manage. We'll all manage.'

When my father took to bed and couldn't stop drinking, my mother called the doctor to prescribe him Valium.

'I think I'm dying, Susie,' my father choked beneath sour-smelling blankets. The doctor left a pot of pills with a curt nod at my mother. I sat on the kitchen floor and played with my Polly Pocket, safe in her plastic universe.

Josh's inability to communicate made his bones itchy. He screamed around the clock and never left my mother alone. He was always pawing at her and hanging from her arms. He was blond and button-nosed and his skin was sweet like sugar paper. She stroked his cheeks to send him to sleep and tried to make up with kisses for the mistakes she thought she made in her womb.

They went from doctor to consultant to audiologist and

back again. His world was made up of corridors painted in creams and teals, machinery that he couldn't hear clicking and whirring behind closed doors. We learned to think differently; outside of the language of our thoughts and the language of the family we thought we had. We had to think outside of language altogether.

83

Donegal is teaching me a new vocabulary. There are words for different kinds of mud and bracken, lots of different words for 'wild' and different words to mark the passing of time. You can learn a lot about a culture through the words that people use most regularly. I want to drop my new words into conversation, in the post office and at the grocery shop down the road, but they are chewy in my mouth like peanut butter. I don't know if I have a right to this language, spoken by my Irish family and butchered by the English on my father's side.

84

Once we were driving home from school listening to the local news on the radio. There was a story about a woman who jumped from the viaduct in Chester-le-Street with her autistic son, killing them both. My mother pulled over on the hard shoulder. Her mascara leaked.

'What's wrong, Mam?' I asked, not daring to touch her.

'I don't know,' she cried. 'I can't explain.' She couldn't form the words to tell me she knew exactly why that woman had jumped. She felt the weight of the hopelessness that had overwhelmed her. I tensed as lorries rattled by us on the motorway, threatening to topple in the wind.

85

So many words. To be pursed on my lips or shaped with my fingers. I am choking on syllables. Some are harder to swallow than others. We learn new ways to hold the smell of strawberry laces and dirt in the garden. Teddy-bear fuzz all skin and fluff. Lampposts and cul-de-sacs. Clouds low and saggy. Dirty caravans in driveways. The snooker hall in the rain. The saccharine shiver of the ice cream man all skipping rope smack and disco dancing. You trace your fingers around his knuckles with your face all yellow. We three bound together in a place more deep than where words can reach.

86

I think that one of the reasons I am calmer here is the power to choose my own words. In London, I was constantly bombarded by adverts on the tube and billboards and posters and music and announcements and snippets of other people's conversations. Here there are fewer words. There are no advertisements at all. I cannot absorb any news by osmosis. I have to actively seek the rest of the world out in order to remember that it exists at all. I have autonomy to choose which kinds of words go into my head. There is less extraneous noise.

I am thinking about insidious words; the way that branding and packaging get inside of our brains without permission and make up our psychologies accidentally, like second-hand smoke. I am interested in images and patterns and the way that sometimes when I go to sleep at night I see logos flash behind my eyelids; fluorescent kebab shop signs and teabag boxes. In the city everything jangles and my nerves are wrought by caffeine and clouded in overheard phone calls. It is difficult to concentrate on anything at all.

87

There is silver in the back of your eyes. Glinting, dangerous. A hard, tinny feeling you do not want me to know. You hide it during Coco Pops and on the walk to school but later when you are alone and staring at the window it leaks out. I want to feel everything you do. I want to know the silver too but you draw me close and squeeze me tight and I can't make the words come. The metal lurks between us, cold and dazzling.

During the days when I was at school and Josh was asleep, my mother cleaned the house frantically. She polished the wooden fireplace with her tongue between her teeth and scrubbed the windows with balls of newspaper. When I came home I walked my feet along the lines left in the carpet by the Hoover, as though it was a lawn that had been freshly mowed.

'Get out of the kitchen!' she shouted, as I attempted to dart across the damp floor in my red tights to the biscuit barrel. 'This room is closed!' She slammed doors and turned off lights determinedly, reducing our lives to the rectangles of our bedrooms so that we couldn't fingerprint the ornaments and spoil the shiny chemical perfection of her afternoons.

We learned sign language. My mother pulled out her heavy Kodak camera and took pictures of everything. Tiny pairs of baby shoes and bottles filled with formula. Plates of breadcrumbed dinosaurs and tins of beans. Her red Panda parked on the street corner. The ivy that grew up the front of my nan's house. Josh learned very quickly. My mam took photos of everyone we knew and stuck them to the kitchen wall, so Josh could learn the signs that meant their names.

My dad's picture was taken in the porch when he came home from the sweet factory where he worked as an electrician. His eyes were lined and his T-shirt hung too big from his shoulders. He seemed distracted, as though he was thinking of something else. He was so afraid of permanence.

I loved the sting of oil and metal on his skin when he came home from work, kicking off his boots in the hallway and scrubbing the oil from his hands in the bathroom. Sometimes his toolbox was stuffed full of cracked Caramac bars and we plunged our hands in with shiny faces. I soared when he came home in a good mood, singing songs at the top of his voice and dancing loops round my mother as she tried to make the tea. She sighed and elbowed him out of the way. She was left to tie our shoelaces and wash our dirty clothes, while he drifted in and out on the wind.

They went to the local college together to sign up for sign language classes, but my dad enrolled on a computer course instead. He didn't learn the colour of my raincoat, or the sign that shaped my little brother's name. My mother and I spoke in symbols. With a fluid twist of her fingers she warned me whether it was safe to trail around him in the kitchen and pester him to take me out on my roller-blades, or whether I had to leave him be and let him crawl into bed with a stink in his hair.

'Stop talking about me,' he snapped, as we weaved an invisible world above him, one that he couldn't understand.

89

When he was old enough, my brother was given a cochlear implant. The doctors sliced open his scalp and put a computer part inside of it that would allow him to hear. He had to wear a little belt with another computer on it and a wire that connected the exterior part of the hearing aid to a magnet under his skin. The operation was four hours long. There was no guarantee that it would work.

He was a small, golden person with sticky-out teeth and

a shrill and lovely laugh. I marvelled at his tiny fingernails, unable to comprehend how they could possibly grow to match the size of my own. He wore stripy T-shirts and shorts, his pockets stuffed full of plastic cars.

My mother sat in the hospital with her eyes closed, praying to an uncertain god. I watched the clock slip through Literacy, Numeracy, and RE, picturing the surgeon's gloves as they peeled my brother's skin from his skull, his blood stinging with surprise beneath the operating lights.

We expected a slow and sorrowful recovery. I begrudgingly filled his cot with plastic cats and Barbie dolls, sulking at the mound of gifts from well-wishers piled at the foot of his hospital bed. The day after the operation, he was up on his feet running around the hospital and screaming, his head all wrapped in bandages, like a drawing of a sick person in a children's book. He was the hundredth person in the country ever to have a cochlear implant and a newspaper came to do a feature on him. He posed in the hospital bed with an angelic smile, white-blond curls matted in iodine.

My mother collected me from school a few days later and winced as he raced around the schoolyard as though nothing had happened.

'He looks like Frankenstein,' I said, eyeballing the staples in his scalp from the back seat of the car, afraid to touch something that could so easily be broken.

My mother tried to make up for the years my brother couldn't hear by building a kingdom of sounds and vibrations. He had toy fire engines that wailed, a Tickle-Me Elmo that laughed maniacally, a set of drums, a yellow maraca, and a doorbell that made all of the lights in the house flash when it rang. My favourite was the rainmaker.

It was a cylinder filled with tiny shards of plastic that sounded like rain falling on a roof when you moved it up and down. I sat for hours with my ear pressed against it, watching the beads rise and fall with the tides of our days.

90

I didn't know you could cut open heads and put things inside of them. There are staples and bandages and hard, horrible things that aren't supposed to be inside of babies. He was inside you and now he is not. Is there a space in you where he was? Is there a space in you where I was? The hospital chairs stick to the backs of my thighs and I slot my feet into the squares on the floor and kick stamp clatter. There is sick in both of us but he comes out living. He is a miracle running and screaming. He can hear now. It must be magic, or maybe god. Is there magic? Is there god?

91

Most nights after dinner I go to the sea. I like walking across the fields in the dark without a torch, invisible in my black jumper. The anxieties that swell beneath my skin during the day seem less significant when I look out at the water, brown and sticky like Coca-Cola.

When the mist moves across the sea, shrouding the mountains and obscuring the stars, it is easy to believe in a force that is bigger than myself. There are so many intricate ecosystems at work that I can understand why people believe in gods and enchantment.

I would like to have something to believe in, but it is difficult. Everything my generation was promised got blown away like clouds of smoke curling from the ends of cigarettes in the mouths of bankers and politicians. It is hard not to be cynical and critical of everything, and yet perhaps there is an opening, too. When the present begins to fracture, there is room for the future to be written.

92

My life was cherry-flavoured. It was filled with red school ties and plastic kittens. I scribbled felt-tip flowers up the walls of my doll's house, cutting my dolls' petticoats with zigzag scissors so they could prance along the roof in miniskirts. I became an expert in imagination, but the purple tones in my parents' voices gathered in clouds and fell into my dreams like rain.

I developed a new range of hearing that picked up on the low, tense voices that leaked under my bedroom door in the middle of the night. I squinted from my pillow as the chink of light flashed black and yellow. Shoes slid on and off and legs paced up and down, uncertain feet stuttering on the laminate floor. I became hypersensitive to the clatter of my mother's heels in the hallway when she was on her way out and the thump of my father's work boots in the porch. I could determine what kind of mood they were in by the weight of their steps.

My father decided to convert the loft in our bungalow into bedrooms for Josh and me. Josh had grown too big to sleep in his cot in their room, and the air in there was heavy and laced with something bitter. I balanced precariously on planks of wood, thrilling myself with the thought of my ankle breaking through the ceiling. I plunged my hands into clouds of fibreglass and cried when an itchy rash puckered my skin.

'I did warn you, Lucy Lou,' my father said. 'That's what happens when you don't do what you're told.'

I figured out how to balance the paint-stained ladder and pull myself through the hole in the roof. I found my dad up there one afternoon, crouched in the corner and shaking. His eyes were out of focus and he smelled of the wrong kind of sweetness, like rotting fruit.

He hammered so many nails into the walls that people joked our attic would withstand an earthquake.

'Building a bunker, are you, kid?' twinkled my uncle. 'You never know, we might need it, like. Country's going to the dogs.' My dad smiled weakly and rattled a box of silver.

'Well, you know,' he mumbled, gazing up at the walls. 'I don't want it to fall down.'

93

Every now and then, when my dad was working away, my grandfather came over from Ireland to stay with us. He brought a black holdall containing his only suit, a clean shirt, some vests and underpants and a bottle of home-brewed poitín. My mother slept with me in my single bed, so my granddad could have her room.

'I envy him, a bit, you know,' she said to me, squashed against my army of teddy bears. 'He moves through his life so lightly. Just packs a bag and goes, without thinking twice.'

94

And then more growing, into a different sort of body. I am a sister and he is a brother and he cannot touch me. People feel pain and he does not understand yet. He pokes his fingers in my ribs and kicks and slaps and I cry out. Where there were two bodies now there are four. Mine must be tucked neatly into school uniform to compare knees and sizes of feet in the playground. I am taller than everyone else and my best friend is small. I want to be small like her but you tell me tall is beautiful. She is Mary in the school play and I am the narrator. I have words to say and she does not. You tell me that is better but I'm not sure.

95

I build a shelf in the kitchen and feel proud of myself. I cut the wood to size with a rusty saw and I drill brackets into the walls, relishing the power of the tools in my hands. I put my smoked paprika on there, and a glass filled with fresh basil. I add my balsamic vinegar, sticky and acrid. I do not have many herbs or spices, but the ones I do are pungent and important. I step back to look at my work and am satisfied. Maybe I have everything I need.

96

Auntie Marie was married to a man who maintained weapons in the Royal Navy. He went to sea for weeks at a time then drove all the way up to Sunderland from Plymouth, where the ship docked. She began to spend weekends down there instead, and we went to stay in her flat.

'I can't bear it,' my mother told my auntie over the phone. 'He doesn't give a toss.' I glued sequins to pink bits of card in front of the telly and pretended I didn't understand.

'They're your kids, too, Tom,' I heard her sobbing late at night.

Josh and I pretended Auntie Marie's scratchy blue sofa was a ship. We spent days pressed against the prow, fighting the pirates and sea monsters swimming through the carpet. My mother fretted around us, trying to puff a new kind of life for us into the polyester cushions.

Auntie Marie came back and we went home. The loft was finally finished and we dived into our new beds, smelling delicious like cheap wood and nylon carpet. I begged for a lime green bedroom and my mother spent days with a paintbrush and a home-made stencil, coaxing shy daisies across the walls.

97

The seasons are shifting. The heathers burn orange and the clouds are singed brown, like the edges of an old book. Autumn always makes me think of the ex-boyfriend I left in London. He is an architect and in all of my memories of our relationship it is autumn, even though I know this cannot be the case. We always seemed to be walking around the city in the cold arm in arm, our breath silver in the sticky Chinatown air, buying beers from corner shops in the evenings and watching the sun bruise the sky.

I sit at the table one night, drinking wine and looking out of the window, at the bald patch in the garden where we had the bonfire, and the bath full of old saucepans and cracked china that we couldn't burn and so don't know how to get rid of. I think about our relationship, and the way that the city eroded our love. I send him an email, even though I know I shouldn't. I write, 'Autumn always makes me think of you, in your long, brown coat.' In the morning I read his reply.

'Sometimes it is nice to hold onto things, instead of letting them go. Isn't it?'

98

The smell of fresh paint lingered in my bedroom. I woke in the middle of the night to my mother's legs prickling against me. I wriggled in confusion and made a grumbling sound.

'Shh,' she whispered. 'It's okay. Can I sleep in your bed tonight?'

'Go away,' I mumbled through sleepy fog. 'I'm trying to sleep.'

I found her in the morning curled up at the bottom of my brother's single bed. He was wrapped up in the blanket. I dragged my duvet from my bed and laid it on top of her.

'I love you,' she murmured from beneath her dreams.

99

The National Deaf Children's Society invited us on a Halloween weekend to Butlins. The morning we were set to leave we hovered around the front door, slurping cartons of orange juice.

'Can we go, Mam?' we whined, sticking our fingers into the keyhole and running our hands along the radiator. She looked at her mobile phone and her eye twitched.

'Alright, then,' she said. 'Let's get on the road.' She fluffed up her hair and frowned at her reflection in the hallway mirror. 'I don't think he's coming. But us three will have fun, won't we?' Josh and I nipped and shoved our way to the car, squabbling over booster seats and throwing our backpacks down at our feet.

'Who's not coming?' Josh asked, fastening his seatbelt and rooting around in the glove compartment for his flashing police siren.

My mother feigned excitement as we arrived at Butlins and skipped through the site to find our cabin, enthralled by the trampolines and arcade games batting their eyelashes at us from every window. We twisted and whined our way to the restaurant where we met the other families, crowded in calm huddles and sharing margherita pizzas. Plastic seaweed hung from the ceiling and the tables were shaped like seashells. I chewed oily cheese while my brother ran from seat to seat, pinching chips from people's plates and upending Cokes with his frantic elbows.

'We're all off to the Space Lounge tonight.' One of the parents smiled. 'There's some kind of entertainment and a disco.' My mother forced a spark into her tired eyes. 'Oh, aye? It's great for the kids, isn't it?'

'It's just a massive playground. Drives you mad. There's a bar at this space place though, so maybe we can have a glass of wine or three.' The woman winked.

'Come on then, you two.' My mother grabbed Josh around the waist as he made a bid for the man dressed up as a cartoon cat making his way towards us. 'Let's pop back and get changed.'

'It's fancy dress!' someone called after us. 'There's a prize for the best outfit.'

My mother collapsed onto the sofa in our cold little cabin, throwing cardboardy cushions to the floor. Josh wrestled a packet of face paint crayons from my backpack and started drawing blue squiggles up my arms.

'Mam!' I gasped. 'Make him stop!'

'Just give me a minute.' She sighed, rubbing her hands over her face. 'Please? I'm a bit tired after the drive. Let's play the quiet game. Whoever can stay silent for the longest is the winner.' We watched her from the floor as she rummaged through her suitcase.

'I don't believe it,' she moaned, upending knickers and toothbrushes onto the scratchy carpet.

'What?' I asked her, sitting on the face paints while Josh tried to claw them from underneath me.

'I've forgotten my make-up bag.' She looked as though she was going to cry. I didn't understand what the problem was.

'That's okay,' I said. 'It must just be at home.'

'We can't go out,' she said. Her lips were pale. 'We can't go.' I come from a line of immaculately turned-out women, experts in dusting make-up over their faces to conceal the tremors that ran through their lives. It was as though my mother had forgotten her armour, and without it all of the other families would be able to see how she was crumbling.

'I can't do this any more,' she said into her hands.

'I want to go to the disco,' I whined, wiggling my hips. 'Please?' She sighed.

'I'll ring Leanne's mam from the pizza place. She was nice. She'll take you. I'll stay here with Josh.'

'But. No! I want us all to go *together*.' Josh wailed like a fire engine. 'I know!' I brightened, pulling the crayons out from underneath me. 'It's Halloween! We can just paint your face instead.' I had a long, black wig in my backpack in preparation for my carefully planned Wednesday Addams costume. My eyes shone with my own genius. 'You can be Morticia!' My mother snorted.

'I don't think so, Luce.'

'Come *on*. It'll be fun.' Josh screamed and lunged for

84

the face paints, knocking over the coffee table in the excitement. My mother looked at us and saw pumpkins and spider webs lurking in our faces. She closed her eyes for a second and sighed.

'Okay,' she said, quietly. 'Okay. I'll be Morticia.' I helped her chalk her face and ring her eyes in black. I traced the outline of her Cupid's bow with the sticky crayon, thrilled by the softness of her cheek under my hand. She looked in the mirror and grimaced.

'You look great, Mam,' I told her. Josh and I dressed and we went to the disco and she sat at the table with the other families while we were ushered onto the stage by eager entertainers.

'You look mint!' Leanne's mam gushed. 'You've really got in the spirit of things. You're braver than me! Younger too though, eh? I'm getting too old for all this carry-on.' My mother smiled and took a sip of beer.

I twirled in circles on the dance floor in my long, dark wig, raising my hands to 'Reach for the Stars' by S Club 7 and half-closing my eyelids as glitter from the disco ball was tossed around the room. The silver discs blurred into stars as I spun faster and faster. I was an astronaut, the room was a galaxy, and gravity pulled everything towards the biggest and brightest planet, stardust caught in her hair and the moon reflected in her bottle of beer. I would forever be in her orbit, moving towards her and pulling away while she quietly controlled the tides, anchoring me to something as the universe expanded further and further away from us.

Part Two

1

A fresh kind of freedom between my bones. Denim shorts on the washing line; yours bigger versions of mine. Grass streaked up my legs and across my face, mud beneath my fingernails and barefoot in the marshes. Sludge horrible delicious between my toes. Red lemonade bubbles make us prickle-tongued. Midge bites and jellyfish stings. Angry kisses reminding me that I am a body. Blisters and jelly shoes, bruises in the afternoons. We curl into bed at night, all peat smoke and sunburn. Hair strung up in salt and brine. You stroke my arm hairs in the same direction, tiny and golden, soft with sun.

2

One night I take a walk down by the old fish factories. It is overcast and swathes of mist drift over the water, obscuring the lights on the islands from view. I walk right out along the rocks to the edge of the land and look down at the sea. It is black and churning. Watching the waves shatter is like dancing at a punk gig. There is catharsis in noise and violence.

3

My grandfather moved back to Ireland when my grandmother died. He inherited his Auntie Kitty's small stone cottage and went to live in it. There was no hot water and the wardrobe was riddled with moths and worms, but he didn't mind. He walked three miles to town and back again every day and refused to accept a lift from anyone. He swam in the sea and picked seaweed from the rocks, drying it out on the roof of his shed so he could snack on it later, licking the sea from his lips. He spent his days tending the fire and listening to the radio. He read Brian Friel stories and walked down to the port to collect fresh fish to fry for his tea. In the evenings he went down to Jimmy Johnny's pub and shared whiskeys with men he knew from his childhood.

4

The coastal air is damp and goes right through my bones. I pull my turtleneck up to meet my mouth and fasten the top button of my jacket. I didn't have a winter coat to bring with me to Donegal and I don't have any money to buy one. It is getting dark quickly and as I turn to leave a set of car headlights swing towards me through the fog.

'Jeeeeeysus.' A man's voice drips through the open window into the night. He sticks his head out. 'I almost did away with you! Sorry, didn't see you through all this cunting fog.' I blink in the glare of his headlights, squinting to see his face through the dusk. He seems young.

'Where you off?' he asks. 'Can I give you a lift?'

'Yeah, alright. It's freezing. I'm just up the road.' I slide into the passenger seat. The man cranks up the heat. Chart music throbs through the speakers.

'What you doing down there in the dark?' I turn to look at him properly. He is swaddled in a black sweatshirt, the hood pulled up over his head. He turns to face me, then winks as though we have a secret.

'I was just out for a walk, actually.'

'A walk? On a night like this? Fucking header, you are.'

I roll my eyes at the road. 'I like walking.' My lips curl. He drives up the road without looking out of the window or touching the steering wheel, his fingers texting frantically. I am always putting my life into the hands of strangers. We have the inevitable conversation about who I am and where I'm from and what I'm doing here.

'What about you?' I ask him.

'Oh, I'm a port man meself. Born and bred.'

I look at him again. 'How old are you?'

'Twenty-five. How old are you?'

'Twenty-five, too. I wonder if I would have known you when I was a kid. I spent a lot of time over here.' He brushes off his hood and looks at me properly. We seem to be avoiding each other's eyes.

'Fuck off! I know you. You used to stay up beside the Skipper's.'

'Yeah!' I laugh. 'Have you got a brother?'

'You mean Declan? Aye, so I do. Right stuck-up little English cow, you were.'

'I was not!' We drive on in friendly silence.

'I'm just up here,' I say, as we turn onto my road.

'Aye, I know who you are, now.' He swings deftly into my driveway and spins around so his headlights light my path to the front door.

'Well,' I say, opening the door. 'Thanks for the lift.'

'No bother, pal. You should pop down to the pub some-time. You must get lonely here all on your own.'

I make a non-committal noise.

'See you, then.' His car careers off into the night.

Later, in bed, I think back to his jerky driving and the awkward angles of his limbs. I feel something cold and wet settling in the bottom of my stomach like fog. I close my eyes and see the sea spitting white lace onto black rocks.

5

The simplicity of life in Ireland appealed to my mother. She spent summers visiting Auntie Kitty as a child and in the uncertainty of her adult years she started looking for places that held an echo of the person she used to be.

Every school holiday we packed up the car. We crammed bodyboards and fishing nets into the roof box and stuffed our favourite clothes into straining suitcases. We left in the early hours of the morning to make it up to Scotland in time for the ferry. My mother always had cartons of juice and Rice Krispies cereal bars ready for us on the back seat.

We spent every day swimming in the sea, climbing onto

rocks with the local kids and jumping into the water with a splash, dodging the jellyfish that flowered around us. We ate sausage sandwiches and pink marshmallow biscuits when the sun went in and fished in rock pools for shrimps and tiny crabs that we carried all the way home in seawater buckets. We searched for fairy rings among the bracken and the heathers and stayed up late to look for nymphs in the grass. We lay on our stomachs and watched the boats clink in and out of the harbour with the tides. The air tasted different away from the schools and suburbs and low-slung clouds. There was so much sky to get lost in. It felt as though we were at the edge of the earth, away from the order of things.

6

Yesterday afternoon, I went for a walk along the cliffs. I remembered the afternoons when my brother was smaller than me and we crawled in the yellow grass together. I thought about London moving without me, the network of trains hurtling underground and the pubs spilling punters into the gutters. I pictured all of the girls in the city like me, with winged eyeliner and bitten fingernails, stepping out into the fray in pursuit of unknowable things.

Time passes differently here. The cliffs and the sea and the long, sandy beaches move infinitely slower than life in the city. The constant rhythm of the water makes the clatter of the tubes and the endless sirens seem trivial and meaningless. The difference is that the cliffs and the beaches will exist for much longer than me. I don't have time to move so slowly.

I sat in the grass for a while and looked out at the sea and the curvature of the earth shimmering in the distance. It seems inconceivable that there is no land between Ireland and America. It seems inconceivable that I ever cycled around Elephant and Castle roundabout at rush hour, or subsisted for weeks at a time on instant coffee and cereal. Sometimes, in order to move forward, you have to go to the edges.

7

There was a music festival in the summertime and an old lorry was parked in the fishing port with the sides taken off. Bands played on the stage and we stayed up late, running around in bare feet as drunken adults clasped their hands over our ears during the final verse of 'Seven Drunken Nights.' The music got under my skin. I twisted and wriggled in my seat, desperate for the moment when my mother would appear in the dark and tipsily spin me around on the end of her arm, twirling me faster and faster. Men's eyes snagged her from across the room, making me feel strange.

8

One evening I walk down to Jimmy Johnny's to have a glass of wine and read a book. Usually I can't bear the curious stares of the old men but tonight I am feeling defiant. They turn around and nod at me when I walk in then sink back into their bodies, absently watching horses race across the television screen in high definition. I choose a seat next to the fire and settle down to read. The door swings open and a hooded figure storms through it, letting in the cold night. It is him, of course. I focus on my book and take a sip of my wine. He greets the men at the bar and pretends not to have seen me.

Eventually, he comes over.

'Where've you been hiding, then?' I shrug.

'I haven't been hiding. I've been around.' He smirks at me and looks at my book.

'What you reading?'

I put my arm over the cover, feeling exposed. 'It's nothing.'

'Read a lot of books, do you?'

'I suppose so. Do you?'

'Fuck no. Can barely even write me own name.' There is a small silence. Our difference hangs delicious in the air between us.

'Want a drink?'

'Yeah, go on then. Thanks.'

9

We sit side by side. The streetlights leak in through the windows. He offers me a cigarette. They are cheap and nasty and scorch the back of my throat. Old men watch us through an amber haze. I look at his arms resting on the bar, strong from carrying bricks and cement, and am surprised by the force of my desire. It is still a revelation to me that I can sit with a person with all of the ordinary boundaries between us, and then with a few carefully chosen words we might end up somewhere else together, all fingers in mouths and hard, wet nipples.

10

There was a hole in the sea off the coast of our favourite beach, known as 'The Black Hole.' It was a dark circle of water rumoured to have currents that could pull you right down into it. There were white wooden crosses peppered on the rocks above, in tribute to teenage boys who dived into the water and were sucked under, never to be seen again. I developed a secret horror of the hole and kept well away from it. Instead, I put planks of driftwood across the bellies of washed-up jellyfish and walked across them in my bare feet as their insides burst and oozed beneath my toes.

11

The pub closes and the barman gives us a water bottle full of whiskey and a plastic money bag pulled from the till, filled with dried cloves, to make hot toddies. He drives the man and me up the road in his van and drops us off at my house. I suddenly feel shy. I have been spreading myself out across the cottage walls. There are letters from friends and lines from poems tacked to the mirror. Paintings and scraps of drawings litter the fireplace. My collection of shells and teeth and bits of plastic from the beach is strewn across the table. I have wreaths made from wildflowers drying out on the hearth. I haven't thought about how any of this will look to someone else. My identity is my own here. He walks around slowly, smoking and taking it all in. I shiver.

'Cold, isn't it?' I mutter, pulling the sleeves of my jumper over my wrists. He isn't paying attention. He picks up a letter and a few others float into the fireplace.

'You seem like kind of a lost person,' he says to me. I frown at the wall, unsure of the correct reply.

'Can I kiss you?' he asks, reaching for me.

'Okay,' I reply, caught in his body heat.

12

We often went to the pub after tea and Josh and I would race up and down the port with the other kids while my grandfather supped Jameson and men with rough hands and lined faces lingered around my mother, savouring her English accent.

I befriended two brothers who lived in the fishing port. They stole money from the barman's tip jar and pushed it over the sweet shop counter with sugary smiles. We sat on piles of bricks behind the abandoned coastguard station and they pressed squares of Fry's peppermint chocolate into my hands. It tasted sweeter because they had stolen it for me.

One afternoon they magicked an unsupervised beer keg from somewhere and we hit it with bricks until we broke the seal on the top. It spurted from the mouth in golden arcs and we shrieked and pushed each other under the spray, delighting in the sticky, hoppy thrill of it.

13

One night a strange man turned up at our rented cottage in the middle of fish fingers.

'How's it going?' He smiled at us awkwardly from the doorway. 'Just came to see if the wee'uns might fancy a trip out on the boat tomorrow.' My mother ran her hand through her hair as we eyeballed him behind mashed potato mountains.

'That would be lovely.' She cracked open a bottle of beer and handed it to him. 'What do you think, Lucy? This is Patrick. He's a fisherman.'

'Yes, please,' I mumbled. Patrick winked.

'And what about the wee man?'

'Say hello to Patrick, love,' my mother said with her lips, kissing Josh on the top of his head. 'Be nice.' She signed in secret with her hands. Josh blew a raspberry. I liked the look of Patrick. He had naughty eyes and a tobaccoey kind of softness. Showing off in front of him, I poked Josh in his side. He knocked his plate over in a rage and orange beans splattered across the tablecloth. I snorted. Josh slipped from his chair and made a dash for the back door.

'Oh, no you don't!' quipped Patrick, slipping his hands under Josh's armpits. Josh screamed a white scream and my mother dropped the dishes in shock. Patrick paled and tossed his cigarette into the garden. He had accidentally stubbed the smouldering tip on my brother's arm. We all looked at it for a second, until my mother swooped down and scooped Josh up, jamming him under the cold tap. He screamed louder. Patrick hopped from foot to foot.

'Fuck,' he said. 'I'm so sorry.'

'It's okay, baby,' my mother said to Josh, holding his trembling body close to hers. His skin puckered like a surprised kiss. There was a strange feeling in the kitchen, as though something had happened that could never be reversed.

14

I think of the day we stole the beer keg. I remember how afterwards my T-shirt stank of lager and I was scared to tell my mother because I thought I'd be in trouble. I went into the pub and saw her standing at the bar. A man had his arm around her waist and the afternoon light fell in shafts through her hair, turning it copper.

15

'Do you remember the beer keg?' I breathe, as we move gently to the cottage floor. I can taste the bitter chocolate and feel the fountain of gold raining down onto me. I picture a hairy hand hooked under my mother's belt loops. I think of the sunlight dripping through the beer and remember how illicit it felt, and how exciting.

16

Things were different when Patrick was around. My grandfather came over to watch us in the evenings, his pockets stuffed full of clove sweets. I relished the bitterness of them, the way they tasted medicinal and lovely all at once. They made me feel grown-up, which was a feeling I was beginning to crave. My mother locked herself in the mouldy bathroom and steams and creams seeped under the door, smelling of faraway places. She did her make-up in the hallway mirror, her face shiny from the shower.

'Which shoes, Lucy pet?' she wondered, pulling up the cuffs of her boot-cut jeans to reveal a chunky mule on her left foot and a delicate sandal on her right. I lay on my stomach beside her feet, tracing my fingers along the gold straps and polishing the nail varnish she had pasted over the cracks with my spit.

'The sandals,' I declared, fingering a buckle. A car horn sounded outside and she shooed me away, shrugging her denim jacket onto her shoulders.

'I'm off, Dad,' she called in the direction of the sitting room. 'Call me if Josh needs anything. Bed at nine, remember, Luce. I won't be back late.' My grandfather raised his eyebrows and kept his mouth shut. I heard the car pull away and lingered in the cloud of her perfume.

My mother and father didn't sleep in the same bed any more and the boundaries between them seemed blurred. I wasn't sure whether or not they were together, or what that meant, or whether it mattered. My mother's freedom made me light but the spell was punctured by the thought of my dad passed out somewhere, his calloused, dirty fingers twitching into sleep.

17

I think about the man when I am home alone. He is Red Bull and cheap cigarettes. He swirls my thoughts in his glass with a straw and they dissolve into the night. All the tight, closed parts of myself drift away in his mouth like sand in the wind. I listen to my body and I let her do what she wants. Here is a space for her to grow, up into all that sky.

18

Hands raw with mooring rope and stubble rashes on soft cheeks. Aftershave and morning sweat and smells that are not our smells spilling onto bedsheets. Creaking springs and strange gasps in the night seep scarlet through my summer. The sun coaxes sunspots from your shoulders and strange lips kiss them in ways that are unfamiliar to me. He slips his fingers into our days with a pace that makes me green. I want your skin soft just for me. His hand falls in and out of yours too easily. I know he is not hungry enough to hold onto us.

19

News travels fast in this small place. Neighbours rustle curtains and turn on driveway lights in the night. They take note of cars, and hours, and at what time the blinds are rolled up. They see us drinking whiskey in Jimmy's, note my unkempt hair, the candles flickering at my window well into the dawn.

There are smirks in the post office and eyes lowered in the street. The owner of the shop across the road twinkles at me in the morning. Paranoia pricks my edges.

'Like mother like daughter,' I think I overhear someone say, but I cannot remember exactly who, or where, or when.

20

Types of fish I'd never heard of started creeping onto our kitchen table in the evenings. We tasted monkfish, light and round on our tongues like balls of cotton wool, and briny mackerel that left a sheen of oil streaked across our lips. There were crab shells served with teaspoons whose insides we scooped out and soft salmon that fell apart on our tongues without chewing. One night Patrick turned up with a live lobster and popped it into the pan, laughing at my horrified face as it squealed in the boiling water, struggling to free itself from the elastic bands tied tightly around its claws.

'Pass us the salt, will you, babe?' Patrick winked at my mother. She passed the jumbo-sized table salt over to him, its lid crusty with ketchup. He leaned over and kissed her and she pulled away, looking meaningfully towards me. I stared at the lobster as it stopped struggling.

Patrick showed us how to break the shell and slurp the tender meat from the bottom of the claws, where it was the sweetest. The kitchen was steamy and our faces were pink.

'What do you think, Lucy baby?' My mother stroked my hair.

'Delicious,' I told her. Bile rose in my throat. Bits of lobster shell littered my plate, broken and inconsequential. I couldn't imagine how it could ever have contained the lobster, scuttling from predators beneath the sea. It seemed too fragile to keep anything safe.

21

He leaves traces of oil and dirt on my sheets. I like smells that are heavy and industrial, reminiscent of building sites.

I wrap myself up in his smell for nights on end. I dream of chimneys with smoke billowing out of them in grey clouds and feel safe.

It is not lost on me that I desire this man who smells of oil and metal, a smell that has always coated the edges of things. It is the smell of the north-east, of the factories and the warehouses, the cobbles and the terraced houses and the low, heavy skies. It is the smell of my dad at the end of the day. I think of my mother growing up by the shipyards and marrying an electrician. I think of Patrick tying his boat to the dock and my grandfather building tunnels beneath the sea. I imagine their hands reaching out across the years to grab her, silvered and sore.

The man reaches over to hold me in the night and I roll away and sleep against the damp wall. My life is very removed from the cogs and machines that brought me into being but they are somewhere deep inside of me, scaffolds stacked around my core.

22

This afternoon, I go to buy some milk from the small shop by my house. As I am standing in the queue, I realise that Patrick is standing in front of me. I study him closely. He still wears the same old work boots with faded orange laces. I look at the tattoo of a Hawaiian dancer sticking out of the sleeve of his T-shirt; the same figure I ran my small fingers over in fascination countless times as a child.

When he flexes his bicep he can make her dance. I breathe in his smell, oil and cigarettes. He brushes my shoulder accidentally as he leaves.

'Sorry,' he mutters, without recognition.

23

We sit in Jimmy's watching the day die through the window.

'Are you hungry?' he asks me.

'Mmmm,' I say. 'Not really. Are you?'

'Starving. Chuck us a menu.' I hand it over to him and he scans the list with his eyes.

'Crab claws,' he declares. 'Have you had them before?'

'Yeah,' I tell him. 'But years ago. I don't eat fish now. I'm a vegetarian.' He rolls his eyes.

'Suit yourself,' he says, and goes up to order.

The crab claws arrive arranged in a flower and seasoned with garlic. He holds one up to my face.

'Have one,' he tells me. 'Go on.' I look at the crab claw and I look at the delicate hairs on his arms. I think about my dinners in London; sad bowls of lentils and chickpeas seasoned with vegetable stock. I want to learn abundance; how to have things without fear.

I meet the man's eyes and take the crab claw from his fingers. I bite into the flesh and tear it with my teeth. He looks at me with interest. I suck and chew and it is like the sea in my mouth. A whole world comes flooding back to me, a time when I ran freely over beaches in shorts and T-shirts and was hungry for things and ate sausage sandwiches, ketchup dripping down my chin. I remember the giddiness of my mother growing young and alive again.

'Well?' he asks, smirking.

'Good.' I blush.

'Have another.' He pushes the plate in front of me. My bare arm brushes against his and both of our hands are dripping garlic and something is shifting with the tides.

24

I am weightless in the water. Light falls in shapes and salt stings my eyes, wet-cold and sun-dappled. I spit silt from my lips and feel the ocean floor under my feet, hard and reassuring. Scrape my knees over rocks and soothe nettle spots in the spray. Fingernails digging into bodyboard foam and the giddy of the waves moving under me. Eyelashes leaking light prisms and limbs trickling gold. I run straight to you from the water. Brush my feet before socks with my Ariel towel. I shriek at the grit of it but I like the safe of your fingers, slippery warm between my toes.

25

My mother leaped out of bed in the mornings with an itinerary of things to see and do; beaches to lie on and great-aunts to visit, the sunlight caught in her hair and on the glittery letters emblazoned across her T-shirt. Josh and I sneaked Nutella for breakfast and drank Coca-Cola at teatime, getting caught up in the sweet heat that seeped from her as she pencilled her eyebrows at the table next to us, pursing her lips into a hand-held mirror. Something ached in my belly when she kissed Patrick chewily on our beach towels, his big hand resting on the small of her exposed back.

'How would you feel about moving here, Luce?' she asked me one afternoon as we walked back from the garage with 99 ice creams, balancing sherbet sprinkles and monkey's blood expertly along the dirt path to our cottage.

'Moving here?' I looked at her. 'But what about school?'

'You could go to school here. You'd get to learn Irish.' I made a thinking noise and bit off the end of my cone, sucking the ice cream down through the hole.

'Could I get a dog?'

'Yeah, I've been thinking about that. A nice sheepdog, maybe. You and Josh could take her for walks on the beach.'

'And what about Dad?' Hurt prickled my mother's face like a rash. She pulled a wheatgrass stem from the ground and shed its head into her palm.

'I don't know, Lucy,' she said, sadly. 'He'll always love you though, you know that, don't you?' I shrugged and crunched my Flake between my teeth.

'Come on,' she said. 'We'd better get back. Josh's ice cream is melting.' I trailed after her through the long grass, wondering how it would feel to have a sheepdog bounding along next to us. I thought of bungalows in cosy cul-de-sacs, of ballet shoes on cold Saturday mornings, and of my new secondary school uniform hanging inside my wardrobe at home, waiting for me to slip into it.

26

In my life in Donegal, I am learning how to take what I want. There are unfulfilled desires, curdled inside of me. I have buried things; swallowed them down and turned off the light. I must learn how to listen to my body again. I must learn how to need, how to ask, how to want.

27

My grandfather didn't understand Josh. Left alone in the world by his parents and raised by nuns, he resented the sensitivity with which we treated my brother's outbursts.

'You need to show him some discipline, Susie,' he said from his wooden chair during one of our visits, as my mother dealt with a tantrum.

One afternoon, we all went down to Jimmy's. Josh and I played with bubble guns in the car park outside, showing off to the local kids as Fairy Liquid rainbows burst over us. After a few pints, my granddad turned sour and started to berate my mother for her treatment of Josh.

'You're not hard enough on him,' he told her. 'He can sense that you're weak and he takes advantage of it.'

'But Dad, he's got difficulties,' my mother answered. 'He needs my help.'

'He needs a firm hand.' My grandfather slammed his palm onto the table. 'A different kind of mother could handle it. You're much too soft.'

My mother looked at him in silence. She thought of the weeks and months she had spent alone in hospital waiting rooms with Josh. She pictured my dad, sleeping under a tree in the park. She remembered her mother hiding in the bathroom, as curses seeped through the lock. She picked up her pint and poured it slowly over my grandfather's head.

'Susie!' he spluttered. 'What the bloody fuck?' My mother got to her feet and came outside to find us. The men at the bar cheered as she walked out.

28

I can remember far more of my childhood during those summers in Ireland than at home in Sunderland. I remember our summers with startling clarity, like the edges of polished quartz, whereas my schooldays are blurred beneath rain-clouds and climbing frames. An undercurrent of darkness, gilded in magic. I believed in both of those things.

29

Rutland Island is visible from the fishing port. There are a few stone houses huddled together, forming Duck Street. For one day and night every summer there was a party on the street. People piled into boats and were ferried across the water by old men in yellow overalls and teenage boys in tracksuit bottoms, their bare chests shallow in the sea spray. The festival folk band showed up with top hats and magic crystals, wielding guitars and fiddles. They set up their drum kit in the middle of the street. Everyone flung their front doors open and people went from house to house, necking shots of whiskey and winking their way through cold beers, their smiles slipping and sliding across their faces in the summer fug. My mother and Patrick chatted with friends arm in arm as Josh and I hung around the band with the other kids, dying for a turn on the drums. Someone released a bunch of yellow balloons across the island and they floated into people's houses.

Tents were put up as night began to fall, and everyone huddled in someone's kitchen to keep out of the cold. A drunken silence fell and people began to sing and play instruments. An old man recited a poem about a fishing boat lost at sea and everyone clapped. The band sang a capella and people grew pink and misty-eyed. There was a lull in the entertainment and my mother piped up.

'Lucy can play the fiddle.' I was having lessons at school. I looked at her in horror and shook my head.

'Come on, wee'un,' someone called from an armchair. 'Let us see what you've got.' I sucked a sherbet lemon and brushed sleep from my eyes.

'I haven't got it with me,' I mumbled. Patrick winked.

'There's one up at the pub,' he said, pulling on his jacket. 'I'll take you over on the boat to get it, sure.' I looked at my mother uncertainly.

'Go on,' she urged, smoothing my hair away from my face. I buttoned up my cardigan and walked with Patrick into the dark. He swayed unsteadily on the rocks at the edge of the island as he untied the boat. The lights from the fishing port spangled in the distance.

'In you hop!' he said, helping me over the side as it bucked below us. He started the engine and we took off without speaking, listening to the water bubble and gulp as we cut across it. The sky was thick and heavy and there wasn't a single star. I shivered at the scope of the darkness, enjoying the weight of Patrick's jacket around my shoulders, warm and smelling of cigarettes. The sea was spilt syrup and the night was ours.

30

The man and I go for a long walk along the beach. It is wet and windy and we hope the cold air will blow our hangovers away. It is getting dark and everything is a different shade of grey. It becomes hard to distinguish grass from rocks and sand and sea from sky.

'Do you feel like we're walking on the moon?' I ask him.

'If we were on the moon then we'd be walking like this,' he says, taking wide steps along the shore. We moonwalk all the way back to the car as stars appear around us.

31

There is something between us that was not there before. Loose secrets in the dark and the snag of you pulling away from me. His hands threaded through yours in a shade of red that is strange. Your body, puckered and sore. His lips, chapped and hungry. Things you do not want me to know. You are turning away from me, tucking us into places I do not want to go.

32

At the end of the summer we packed up our car and drove home, shyly leaving sticky kisses in my grandfather's stubble and promising to call him on Sundays.

'You be good now, Lucy,' he called to me as we pulled out of his drive. 'You're our wee hope.' I drew angels in the condensation on the car windows as Josh snored in his booster seat.

'Stop it, Lucy love,' said my mother. 'You're only making more work for me.'

It was a long drive from the ferry and we passed the time by playing 'The Mile Game.' My mother watched the miles slide away on her milometer and it was my job to shout when I thought one had passed.

We were less than a hundred miles from home when it began to get dark. My mother saw the sign for Scotch Corner and she pulled into the services and turned off the ignition. Josh woke up and blinked in the dusk.

'Can we get McDonald's, Mam?' he asked from the back seat. My mother put her head on the steering wheel and started to cry. I watched the freckles on her arms quiver with the force of her sobs.

'Mam?' I pulled at the neck of my T-shirt and looked at Josh. She wiped her eyes and spoke from behind a tissue.

'I don't want to go back, Lucy love,' she mumbled.

'It's okay, Mam,' I said, smelling the end of the summer through the open window. 'We can go to Ireland again, next holidays.'

'I want to go back now,' she said. 'Come on, let's turn around. We can get back on the ferry. We could stay with your granddad for a while. He won't mind.' I looked at her.

'But we've driven all this way.' Josh undid his seatbelt and started to clamber over the gearstick and onto my knee.

'Josh!' I groaned as his fingers slipped between my ribs and jabbed at my soft insides.

'I want to go home, Mam,' I said quietly as she checked for smudged mascara in the rear-view mirror. She exhaled through her nose.

'I know, Luce,' she said, sadly. 'I know. We've got to go home, really. Come on. Josh, get back in your seat.' We shoved and squabbled back onto the motorway as the cat's eyes spluttered into life. I kept my eye on the milometer, silently counting the miles as they fell behind us into the night, leading us closer to home.

33

There is a wind turbine at the end of the fishing port. I like that wherever I am, whether in town or at the beach, I can use it to orient myself. In the early days when I was drunk in London, I used the Strata tower with the windmills in Elephant and Castle as my marker. Later, it became the Shard. I feel an affinity with the Shard, even though it is a symbol of the wealth and status I am so far removed from. It was just an idea when I first arrived there and it grew up into the city at the same rate I did. I like that I can remember a time when it did not exist. It is proof that time is moving forward, especially during those days when I am sliding backwards.

34

My mother started disappearing. She pressed a wad of five-pound notes into my palm, 'For lunches and anything you might need. No sweets, mind.'

'Where are you going?'

'To a wedding with your Auntie Marie. Your dad'll be here. Look after Josh. You can call me any time, day or night.'

'Even the middle of the night?'

'Even the middle of the night. But you should be asleep by then.' She pulled me close to her and I gulped down the smell of her Elizabeth Arden make-up.

When my mother was away the rules were relaxed. I could wear whatever I wanted and we were allowed to eat chocolate for breakfast. My father picked me up from school with his sunglasses on, blasting the Beautiful South from the wound-down windows. The other kids watched jealously as I flung my lunch box onto his back seat.

One night as we sat down to eat our tea, my father solemnly served himself my brother's hamster onto his plate. He picked up his knife and fork and made as though to cut off its head. Josh began to scream.

'Lucy!' he shouted. 'Lucy! Make him stop!' I rolled my eyes at them but inside I was uneasy. My dad snorted.

'Hamster is a delicacy in loads of countries, you know.' He held the quivering ball of fur in his palm. Josh's wails made my brain pulse behind my eyes.

'That's not really funny, Dad,' I said, lowering my eyes. I took the hamster from him and held it close to my chest. I felt its frantic heart thudding against my own. I returned the hamster to its cage haughtily and signed to Josh that it was all a joke. That tiny heartbeat settled in my bones for the rest of the evening, making me dizzy.

I woke in the middle of the night to go to the toilet and found my father passed out on the sitting room floor in front of the fire, a can of Carlsberg leaking into the carpet. I picked it up and quietly stood it on the fireplace, leaving the spillage to seep into the rug.

35

I am becoming a person who does her own things. Things that no one else knows. Roller-skating down hills on one foot like a pink flamingo, daring my bones to shatter. Hiding in other people's gardens, peeking in at the yellow fuzz of their teatimes through half-closed curtains. Scribbled stick-men on skirting boards and earrings stolen and tucked under pillows. I do things alone now, without you. I want to be close and I want to be distant. I push my fingers so far into the soil in the garden that the fleshy webs between them ache. I am seeing how far I can go.

36

When I go into a shop or garage to pick up firelighters or matches, people realise that I am a stranger. They zip up their raincoats and rattle their car keys. They look at me with interest and ask, 'Who do you belong to, then?'

Ancestry is very important here. It is something to do with the landscape. Sometimes the wind is so strong that it is a struggle just to walk up the road. The trees and grasses are fat and rubbery. It is impossible to snap their stems with your hands. They have evolved to be tough in order to survive. If people didn't anchor themselves to something it would be easy to get lost in the scope of the sky and the sea. The links between families are lights strung through the trees in the dark.

Most people I know in London are preoccupied with reinventing themselves. It is difficult to do that in a place where everyone can see your lineage. Are ownership and belonging inextricably bound? Can I belong without being owned? Do I have to own the things that belong to me?

37

I called my mother from the house phone the night she was due back.

'When will you be home?' I asked her. I could hear the thrum of music and glasses clinking in the background.

Strange laughter leaked silkily into my ear as I strained for the sound of her voice.

'Mam?'

'It'll be late tonight, Lucy baby. Tuck yourself into bed and I'll be there in the morning. I love you. See you soon.'

'Love you, too,' I mumbled to the dialling tone.

I burrowed into the centre of my bed and watched patterns bloom across the surface of my eyes as I strained to see in the purple-dark. I could hear my father crashing around, opening and closing cupboards. It made me uneasy. He usually spent his evenings smoking quietly in front of the fire and taking gadgets apart then putting them back together, listening to the Specials with the telly on mute.

I got up.

'Dad?' I started, hovering around the kitchen door in my nightie.

'What is it, Luce?' he asked, rustling bin bags.

'I can't sleep.'

'Go back to bed and give it a try, eh? Your mam'll be back soon.' A lit cigarette dangled from his lips. My mother never let him smoke in the house. There were coat hangers splayed in the hallway at awkward angles.

'What are you doing?'

'Just having a bit of a clear-up before your mam gets back.'

I lingered.

'Off you go, Luce.' There was an unnerving brightness in his eyes. I felt something settling in the air.

I woke to my mother's hand on my cheek, cold and smelling of aeroplanes.

'Lucy?' she whispered, stroking my nose. I untangled myself from my sheets and turned to look at her. Her face was creased. 'Where's your dad?' she asked. I shook dreams from my hair and squinted in the dark.

'What do you mean? He was in the kitchen. I don't know. I've been asleep.'

'He's not here, love,' she breathed. 'What time did you go to bed?' I threw off my duvet and gave her a hug.

'I can't remember.' My mother sighed and left my bedroom. I followed her, hankering after her softness.

The hallway was bright after the dark in my room. The front door was open and the night crept into our house and filled it. I went to close the door and my mother came after me.

'I'll get it, Lucy—' she started, but I was already at the handle. I looked out at the street. My father's car was gone. In its place in front of our house was a pile of bin liners, dark and heavy in the moonlight. I looked at my mother. She seemed older than I remembered.

'Come on, then,' she whispered, taking my hand in hers. 'Help me get them in, eh?' I padded after her into the street in my bare feet, enjoying the tingle of the pavement between my toes. As we got closer to the bin liners I saw that some of them were split open. Her lacy knickers were in the gutter with the moss and the crisp packets.

'Your clothes!' I gasped. She nodded, sadly.

'Yeah,' she said. 'All my things.'

I squeezed her hand. 'They look so sad.'

'Don't be silly.' She picked up her knickers and stuffed them into her pocket. 'Clothes can't be sad. It's only stuff, you know.' I helped her carry the bin liners into the house and hung her flowery dresses and turtleneck jumpers back in the wardrobe where they belonged.

38

I started secondary school, self-conscious in my too-long skirt with my too-smooth ponytail. I watched my reflection in the dining hall window as hundreds of kids shouted and pinched limp chips from plastic trays.

Having a school bag was uncool. You were supposed to fold your exercise books in half so that they would fit in your blazer pocket, leaving your hands free to unwrap cherry drops or smoke cigarettes behind the science block. Rockport boots were for kicking people in the ankles as you passed them in the corridors, or if you wanted to be subversive you could wear a backpack with the straps lengthened to capacity so it banged against the backs of your knees. Charver or Sweaty, Griebo or Goth, Spice Boy or Skater. You had to choose your tribe and stick with it.

Rosie and I lurked around the hippy shop in the shopping centre after school and bought a smattering of star-shaped studs to press into our tote bags to declare our side. They wouldn't fasten into the fabric properly and they caught our skin, tearing fresh wounds in our hands whenever we reached down to get our Maths books.

The PE changing rooms required a different language altogether. Shy of each other's bodies, we kept our eyes on the ceiling, not wanting to be accused of staring at another person, even though we were all dying to. Girls with soft bellies pranced flagrantly in neon bras while others with cautious mothers changed in and out of sports tops. Some girls took their clothes into the toilet cubicles and changed in there, while others rolled their eyes and whispered about them.

Our PE lessons were comprised of shivering on the

netball court, fingertips throbbing when the ball inevitably bounced off them or traipsing around the park at the back of the school wearing pedometers to record our progress. We quickly figured out that you could increase the step count by shaking them, so instead we sat on the benches in the cold, munching Discos and pinching tokes from each other's tabs. I got into the habit of conveniently forgetting my kit every week so that I could sit in a warm classroom and dash out my punishment essay in ten minutes and spend the rest of the hour doodling flowers and surreptitiously reading my *Kerrang!* magazine, hoping that one of the boys in the year above would walk past the window and notice.

39

So many bodies. Bulges and lumps in places I didn't even know about. My body is prickly and we are finding new ways to define ourselves. We cut our hair and roll up our skirts. We paint our nails and play with clear mascara, all eyelash curlers and lip gloss in the toilets. There are so many things we can and cannot do. You take me bra shopping and I pull off my top for the lady. My nipples are round and soft. I am measured by cold hands and we choose little blue bras to match my school blouse. No underwire for I am too new. You tell me no one ever did this for you, so you want to do it for me. Afterwards we share Thorntons toffees. We suck all the chocolate off in the car, our hands touching in the bag by the gearstick. You always let me have the biggest piece.

40

My friend Alex calls me from London. He swings his legs over the windowsill of his single room and smokes as he talks to me. I can hear traffic hurtling by on the road beneath him and his neighbours laughing and calling to each other. I sit in my garden so I can get a signal. It is so cold I am wearing three jumpers. London seems artificial and trivial when juxtaposed against the gnarled trees and the heavy, unmoving rocks. The sounds from Alex's world set my nerves on edge, like a television left on somewhere, just out of reach. Alex tells me about his latest romantic endeavours, and I try to tell him about mine, but I feel strangely guarded. My world here is my own and I don't want anything to shatter it.

41

At Easter we went back to Ireland. Josh and I watched cartoons from the carpet as Patrick glowered in his armchair, a nicotine stink coating his hair and settling in the lines on his face. Everything in his house was brown. The carpets were patterned in rotten flowers and the curtains hung heavy and tired at the windows. His furniture was made from cheap stained wood and crucifixes hung askew on the yellowing walls. I tensed my muscles under a scratchy blanket at night as their bed creaked and damp seeped through the walls. I read Jacqueline Wilson books under the covers until my eyes ached, painstakingly copying the illustrations into my fluffy notebook.

During the day, Patrick sulked in front of the telly nursing cans of Guinness while my mother took Josh and me for long walks on the beach, zipping our coats against the wind and determinedly lighting a disposable barbecue in the drizzle. We sat in the boot with our legs dangling into the car park, eating sausages wrapped in sugary buns, our ankles prickling with goose pimples. We stayed out as long as we could and then crept into the brown house, clamouring for bubble baths to wash the cold away.

42

Things can break inside of me without me knowing. There is pain in places I have never felt before. I am brown and earthy and we are back in that deep, dark space together. You hand me sanitary towels, soft and strange, and tuck me up gently and explain about bodies. I am hot and sore all over. People treat me differently, in shops and pubs and post offices. They can smell the bitter redness in my knickers.

43

My friend Alex says that when he is romantically involved with a person, he gives them small pieces of himself to keep. He says he gives away too much of himself to others but I think that perhaps I do not give enough. I do not have a surplus of self. I cannot afford to give parts away.

44

One night Josh got carried away with his plastic boat and let the taps run for too long. The water spilled over the sides of the bath and pooled on the bathroom floor. It seeped through the floorboards and dripped guiltily into the sitting room where Patrick and my mother sat on the settee. My mother rushed upstairs and tried the bathroom door. It was locked and Josh couldn't wear his cochlear implant in the bath, so he didn't hear her. She rattled the handle, tensing at the sound of Patrick behind her on the stairs.

'That's fucking enough!' he shouted, ramming the door with his shoulder. It burst open and Josh looked up at them from beneath wet curls, his pink mouth puckered in surprise. Patrick yanked him out of the bath by his arm and marched him into his bedroom. His slippery body slithered out of Patrick's grasp.

'Patrick!' gasped my mother. Josh started to scream. Patrick slapped his bottom and the sting of it filled the whole house. He banged Josh's bedroom door and turned the key in the lock, leaving Josh in there alone. My mother flew down the stairs after him.

'How dare you!' she shouted. The front door slammed and Patrick was gone.

We packed up the car and left the next morning. When we were seatbelted in and ready to go, my mother handed me a small blue jewellery box. 'Pop that through the letterbox, will you, love?' she asked me.

'What is it?'

'Never you mind.'

I did as I was told then buckled myself in, my stack of books for the journey heavy in my lap. My mother was thin-lipped. I knew better than to ask questions. I swallowed and opened my notebook as the pubs and bogs blurred into mountains.

45

I walk past the house I stayed in as a child, when I came on holiday with my mother to visit Patrick. It is empty now. There are broken Christmas lights hanging from the gutters and the garage door swings in the wind. Grimy lace curtains are heaped on the windowsills. I walk up the driveway and around the corner into the back garden. When I was small, there were wild kittens living in the turf shed and I balanced saucers of milk in my hands as brambles tore my pedal-pushers. The garden looks exactly the same. There are mouldy ropes lurking in the grass like snakes and a mildewed tea towel caught in the bushes, swollen with rainwater.

46

What is this little flower? White and creamy. Hard and guilty. Into the swimming pool where the sunlight dances, caught between schooldays and weekends. Caught between me and someone new. Surplus skin spills from the tops of school trousers. Little muffin tops. I didn't know bodies were important until now. In the spaces where you and me used to be there is a new language. I watch you flick your hair and I push out my chest and you stand me straight against the kitchen wall to improve my posture. You explain ladies' sizes and teach me how to hide things in layers. My nipples prickle inside of my T-shirt, pink with possibility.

47

I carefully noted my mother's movements, storing them safely inside of me. I sensed that I would need them somewhere in the future. I watched the downward slope of her eyebrows as she checked her reflection in the rear-view mirror and the nonchalant arch of her hand in her hair as the guards at the ferry port checked our car for stowaways. I memorised the curves of her calf muscles and the Coral Kisses on her fingertips, chipped and bordered by hangnails. There was a wildness in her that scared me. I envied it. I breathed in her skin as she reached over me to grab her bottle of Diet Coke, flat and sour from too long in the car.

48

I try to remember what we were like here. My mother younger and full of fire and Josh with his angel curls. I think of Patrick in his lighter days, chasing me around the garden with a cigarette in his mouth, skinny and funny and spluttering expletives. I look for the remnants of my younger self through the window, curled up on a bed scribbling in a notebook or turning cartwheels through the grass in a pair of denim shorts. I cannot find her.

49

When we arrived home, my mother couldn't fit her key in the lock on our front door.

'What the...?' She jiggled it around, but it was no use. 'I don't believe it.' We munched Skips in the car until the locksmith came. Josh and I squabbled on the back seat.

'Christ,' said the locksmith when he finally turned up. He looked my mother up and down. 'Some bastard's gone and filled it with superglue.'

50

I walk along the beach and watch the waves drift forwards and backwards then backwards and forwards. I don't have a job. I don't have a partner. I don't have anything to anchor me anywhere. I make my decisions based on chemical impulses. I feel the pull of particular places in the lining of my stomach.

Sometimes I ache to watch the afternoon leak onto a particular street or crave the sticky smell of a specific corner of a certain pub in a particular city. Sometimes, places I have never visited before take hold of me and I imagine I can see the light on the paving stones and taste the water from the taps. There is a lot of freedom in not having anchors, but sometimes I think it would be nice to have a reason to be somewhere.

51

I came home from school one day with something bubbling beneath my blouse. I twirled my hair in the steamy kitchen as I pushed my lips into shapes, trying to figure out how to frame the words that would give me the answer I wanted. In the end I just blurted it out.

'Can I get my belly button pierced?'

My mother gave me a long look. I licked lip gloss from my lips with a nervy tongue. She raised her eyebrows.

'Yeah, alright,' she said. 'Should I get mine done, too?'

We made an appointment at a cheap beauty salon and held hands as a stern woman with orange fingers pushed a large needle through the soft centres of our bellies.

'How old is she?' the woman asked my mother afterwards.

'Thirteen,' I replied, quickly. She flashed an understanding smile at my mam and I felt left out. We walked out of the salon with our tops rolled up, midriffs winking at the passing cars. Our belly buttons stung as we climbed onto the high stools in McDonald's. My mother touched my arm as I dipped my fries in ketchup.

'It seems symbolic of something, doesn't it, Luce?' she said, rolling down her T-shirt. 'It's a new start, isn't it? Me, you, and Josh. Just the three of us.' I smiled at her as I stuffed the empty wrappers into my Happy Meal box, leaving the free toy to be thrown out with the rubbish.

My belly-button piercing coincided with the stares of boys from school lingering on my skin when I boarded the bus, as though they could see right through my school blouse and into my navel to that small precious promise of the future.

52

There are parts of you I want for myself. I want to feel the shape of your hips fill out mine. I run my fingers along the lids of your nail polishes, craving Peach Sunset and Tropical Bliss. I slip your bracelets on and off my wrists; bigger and better than mine. I want to drip the eyes of strangers down my spine the way that you do. I want to paint myself new in Revlon and Rimmel. I cram your blusher brushes in my pockets, rosy with secrets.

53

All over Donegal there are abandoned, overgrown cottages. Some of them are shells built from crumbling stones and others are intact with vases and bottles of holy water rotting on windowsills and brambles creeping into crevices.

Often, they are run-down family homes. Their newly built replacements stand beside them, freshly plastered and insulated with flat-screen televisions winking through the double glazing. Others seem much more desolate, as though a lonely old person passed away and their families live too far away to make returning worthwhile. When I first arrived here I was puzzled by these houses, rusting in the wind. I wondered why they weren't demolished. I thought that it was better to get rid of old things, rather than letting them loom in the present like mournful relics.

The answer is space. There is so much space here that there is no need to reduce old things to rubble. There is sentimentality somewhere in the history and there is something important in observing the way that nature takes over. At first, I thought that a reluctance to relinquish the past was a refusal to acknowledge the passing of time. Now I understand it more as a symbol of temporality and a reminder that there are layers of lived experience criss-crossing the surfaces of our lives, invisible to us. There is room for everything here. There are traces of the past in the present and there is space for the future, too.

54

The internet moved at a rapid pace and everyone I knew rushed home after school to sit in front of the peculiar electric of their dial-up connection to gossip through Myspace and MSN Messenger. I trawled through profiles for the kind of person I wanted to be, saving pictures of emo scenesters with leopard-print hair and cutting and pasting sepia indie girls with dolly beads clasped around their necks. I figured out the right brands of skate shoes and impatiently downloaded discographies on LimeWire, gleaned from trawling through someone's 'Likes' section. Music assuaged some of the chaos brewing inside of me and the boys wearing girls' clothes made me excited, as though boundaries were something that could be broken.

55

Sparks in the air everywhere I turn. Hair cropped on the back of a neck and a trembling hand. Blushing cheeks. Skin is shiny and armpits are sweaty and eyes are lurking everywhere. The boys at school play a game where they run their hands up our thighs and we try not to flinch. I am the best at this game. I can go very far without moving even though I am jelly inside. Can they sense the prickly heat in my knickers? I even think I like it. Breasts quiver under school shirts and everything feels tight. We are bursting into new shapes. The brush of a finger and I'm neon all over. You try to hold me but I will not let you now. I am on fire. Do not come into the bathroom when

I am having a bath. I am all locked doors and hours in mirrors. I shave my legs and pluck my eyebrows into nothing because that's what ladies do. You teach me to look after my body. Face wash and creams and deodorants. Spots are bad and sweat is worse and we must keep our bodies under control. There is a girl in our class who smells. No one has told her to wash under her armpits. She has no one to iron her clothes. We keep away from her and titter in corners. We don't want to end up like that.

56

I don't get much phone signal in my cottage due to the thick stone walls. My friends and I communicate through Whats-App voice messages. There is something nice about having their voices stored in my palm, to be turned on at will. Hearing their words fill the room makes me feel less alone.

It is interesting to listen back to my own replies. I notice the pauses and repetitions and colloquialisms I use, and how I often seem to have trouble expressing what I want to say. It is similar to looking at your own Facebook profile, which seems narcissistic but is actually just a way of trying to find a sense of yourself and comparing the way you feel to the way that others see you.

There is something nostalgic about listening to the voice notes. I smile and laugh as my friends tell me anecdotes; instinctively, as though we are having a conversation. My facial expression changes according to their joy or sadness and it is as though we are experiencing the emotion together, even though for them it has already passed.

Sometimes I can hear the sound of traffic and people in the background. More than once, I have moved out of the road to make way for a passing car, only to realise that it is the recording and I am moving out of the way for a car driving in the past, hundreds of miles away.

57

I watched the boys in the year above as they skulked around school with guitars on their backs. Girls with dyed hair and heavy fringes carved shapes into their arms with compasses stolen from the Maths classroom. They held lighters to their wounds so that when the scabs fell off their skin would scar in heartagrams. I begged my mother for a pair of pink Converse All Stars. We went shopping one night after school and the next day I raced home from the bus stop to open my wardrobe and look at them in their box all rubbery with promise. They were a passport into a different kind of life.

I got into trouble at school for wearing nail varnish and drawing all over my exercise books, but my grades were good and they redeemed me when I was called out too many times for chatting in class. I counted down the periods to English in secret. Books sent a terrible heat through me that I didn't want anyone to know about. When I was asked to read out loud I struggled to feign disinterest and keep my voice at the socially acceptable monotone. Writing essays and stories took the knot out of my stomach and unspooled it across the page. When I wrote, it was with an invisible part of myself; a lambent secret that only my teachers knew about. Reading made me feel like I was standing on the precipice of something very tall, and I suspected that one day I would jump off the edge of it.

58

For a time in London, I spent most days with the architect. He sat up late at the kitchen table designing buildings on his laptop. His strong lines and sharp corners slotted into place. They grew upwards and outwards, night by night, while I pulled pints and turned in on myself, like an ingrown hair.

Once, he took me to see a school he designed. When he wasn't looking, I pressed my palm flat against a wall and closed my eyes. I imagined the cold, heavy plaster seeping into me and filling my body, making me impenetrable. The floors and ceilings made me feel far away from him. It seemed unfair to me that he had so much proof of his existence, while I was getting smaller every day.

59

I spent lunchtimes in the art and music rooms and break-times with the tough kids on the school field. I wasn't sure where I fitted in. I felt intimidated by make-up and the cool girls in scrunchies and push-up bras who gave boys handjobs under the desk during Geography.

60

Now I understand that words are precious because I can carry them all around inside of my head. The architect needs computer programs and contracts and laws and builders and bricks and mortar and light fittings and skirting boards. All I need is myself.

61

The toughest girl in my class got her period on the seat in the Science lab. The boys behind her showed no mercy.
'Sarah, love!' they cawed, swinging on their stools. 'Someone's got fucking jammy knickers!' I died inside for her as she swivelled around to face them, blushing beneath layers of orange foundation.
'That,' she said, looking each of them in the eyes, 'is what you call The Facts of Life.' She stalked out of the classroom, leaving wet blood smeared in her wake. I treated her with reverence after that.

62

My body is the wrong kind of body. I have full breasts and a small waist and grown men stop and stare in the street. At first it is thrilling when boys from school touch my bum on the stairs but soon it turns sour. I want it and I do not want it. I want to be visible and I want to be invisible, or perhaps I want to be visible to some people and not to others. It seems unfair that I can't choose. I let some boys touch, slowly. Maybe hands in knickers but no more. I go home all tingles up my arms and in my chest but still I am wrong. It is my legs I think, too thick in my school skirt. I look at your legs and they are perfect. Sculpted in fake-tan shimmer. Things get better with age, you say, but I don't have time to wait.

63

On the bus one morning, me feeling shy in a short skirt, two boys with their feet on the seats licked me lazily with their eyes.

'Aw, yeah mate,' they said in voices that were too gruff for their small faces. 'I'd do them both, like.' They craned around to get a better look at me and another girl around my age who had got on afterwards.

'What about her head,' said one, nodding in my direction, 'on her body?' he said, gesturing towards the other girl.

'Fucking rights,' agreed the other boy, salivating in his seat. 'I'd bang the fuck out of that.' I put in my headphones and pretended not to hear. I tugged my skirt over my knees and spread my palms across my thighs, trying to ascertain their width in comparison to everyone else's. I sneaked a look at the other girl out of the corner of my eye; small and skinny in jeans and a crop top. My skin felt prickly, like a mohair jumper that was too small for me, stifling me as I tried to stretch beyond it. The boys blasted New Monkey from their mobile phones and old ladies tutted and tsked among themselves, too afraid to do anything about it.

64

We don't leave the house for three days. Our lives take on a timeless quality, punctuated by coffee in the mornings and hot whiskey in the evenings, blurred with limbs and duvets and thick, strange sleep. We share cigarettes in bed and I watch as the smoke curls in the curtains, coating everything in its stink. I leave the windows closed. We are snails leaving trails. I want there to be a reminder, the essence of what we did lingering here. We giggle our way through the hours and make paintings spread out on the living room floor. We burn candles to the bone and play each other music. We like to bite and scratch.

'I'm scared I might hurt you,' he says, holding back.

'I'm pretty strong, you know,' I reply. Pleasure pools in my stomach like warm honey. I trace my fingers over the outline of his tattoo; a dove and a wooden cross.

'A good Catholic boy,' I tease with my head pressed into the pillow.

65

Springtime brought gypsy skirts and white linen trousers. My mother was young and beautiful with a whole life behind her but a whole possible life ahead of her, too. She had dancer's legs and everyone swore she looked just like Rachel Stevens from S Club 7. She got blond highlights in her hair and bought tiny brown miniskirts with plastic medallions from New Look. She came home from the shops rustling bags filled with vest tops, cork wedges, cropped denim jackets and Rimmel Good to Glow instant tan, shimmied down the legs for a glimmer across cobbles in car headlights. I bought her *Life for Rent* by Dido for her thirty-ninth birthday. We took the lyric sheet out of the CD case and looked at the pictures of Dido with her feathered hair and boot-cut jeans and dreamed that was what our futures would look like. We ripped a topless picture of Enrique Iglesias from the *Top of the Pops* magazine and stuck it on the fridge.

66

There is a smell in your skin that scares me. Sweet. Sour. A smell that thrills me and makes me sick. I note the gentle ooze of your hips over your jeans, the molten, gorgeous spill of you. The world is full of eyes on fire in ways I could not see until now. I dye your hair copper brown in the kitchen and I do not wear the little plastic gloves. You frown at my stained fingertips but I am pleased. You: streaked across me in semi-permanence.

67

She started hanging out with her father's old friends in Luma Bar in Sunderland in the afternoons. There was Harry from Londonderry who played the spoons. There were the chefs who joined them after work, their arms coated in burger grease, clutching cheesy chips in tinfoil cartons, fat congealed around the edges. There was Toni who owned the caff and his 21-year-old girlfriend, Jane. Their landlady told Harry that they never ate anything and stayed up all night doing coke and drinking champagne naked in the kitchen under a giant umbrella. Jane sometimes did sex work when the money got tight and Toni pretended not to notice as strange men shuffled upstairs in the dark, touching their way around the door handle because the bulb had blown and no one cared enough to buy a new one.

An army of joiners from Glasgow descended on the scene, sweating over girders and wires during the weekdays, building a nightclub and casino in the centre of town. They hit the bars in Park Lane after their shift, easing out the knots in their muscles with cheap pints of lager and casting oily eyes at the local ladies. They were nicknamed 'The Meerkats,' on account of the way they craned their necks to get an eyeful of the women walking past.

I envied the ease with which my mother existed in her body. I slouched uncomfortably in my ripped jeans, pulling at my jumper, trying to obscure my breasts, while she perched at the pub table, jangling bracelets and reapplying her lipstick in the back of a silver knife. Sometimes I could actually sense my skin growing and stretching. Shooting pains stung my limbs like electric shocks.

The joiners' gaffer was Gordon. He drove a Jaguar with tellies pressed into the backs of the front seats and kept a loose change jar on his kitchen counter filled exclusively with two-pound coins. My mother was full of something special and traces of it lingered in the air when she turned her head to give whoever she was chatting to her full attention. Gordon offered her a lift home one night. I imagined her crossing her legs over his leather seats as they took off into the streetlights together.

68

I can feel something new inside of me. The desires of others break over my skin like the coloured flowers shone onto walls of clubs I used to go to. I have twisted myself so far into uncomfortable shapes to please other people that I have forgotten my most natural form.

This is a place that shaped my family. Living here, in the smallness and the silence, I am learning how to listen to myself. I am cycling through mountains and playing my favourite albums on repeat. I am reading and thinking and watching films, wrapped in a duvet by the fire at night. I am writing letters to my friends and teaching myself how to cook slow, careful meals, creamy curries and thyme-speckled vegetable bakes, goat's cheese seeping through my layers, salty and soft.

Some days I am very raw, as though my outer layers have been peeled away, exposing the new parts of myself to the wind and the sea spray. When you have been distant from yourself for some time, coming back into your body is alarming. Acknowledging that your desires are plural and even contradictory is a difficult realisation, but it is necessary if you are going to live in a way that is true to yourself.

I feel very sensitive to different consistencies of light. The speed of the wind. The pull of my clothes against my arms. Everything has a texture. I had stopped noticing it. I have a new pleasure in holding objects. A cold, round apple is solid in the palm of my hand. I stroke the smooth, hard squares of Scrabble letters. I run my fingers over the rough wooden surface of the table. I wonder if this is how my mother felt when we came here during those long, brooding summers.

69

My father moved into a house in a different part of town. Occasionally he picked Josh and me up and whizzed us to Frankie & Benny's or the cinema. We sometimes stopped by his house on the way home and I wandered around it, wondering at the emptiness. He slept on a mattress in the corner of the room and an empty IKEA shelving unit covered the back wall.

'Why don't you get some more things, Dad?' I asked him, sitting on the floor. 'There's too much space in here.'

'I dunno, Luce,' he said, looking around. 'I don't see the point. It's just a house, this is. It's not my home.'

One night he cruised the streets looking for my mother.

He borrowed a friend's car and wore a wig and thought that she wouldn't recognise him peering in at her new life through the pub window.

70

Here in Ireland, I am often asked, 'How long are you home for?' which means 'How long are you staying here?' I resented that as a child. When the weather was bad the summer days stretched on into nothing, lumpy and bitter. My mother sometimes got an ocean look in her eye and I feared that we would never leave and the north-east would dissolve in the rain, my friends forgotten. I feared this place becoming my home and now, I suppose, it is.

71

I wandered around the shops at the weekends after drama club, catching the shock of my body under the lights in the Topshop changing rooms and learning the shape of hate. I bit my lip as I tried my best to memorise fashion rules and wriggle into the sliver of space I was expected to occupy.

When the shops shut I went shyly to the pub to meet my mother and her friends, sipping Coke through a curly straw and fingering the gummy strawberries in my jeans pocket.

'Sit down with us, darling!' Toni cooed. 'What a pretty little thing you're turning out to be. Just like your mother.'

'Ah, Tone, you're embarrassing her, man.' Jane took a gulp of her white wine and soda, her lip gloss coating the edge of the glass. Toni licked her cheek and she squealed and tottered off to the toilets to get changed. Jane always brought a tiny beaded handbag with her with an outfit change stuffed into it by some kind of magic. When afternoon segued into night she nipped into the loos and came out in a different dress or blouse, with eyeshadow to match.

'Give us a twirl, Janey!' Toni squealed, squeezing her bum. My mother was radiant among the half-drunk pints and the smattering of coins that people pressed into my fingers, streaked with make-up from the Collection 2000 samples in Superdrug.

'And what do you want to be when you grow up?' loomed Harry as the street lamps sputtered on.

'A nurse!' trilled Toni. 'A perfect little nurse! I think she'd be a wonderful nurse, just like her mother. Can't you see her in the uniform?' I grimaced and my mother caught my eye.

'I'm not a nurse, Toni,' she warned. 'I've got Josh now.' I held onto the legs of my mother's bar stool, drinking in her DKNY perfume and watching her laugh through the cigarette smoke.

'Do you want to call a taxi, pet?' she murmured to me. 'Go on. I'll pay. Josh'll be home from your nan's soon. You'd better get back for him. I won't be long.' I took the crumpled notes and shoved them into my backpack. 'You're my little star,' she crooned into my scalp.

When I came home I called Rosie and she rushed over. We barricaded my bedroom door so Josh couldn't bother us, playing my dad's old Travis album at top volume and cutting the feet off our tights to make them into footless leggings. When we got hungry I made pasta for the three of us, trying not to get ketchup on my glittery vest top as I squirted hearts and smiley faces onto the middle of our plates. I plonked Josh in the bath and he splashed water everywhere, soaking our wood-panelled bathroom until it began to decay. Months later my mother and I hacked it off with hammers and found smelly black mulch rotting beneath it.

72

Toni died unexpectedly one Saturday afternoon. He had been up all night on a cocaine bender and did a charity bike ride the next day. He had a heart attack before he reached the finish line. Jane packed up her things and went back to her life. She was only twenty-one. She applied to university and pretended none of it had ever happened.

A few years later, when I was almost old enough, I went to a pub in Sunderland with my boyfriend. Jane was working behind the bar.

'Jane?' I said. She didn't recognise me. 'Susie's daughter,' I explained. Her eyes widened in recognition. 'I'm so sorry about Toni.'

A shadow of a sadness passed across her face. She looked so young beneath her make-up. 'Oh, thank you.' She emptied the dishwasher without meeting my eyes. 'It all seems so long ago now, you know?' She was just another student working in a bar, on her way to other things.

73

When I got home from school, my mother was often out collecting Josh or doing a food shop. She left me lists of jobs to do signed off with a blue biro love heart. I collected the washing from the garden in my bare feet, dropped the clean bedsheets in the mud, and then ran myself a bubble bath.

Sometimes I pushed open the door of her bedroom and walked around it, breathing in the hot smell of her hair where it lingered after a blow-dry. I opened her wooden jewellery box and fingered her hoop earrings in their nest of hairgrips. I opened her wardrobe and stroked her dresses; the bobbled ones with supermarket labels and the glitzy, floaty ones she ordered in secret from the Next catalogue. My favourite had a band of gold sequins around the middle and we called it the Cheryl Cole.

If I stayed in her room long enough, the objects in it began to seem divorced from meaning. A lipstick was just a lipstick without her fingers pushing colour to the surface. I felt scared that the things I admired became static and meaningless without her to breathe life into them. Before I left, I slid my tights over the carpet to brush away any traces of my feet. I always made sure everything was exactly as she left it. I couldn't let her know how much I craved her when she wasn't there.

74

School lunchtimes are steamy hot and greasy. Crammed into rooms smelling of other people's sandwiches. We sit together with lunch boxes and scrutinise. That girl is a swimmer so she eats lots and that girl has cottage cheese, a healthy thing, and we all sit in circles breathing in. Is there too much chocolate in mine? We are all blushing. We should have yoghurts and raisins, not milkshakes and pizzas. We compare our thighs in the reflection of doors and people tell us that's where our value lies. Fat is bandied around like a swear word and we learn that it is the worst thing we could ever be. We look at pictures in magazines and watch music videos in ICT and someone says that nothing tastes as good as skinny feels and we scoff at that but somehow it gets in.

75

There have been times when my skin has been so thin it is as though the morning light might leak through me. Like those IKEA paper lamps that started off cool and ended up crumpled on the floor, red-wine-stained and sagging from cheap skeletons in sad student rooms.

I have stood on the tube as the doors opened and held onto the bar until my knuckles turned white in fear that I might get blown out onto the tracks with the rats and crumpled crisp packets.

That is the wrong kind of lightness. It is better to have

weight and to be able to pull stars and planets towards you. I can see that now. The beaches here are vast and empty and on a clear night the Milky Way is visible from my garden. I have been avoiding the sea and the stars because they make me feel small. I am trying to grow bigger.

76

Sometimes Rosie and I hung out in Durham with her friends from dance school. They had brown limbs and leathery handbags and names like Jojo and Bebe. They toted skinny Vogue cigarettes from the cuffs of Jack Wills blazers and I felt pale and dirty around them, my syllables clumsy and lumbering.

One evening we missed our bus home. My flip phone buzzed and flashed, coated in silver nail varnish.

'Where are you, sugarplum?' my nan's voice cooed. 'We're about to pass your house. We're dropping off Josh.'

'Shit.' I tugged Rosie's ballet cardigan. 'We've got to go.' Bebe and Jojo rolled their eyes.

'Oh, stay,' they pleaded. 'We've got a bottle of vodka for later.' I made wistful eyes at Rosie and she shrugged them off.

'Next time, bitches!' she called over her shoulder. We walked along the side of the motorway all the way home. My phone rang into the traffic as Rosie whimpered and cars tooted at us as they flashed by our small bodies, joined at the hands.

77

The buzz of hunger wears away at hate. Skirts too tight and skin dimpled in changing room lights. We get bad haircuts and put toothpaste on our spots and we learn the opposite of love. I cannot tell if I am a pear or an apple or an hourglass or even which one I am supposed to want. You tell me it doesn't matter but I know that it does, even to you. Boyish seems best because boyish means exempt from these things. I am not boyish. I do not want my body to cause a stir. I don't want it to be the first thing that speaks. I think of sex, of course, but I think of other things, too. People look but they do not listen.

78

'You can't wear them shorts around the house any more, Lucy pet,' my mother said one morning over toast. They were pink silky hot pants with a matching pyjama top.

'Why not?' I pulled them down so they covered my bum cheeks.

'They're indecent. Poor Gordon doesn't know where to look.'

79

'Look at the moon,' the man and I text each other at night, and sometimes I can see it and he can't, and sometimes he can see it and I can't, depending on the weather. We try to send each other pictures on our phones but it is almost impossible to photograph the moon without proper equipment.

80

My friend Lauren's dad was an old punk. He wore a Harrington jacket, subscribed to the *NME*, and bought us tickets for gigs at the local student union. Those frantic evenings were a portal into another world. Gigs were a space where the rules and norms of everyday life were suspended and anything could happen. The grease and glamour released some of the weird energy spiralled inside of me.

Lauren and I linked arms to stop each other from going under as the crowds pressed in. We twisted with dads at Supergrass and laddered our tights for Funeral For a Friend. We lurked around the merch stall to ask Bullet For My Valentine to sign our knickers after their supporting set.

'Is this even legal?' they drawled, swigging beers and exchanging glances. Big men without shirts spun the crowd into whirlpools as circle pits whipped us faster and faster into the centre.

81

The man and I become obsessed with the moon. We drive out to the mountains at night to look at it. We measure the passing of time through its fragments. I read obsessively about the links between tides and emotions and circadian rhythms. I discover that more babies are born when the moon is closest to earth and the gravitational pull is strongest. I wonder if the moon could pull things out of me.

82

We slouched into school the next day with pink dye streaked in our hair and the smell of spilt beer wafting from under our uniforms. It seemed incredible to me that anything as dreary as a Maths class could possibly exist when hot lights flashed behind fire doors in unassuming parts of town.

Musicians became our role models. We knew there were other lives beyond the chip shops and the bus stops but we didn't know how to get there. We didn't know anyone who was a doctor or a lawyer, but most people had a brother or an uncle who played in a band. My mother was proud that I knew all the words to 'Wonderwall' before I learned any nursery rhymes, belting it out at playgroup while the other kids sang ditties about sheep and lambs.

When I was at school we were swamped by bands like

the Arctic Monkeys; working-class lads who cut their lines with offhand Shakespeare and made it big on Myspace. The internet made art permeable. We could download songs illegally and send them to each other over MSN for free. We danced at indie discos to bands like Art Brut and nursed cans into the early hours singing Billy Bragg's 'A New England,' spread-eagled on someone from school's stepdad's carpet. We loved the Holloways and Jamie T. for their socialist whimsy and delighted in Tim Booth jangling across music channels in a dress. Women like Kate Nash and Lovefoxxx were special, singing about Escher and bird shit, twirling in trainers and tie-dye catsuits.

I scrawled 'Red Squier Strat' across the top of my Christmas list and in the morning it was waiting for me, a Santa hat hanging jauntily from the neck. I had been wearing a plectrum on a necklace for weeks in anticipation. My eyes were full and gold with plans for my band, the sequins we would wear and the songs we would play: rock covers of Girls Aloud and the Sugababes.

I started lessons in an outbuilding at the back of someone else's school, with a man called Scott we found in the paper who taught me Green Day songs. My mother dropped me off and he watched her car pull away through the window.

'I didn't realise your mam was so lovely,' he said, turning tuning pegs. I shrugged non-committally and pulled my stripy rainbow strap over my head.

The next week he stood at the window as my mother paced the schoolyard on her phone. 'You look nice,' he said, turning his attention back to me. 'You and your mam going somewhere after this?'

'Oh,' I said. 'No. Not really.' His eyes snagged my knees

as he adjusted the music stand, still scabbed and bruised because I wasn't quite there yet.

'I'm not looking at your tits, by the way,' he said, unzipping his guitar bag. 'I'm just reading your T-shirt.'

I smiled uncertainly.

In our third week, while I was packing my guitar away, he came out to my mother's car after class and asked my mother out on a date. She laughed it off until I told her about the T-shirt comment. We stopped the lessons after that. I never progressed beyond 'Basket Case.'

83

One night, I take a video of clouds drifting in front of the moon. The moon itself is not visible but I can see the light changing as it fills the different shapes and textures of the clouds. This proves to be the most effective way of capturing the moon. We observe the way the light is reflected in other things.

84

I started spending my Saturdays at Goth Green in Newcastle. Hundreds of teenagers congregated on the grass by the war memorial, wielding skateboards and instruments and two-litre bottles of White Lightning. Lauren and I smeared red eyeshadow across our eyelids and layered dolly beads before we went out, giggling on the metro as the Tyne flickered by. We skulked around with people from school as they drew faces on tampon wrappers and set their shoes on fire and we ogled Myspace celebrities behind their Scene haircuts. Sometimes we went to Exhibition Park to watch the skateboarders, checking out people's outfits while poppers were passed around and girls got fingered in the bushes.

One afternoon I plucked up the courage to enter the gilded caravan that sat at the edge of the green. A woman sat at a small table among cluttered ashtrays and crystal balls. She had a sausage dog buried beneath the frills and flounces of her skirt. I crossed her palm with silver and she grasped mine in her thick fingers. She fixed her eyes on a spot on the wall and murmured an unintelligible prayer.

'Eat lots of salad,' she finally declared, without looking at me. 'And stick with God.' I thanked her and clattered back down the painted steps, blinking in the daylight. Disappointment sagged in my chest.

A skateboarder cornered me on the green one day and offered to give me a lesson on his knackered-looking skateboard. He had dirty blond curls and a trucker cap covered in marker pen. I smiled sweetly and hopped onto his board while Lauren chatted to his friend and watched me out of the corner of her eye. I poised my feet artfully, swallowing yelps as I smacked the concrete over and over again. He put his hands on my waist to steady me and we sailed across the pavement together.

'Luce,' Lauren called from the grass, brandishing her mobile. 'We're gonna have to go. Me mam'll be going mad.' I picked my military jacket up off the floor and explained to the skater that we had to go.

'Thanks for the lesson,' I said, coolly.

'That's okay,' he said. 'I'll walk with you to the metro.' Lauren gave me a look but said nothing. As we waited in line at the machines to get our tickets, the boy suddenly spun me round and kissed me, pressing my body against the ticket machine with his. I tentatively kissed him back. He took off his cap so that he could stick his tongue deep into my mouth without poking me with its peak. We forgot about the tickets and Lauren and I jumped the barrier and ran for the train, spluttering and shrieking.

'I cannot believe you!' She laughed in disbelief as we squashed onto a seat.

'Here,' she said. 'Give us a spray with this, will you? Don't want me mam to get a whiff of the tab smoke.' I took the spray from her and masked our afternoon with vanilla-flavoured Impulse. It lingered on our skin for a long time afterwards.

85

I no longer hunger for your hands on my skin. Now boys touch my body and decide if it is good or not. I am lucky. I have a nice one. He kisses and sucks and licks and fucks but there is a mad, sad thing growing in my belly. I always want more. I do not want to be me for reasons I do not understand. I have read too much or seen too much or had too much of something. I cannot settle. I am itchy all of the time behind my eyes and between my bones. I get so drunk that sometimes I pass out in spangly dresses, purpling headaches on chip-shop floors. I can't remember what I did but I like it that way. I am losing the us and pulling away.

86

There is so much space here. Space to breathe and spread myself out. When I cycle into town I pass bogs and sea and sky that seem to go on forever. The sunrises and sunsets seep in pastels and because there is so much sky they seem like a main event. I love the stretch of brown rocks in the bay when the tide is out. I love the cloud formations. I love freewheeling down the hill on my bike into the yellows and oranges. I go for walks across the beaches and I am the only person around for miles. There is room to grow and to think about things, as opposed to the city where everyone clamours for the same sad vantage point from a dirty train window.

87

My mother and Gordon started going to the pub less. He parked his Jaguar outside of our house and they spent their evenings squashed on the settee watching the soaps. He sighed dramatically and turned the television down when I burst through the door, spilling the dramas of my day into their silence.

'Sounds lovely, Luce,' my mother said absently. 'Are you going to have some tea? There's chili in the pan.' I went into the kitchen and helped myself.

I started eating less, serving myself smaller portions and stopping before I was full. The internet forums I trawled through were concerned with hip bones and clavicles, and

I wanted to give myself the best possible chance of becoming someone different.

88

The endless skies are important but all that space can be claustrophobic, too. There is so much of it. After a while, the pinks and purples start to make me feel seasick. It is all too conspicuously beautiful.

89

My friend's dad ran an Italian restaurant and he gave me a weekend waitressing job. I wasn't allowed to take orders but I ferried pizzas to and from the kitchen and prepared desserts in the tiny back room, where a sullen woman washed hundreds of dishes by hand, night after night.

My mother bought me a card that said, 'Congratulations!'

'You're so independent, Lucy.' She smiled proudly. 'I knew you would be.' I bought a little black dress and old men crinkled when I lugged the heavy dessert board over to their table.

'Is she on offer?' they asked the waiters, twinkling conspiratorially across the restaurant. I hated serving people from school. I put down their Four-Cheese Specials and Half Pasta Half Chips with burning cheeks, dying to rush out to the back step with the waiters Joe and Sam, where they skived smoking joints and I could have a break from the eyes and the chip grease.

Francesca was the manager. She had angel wings tattooed across her shoulder blades.

'I like your tattoos,' I told her when I first started.

'Baby,' she said. 'Let me tell you a secret. If you want to get a tattoo, get it somewhere you cannot see it. That way, you will never get sick of it.' She winked at me and went off to clatter plates.

One weekend we were rammed. Everyone was sweating and I was doing a good job, rushing plates rapidly from the kitchen without mixing up the orders. I ran into Francesca as she came hurtling around a corner, shiny and breathless.

'Baby!' she exclaimed, grabbing me by the shoulders. 'You are banned from that kitchen.' I looked at her.

'What?'

'You heard. You're not to go in there any more.'

'Why not?'

'All of those chefs, they look at you all over with their eyes! All the time! I cannot bear it.' I reddened.

'But how will I take the food to the tables?'

'Your problem,' she said, going to attend to something else. Joe laughed softly into my ear.

'Don't worry about her,' he said. 'She's just jealous.' I wavered, uncertain. I felt hurt but I couldn't explain why. Joe shoved a bowl of hot pasta into my hand, scalding my fingers.

'Take this to table two,' he told me. 'And how about a drink after work?'

We were allowed to order pizzas and chips to take home with us after our shift.

'What are you having, Lucy?' someone shouted from the kitchen when the last customer left in a flurry of garlic and perfume. 'Chef needs all the orders in now.'

'I'm fine, thanks,' I called, cleaning the tables. Francesca glanced at me.

'You are not eating anything?'

'Not hungry,' I told her. 'Ate loads before I came to work.'

'Suit yourself,' she said, breezing into the kitchen to collect her pizza, gold heat seeping through the cardboard.

90

My brother spoke a lot of languages. He understood invisible things that I did not. He felt the cold, clear colour of the sky in the mornings and the taste of worry on my mother's skin. He was fluent in the shapes of strangers' lips and the particular shudder of the car as it passed over familiar tarmac, but he wasn't able to express all of the things that he needed to say. As he became used to his cochlear implant, he relied on sign language less and less. He wanted to be part of the hearing world. He wanted to dance to music and to enjoy the delicate nuance of spoken language. He learned the way that putting feelings into words and out into the world could ease the pressure inside, like letting air out of a balloon.

He went to a school for the deaf but he didn't identify with the other kids there. He wanted to be hearing, but he wasn't. He didn't want to be deaf but he was and so he cut himself off from a world that could have offered him answers. He moved through different cultures speaking different languages, never feeling like he fit into any of them.

My mother explained that sign language users sometimes think in binary terms.

'You've got to explain everything to him, Lucy,' she told me gently. 'It's harder for him to understand meanings that you imply but don't actually say.'

'What do you mean?'

'You know. All the unsaid stuff. The spaces between things.'

I started writing all of my thoughts in my journal, staying up late into the night with white heat expanding across my chest. I wrote until I fell asleep and woke in the morning with my notebook rumpled under my duvet and a fresh calm inside of me.

'What comes first, Mam?' I asked her one morning over toast. 'Thoughts or words?' She was rushing around looking for Josh's exercise books.

'I don't know, Luce,' she said, brushing her hair out of her eyes with the back of her hand. 'Ask me later, eh? I'm a bit busy at the minute.' I stared at my toast until the butter disappeared and tried to think a thought without words in it.

Josh's frustration at being unable to express himself grew bigger and bigger inside of him. He turned wild. His school didn't know how to deal with him. It was in York, which was too far for him to come home every night, so he had to stay there during the week. He hated it. Every weekend he brought the entire contents of his bedroom back in his suitcase: his duvet, his clothes, his books and pictures and even his bedside lamp. My mother hated sending him back on a Monday morning, but she didn't know what else to do.

She was forever getting phone calls that tore her out of her day and sent her down to collect him. He started fights and smashed things. He poured hot oil out of a window onto someone's head and claimed he had been making pancakes.

One night we got a call to say that he had set his room on fire by reading a newspaper in bed, propped up against a lamp. The fire service was called and he had to sleep in a different room for a few days, while they checked his carpet for smoulders.

Another time he ran away. He was ten years old and full of secrets. Nobody knew where he was. My mother sat by the phone saying prayers, chewing the insides of her cheeks until they bled with worry. They found him in the chip shop down the road, warming his hands against the counter.

The tension that built up inside of him led to extreme temper tantrums. He flailed around and punched and kicked and spat and bit until he had to be held down so that he wouldn't injure himself or somebody else. He came home one weekend with bruises flowering across his arms, finger-widths apart, where the care staff had restrained him. My mother put him in the bath and gently soaped the hurt away. I sat on the toilet lid and watched them, feeling a twist in my stomach.

My mother worried about him so much. She was scared that one day he might do something irreversible. I came home from school full of some kind of classroom drama or ideas for an essay or an art project that involved me hanging upside down from the climbing frame and sketching all of our washing on the line.

'Can we chat about it later, Lucy?' She frowned, her face

taut with worry. 'I'm going to have to go and get Josh.' It felt like she was at the opposite end of a very long tunnel and I couldn't get through to her.

'Do you want me to come with you?' I offered.

'No, no. It's okay. It's a long journey there and back, and you've got school tomorrow.'

She sped off down the motorway with stern words from Josh's teachers ringing in her ears and I savoured the silence, drawing and chatting online until the inevitable explosion arrived with a banging and slamming of doors. He went into his bedroom and let out his anger, smashing his toys and throwing them down the stairs. My mother and I barricaded ourselves in the kitchen until the outburst was over.

I knew how he felt. It was as though there were small, sharp springs coiled up inside of him and he needed to scream and scream until everything was gone. Afterwards he curled on the sofa whimpering apologies, while we smoothed out the evening.

'Lovely, lovely Lucy,' my mother crooned when she was in a nostalgic mood, playing David Gray and cradling a cup of tea in the sitting room. 'You're our hope.'

91

We dissected frogs in Biology at school and when we got to the hearts, all soft and wet, I wanted to cry. I shoved mine back into the frog's body with my fingers, away from the callous eyes of my squealing classmates.

92

The man is never still, even for a moment. He is always smoking and texting and driving his car all at once. His whole body trembles.

'Relax,' I say to him, resting my hands on his shoulders.

'I am,' he says. I can feel the raw energy beneath his skin.

93

Bodies are fragile; fleshy and strange. You slather your legs in cream beneath your silky nightie and I look for your most delicate parts; the creases on your elbows and the skin between your toes. I pull your hairs from the plughole and count them as the water gushes down. I want to remember this imprint of your body when it is mine and no one else's. I want to hold the small parts of you tightly. I want to save them and thread you back together.

94

I go for a walk across the fields. It is windy and the coffee-coloured cows stop to look at me. When I first arrived here I was afraid of the cows, but now they seem impossibly gentle, with their long eyelashes and sad mouths. I call Alex to update him on my recent discoveries.

'I'm so stuck in my head all of the time,' I tell him. 'But he is completely in his body. I want to be like that.'

'Maybe he can sense that, too,' Alex says. 'You need to find a language that both of you can speak.' Alex is a painter writing an MA thesis on the way that different artistic mediums convey different sentiments, like alternate languages. We have spoken about it at length together, but I haven't thought to apply it to people.

'I think art is the link,' Alex says. 'Between mind things and body things. It brings them both together, and that's why it's so important.'

'And maybe sex?' I ask him. He pauses.

'Some of the time,' he replies.

95

I plastered my bedroom walls from floor to ceiling with cut-outs from magazines. Kate Moss, Brigitte Bardot, David and Angie Bowie, pictures of my friends, club night posters, set lists from gigs and notes and drawings and plastic flowers. I wrote song lyrics and lines from poems straight onto the walls and scribbled slogans across my mirror in lipstick. I created a world that was simultaneously real and imaginary, of music and art and mavericks; people who were more than the spaces they inhabited.

I became obsessed with clothes. An idea for a perfect outfit filled me with manic energy. I spent all of the money from the restaurant on tiny dresses, the shorter and sparklier the better. I soaked my long blond hair in peroxide, much to the dismay of my mother's hairdresser.

'You'll never be able to stop now,' she sighed, fingering a straw-like strand. I looked at her in the mirror and felt satisfied. I didn't want to stop. I didn't know where I was going but I was moving in a definite direction. I liked tacky, trashy, terrible things. I sighed around the shops touching dresses I couldn't afford. I saved up for a faux leather jacket. I tore old jeans into tiny denim skirts and slithered the belts out of the trousers Gordon left hanging on the bathroom door.

A smattering of vintage shops opened in Newcastle and my friends and I tried on fur coats in musty attics, prancing around in front of the mirror and seeing ourselves differently. I was tall and shiny but I wanted to be rougher; stranger and skinnier. I wanted to be taken seriously and to shake things up like Debbie and Courtney and all of my heroes. I didn't want to be lovely at all.

I bought a fur coat in secret. I skipped school one stale afternoon to get the bus into Newcastle and go to my favourite vintage shop, the weird one that had surfaces cluttered with telephones in the shapes of lips and dolls' heads glued to the mirrors. I picked the fluffiest, most ostentatious coat I could possibly find and bought it with a beating heart, guilt pooling in my mouth.

The shopkeeper dressed like Slash. He had thick dark curls and always wore a top hat. I nervously passed over greasy notes, waiting for him to ask me what I thought I was doing, or to tell me that I wasn't allowed to be there. He winked at me.

'Perfect for autumn, that is, love. You're gonna be a dream.' I hurried the coat home and stuffed it in the back of my wardrobe.

I never dared to wear it in public but later, when I fell in love, my boyfriend did. We went on a trip to Paris and he wore it over his suit as we skulked around cemeteries having loud arguments, pretending we were Jim and Pamela.

96

I get a text message from Alex.
  'Listen to the animal part of yourself.'

97

My mother met an art teacher with a mullet who wore long coats with Chelsea boots. He made her a mix CD and scrawled 'I've Got a Safety Pin Stuck in my Heart for You' across the shiny silver surface in permanent marker. The first song was 'Gordon is a Moron' by Jilted John.

She was dizzy with everything else going on in her life and she listened to the CD once and then forgot about it. I pinched it and kept it in my Walkman for months, learning the words to the songs I believed would help me gain respect in the eyes of the people I deemed cool. Rosie came to my house after school and we put it on and flailed madly around the house to X-Ray Spex, whipping off our tights and munching KitKats at the same time.

98

There is a splitting and a tearing between what was once us but is now me. I want too much. The violence of it scares me. I am oozing with it, unchecked and unbridled. Girls like me are not supposed to want things. Everything is difficult for him and I have it all. I am pretty and clever. I do not have holes in my head or in my heart. How dare I want any more?

99

I have started drawing. I haven't drawn since I was a teenager, but in the cottage in the evenings I am drawing and drawing. Vines and houses leak from my pen, faces and animals and words in unknown languages. Splintered black lines fissure out of me and I can't stop them. My fingers and elbows are stained with ink.

100

My school belonged to an in-between town called Washington. It was technically in Sunderland but equidistant from Newcastle. Our school crest had three stars on it to mirror the American flag. George Washington's family originated there and went on to form Washington,

DC. We were the forgotten beginning of things; ugly and un-assuming, overshadowed by our famous cousins across the ocean. We clung to the story because we wanted to feel like we mattered.

Washington was made up of retail parks and motorways and there didn't seem to be anything natural or organic about it. It was split into numbered districts like a paint-by-numbers picture where someone had run out of colours and swirled everything into a greenish brownish grey.

There were lots of housing estates made up of identical houses with bricked backyards, and there was a river with a couple of pubs and a working men's club. There was a big, brutalist shopping centre where mams pushed prams in velour tracksuits and babies with snotty noses and frilly socks clutched sausage rolls like pasty pastry angels.

It was the site of the Nissan car plant, one of the north-east's biggest employers. Boys at school knew the factory was looming in their future, waiting for them to grow into the overalls.

At the weekends we usually ended up at a party in a council flat rented by someone who used to go to our school. People combed the carpets for spilt drugs with their fingernails at the end of the night and fucked quickly in cold bedrooms, wasting the days away before work or school again on Monday morning.

There was a certain charm surrounding the pebble-dashed houses and the bus stops and the endless drama of our lives played out between cities on bridges and aban-doned railway lines. There was a sense of camaraderie at those flat parties, the feeling that we were all in it together and just looking for a good time.

High-rise tower blocks and the despondency of stale, squat houses are aesthetically pleasing when you are removed from them. Middle-class architects with utopian ideals might be able to appreciate the solidity and the magnitude of a huge hunk of concrete with lives carved unapologetically into it, but when that becomes your reality and you have no choice and no way out, when you're living every day under the shadow of someone else's vision, it becomes oppressive, the weight of their dreams crushing the life out of you.

A set of disused railway lines ran the whole length of Washington, a proud scar from our colliery past. We hung out on them sneaking cider and people climbed onto the old viaduct and snogged in damp corners, daring each other to hang off the edge, legs dangling down onto the motorway below.

We spent evenings trudging through parks and around the perimeters of misty football fields. We pushed each other on swings that we couldn't quite fit into any more and followed the railway lines from one house to another, where we took tokes on joints and listened to heavy metal in boys' bedrooms while they groped our breasts through our T-shirts. The smell of Lynx and weed and socks was a new kind of delicious; getting under my skin and bringing my veins and capillaries to the surface.

101

There are worlds that are different to the one you built us. If I was small enough, I could crawl through the tunnels that lead there. I am so lovely. So shiny. I am soft but I want to be spiky. My skin promises sex and gold but inside I am twisted and shapeless. I think too much about things. I have too much to say. My body takes me places that my mind does not want to go. My edges are beginning to fray.

102

The man and I drive out to Sliabh Liag, a nearby mountain where devastating cliffs crumble into the sea.

'The highest cliffs in Europe, these are,' he boasts. We climb to the top. There are slate steps at the peak. It is drizzling and they are slippery. We grab clumps of heather to stop ourselves falling.

'Fuck!' He slips on a wet patch and sinks into a mound of mud.

I laugh at him.

'It isn't fucking funny, thanks,' he teases. 'Me new trainers! Cost a fortune, these did.'

I roll my eyes at his Nikes. 'How much?'

'Two hundred.'

'They didn't!'

'Sure, they did.'

We scramble to the top, panting. It is dusk and gold lights glow in the valley below us. Everything is blue-grey and slate. It is difficult to tell where the sea ends and the sky begins. The waves crash beneath the cliffs with a force that leaves us breathless.

'Who needs London?' he asks me. 'When you can look out at that.'

I squint at the horizon. I can't make sense of the vastness. My eyes make patterns in the expanding sky.

'Forget London,' I say into the wind.

He looks shyly at me and pulls up his hood. The wind lashes the cliffs. We start to descend.

'Where else would you like to live, then?' he asks.

I am quiet for a little while. Our shoes hit the slate with damp slaps.

'Dunno,' I tell him. 'Anywhere. I feel sort of floaty. Like there's nothing keeping me anywhere.' I look at him sideways. 'What about you?'

'God,' he says. 'Everywhere. I'm gonna go to Australia, then Canada, then maybe South America. The good thing about being a labourer is that you're always wanted, all over the world.'

I look at the cliffs and sea and sky. 'Don't you ever feel guilty?' I ask him. 'I mean, it's beautiful here. Don't you ever feel bad for wanting something more?'

He skips a step. 'It isn't something more,' he says, decidedly. 'Just something else.'

103

Each part of Washington had a parish, and parishes had Catholic clubs, which were essentially working men's clubs attached to churches. We figured out pretty quickly that we could get served in the clubs underage, so that's where we congregated. Working men's clubs really were for working men. On Fridays women weren't allowed in the main bar and we had to sit at a picnic table in a cold little porch with a plastic roof, tacked on as an afterthought.

The first time I got drunk was in a Catholic club. Bands

from school started to play gigs there, and big groups of us descended into carpeted function rooms, having lip-glossed discussions over who should go to the bar.

'You look the oldest, Lucy,' Lauren hissed.

'What can I get you, pet?' I scanned the rows of glass bottles for something I recognised. The woman behind the bar peered at me closely from beneath her Coke-can fringe.

'Vodka,' I blurted out.

'Vodka and mixer? Or just straight?' A long pause.

'Straight? Please.' The woman raised her eyebrows.

'Single or double?'

'Er. Double?' She filled the glass and put it down in front of me. I walked back to my friends feeling victorious. We passed it around and took a sip each until it was gone. My friends coughed and wrinkled their noses. I bit my tongue in secret and finished it without flinching.

I couldn't go home to my mother smelling of vodka, so I spent the night at Lauren's house. Her parents were together and easygoing, and her dad gave us a can of cider to share. I drunkenly raided her sock drawer and threw all of her knickers out of her bedroom window. They floated down to the garden in pastel colours. In the morning, they were strewn across the patio like blossom.

There was a barman at the club who grew to like us. We called him Terry, on account of the Tia Maria and orange juices he slid across the bar.

'Just like Terry's Chocolate Orange,' he remarked sagely every time. We nodded in agreement. 'These ones are on me, girls.' He winked.

We vomited them up later in the church courtyard, frantically chewing spearmint gum before our parents came to pick us up. We backcombed our hair and wore T-shirts emblazoned with bands that our dads listened to. We tore away bits of the fabric, so that our small cleavages would not be outdone by Joe Strummer smashing up his guitar on the cover of *London Calling*. The boys knocked over amplifiers and kicked guitar pedals while we danced on the tables in our Primark brogues, sweating under fake leather jackets.

104

Vodka smells like paint and danger and twists me into a lighter version of myself. Roundabouts blur into merry-go-rounds and I slip in the sludgy silt caught in car parks and on viaducts. All the want and weight of my days evaporates, until the morning comes.

105

Something was happening. Stickers started appearing in strange places. Two boys with rumpled hair, arms emblazoned with the word 'Libertine,' pouted at us from posters pasted over the cupboard in the science lab. They stared at us from fold-down seats and bus timetables, obscuring the routes. Old ladies puffed out powdered cheeks in disapproval as they heaved their pulley-trolleys onto the bus, while we shared earphones and scribbled lyrics on the backs of our hands in blue biro.

Pete Doherty became a vessel for kids who had never heard of Rimbaud to pour their tortured souls into. We trawled forums and Myspace pages to glean his literary references and maybe catch a grainy BlackBerry picture from one of his infamous Whitechapel flat gigs. We were worlds away from London, where the streets were paved with troubadours and Amy Winehouse slunk around Camden in her bloody ballet flats, but we could taste the excitement, from dining chairs plonked in front of computers in stuffy sitting rooms.

'You're wasting your life on there!' my mother exclaimed, threatening to pull out the ethernet cable. 'Go and read a book or something!' Boys recorded songs in their bedrooms and sent them to me, changing the lyrics to fit my name. We chatted about Kerouac and Morrissey and wrote terrible poems and saved them in secret folders on our desktops.

We loved the unpredictability of it. The Libertines played a gig at Northumbria Student Union and kids from school thronged the streets as the police turned up in riot vans. In classic fashion, Pete didn't show up, and we surged past the pubs, throwing orange traffic cones into the crowd and belting 'Time for Heroes' in unison. We had grown up stuffed full of stories from other people's youths and we were desperate to be part of something significant. Our time felt cheap and unimportant.

106

The tanning booths and pawnshops and the awkward shape of my school uniform coaxed something mad and reckless inside of me. As I watched the clock hand slide through minutes and hours from my school desk, I could feel the wasted days of my life piling up behind me. They dug into my back, crushing my lungs and making it difficult to breathe. I felt like a small, shy shard that could easily slip through the cracks in the pavement and be lost in the dirt. I didn't know what it was that I wanted, but I wanted it so badly it sent shooting pains through my ovaries. I retreated further into books and music. Lauren and I started skipping lunch at school, so that we could save our money to sneak out to the pub at the weekends. We shared a Diet Coke and celery sticks, while our friends rolled their eyes and tucked into ham and cheese paninis.

107

The man fantasises about being in an accident. I watch him light a cigarette, his face hungry in the flame.

'I think about it sometimes. How someone would find the car flipped over on the road and call an ambulance. They would have to cut me out. Everyone would know about it. They would take me to hospital, but it would be fine; superficial like, just a few cuts and bruises.'

His cheeks hollow as he breathes in smoke. I imagine his mother's small face at his hospital bed. I picture the horror down in Jimmy's as people retell the story in dark tones, and him, laughing, emerging unscathed.

108

Everyone's parents seemed to have split up. There were empty houses most weekends, as mams and dads went to climb hills in the Lake District with new lovers. We descended on their free sitting rooms, supping their beers and snogging on their sofas. We were mirror images of each other. They were rebuilding their worlds and we were defining ours for the first time, testing our parameters.

My mother and father legally separated. They were still married but they had been living apart for a couple of years. My mother started to reclaim her space. We took hammers to our rotten front door and hacked it off. She painted the hallway turquoise and decorated it with stars and moons. Our bathroom was hot pink and we tacked strings of fluffy fairy lights from Argos along my bedroom walls.

She couldn't afford to redo our kitchen, so she bought a paint-n-grain kit and spent a weekend covering the ugly white cupboard doors in faux wood print. She painted the whole thing light brown, then stencilled faux grain over the top, so that from a distance, with a squint and the lights turned off, the cupboards actually looked like they were made from wood. We were barricaded out while the cupboards were drying, so we couldn't ruin the illusion with our sticky fingerprints.

'Looks alright, doesn't it, Luce?' She frowned and bit her lip.

'Looks great, Mam,' I promised.

I came home one night to her on the sofa, bundled up in her fluffy dressing gown, pink and gold from the shower.

'Lucy love,' she said, drawing me close to her. 'There's someone I'd like you to meet.'

I widened my eyes. 'Who?'

'Have you got plans next Thursday?'

'I'm supposed to be going to a gig with Lauren.'

'Do you have to go? This is important to me.'

I turned around to look at her. She seemed relaxed. I inhaled her satsuma body butter.

'Alright,' I agreed. 'We haven't got tickets yet.'

Ben was a teacher at the local college. He had worked as a fireman, crawling on his knees through thick black smoke, until he got too old.

'Ooh, I hope he's still got his uniform!' my mother's friends smirked when she told them. I was struck by the image of water on burning buildings and strong hands soothing charred bodies.

He came over to cook for us. My mother spent the day cleaning the house. She went through the fridge and threw away mouldy jam jars and furry tubs of cream. She took down Enrique Iglesias and threw him in the bin. She spent a long time in the bathroom, steam leaking into the hallway. I painted my fingernails black at the kitchen table, feeling nervous.

Ben was shy, too.

'Lovely to meet you, Lucy.' He smiled, unpacking ingredients. 'I've heard a lot about you.'

I looked at him from behind my hair. 'Need a hand with anything?'

'No, it's alright, I've got this. Why don't you and your mam wait in the living room? Relax, watch the telly. I'll give you a shout when it's done.'

We did as we were told, pulling faces at each other. Josh was at school and our house was calm and quiet. It was new to us; someone else chopping and slicing our evenings into a different shape.

He made peppers stuffed with goat's cheese and watched us nervously as we tucked in. I had never tasted goat's cheese before. It was bitter in a nice way, a sensation I was coming to associate with grown-upness.

'It's lovely, Ben,' my mother said, smiling at him.

'Yeah.' I swallowed. 'Thanks for cooking for us.'

'My pleasure,' said Ben, refilling his glass with water. I was impressed by the peppers. They were posh and creamy with promise.

109

There is an island just off the mainland called Inishfree. It was populated in the past, but it is so remote that most people were forced to leave to make a living. The last remaining resident was an old man who lived there alone, writing poetry and playing his saxophone. He claimed that the isolation gave him the time and space he needed to make his work, and the lack of streetlights meant that he could always see the stars at night.

He lived on the island for twenty years until his wife, who lived and worked in Essex, persuaded him to go home. The local newspaper turned up to document his return to the mainland. He was carrying one suitcase, three saxophones, a flute, and a clarinet. When the journalist asked him what he was looking forward to about returning to England, he said, 'My wife, Alice, is a wonderful cello player. I'm looking forward to making music with her again.'

110

The tension inside of me twisted tighter. I couldn't bear the smell of the corridors and the whispers in groups in the schoolyard. I was a drifter and felt under constant scrutiny. Gaggles of girls looked each other up and down and boys boasted about who got off with whom and whether or not they were decent kissers. At breaktimes we sat in circles in the cafeteria reading blowjob tips in *Glamour* magazine and taunting each other about our naivety. I found the pressure of getting things right excruciating. I kept my eyes on the clock, desperate for the bell that signalled the end of the periods that slowly trickled into evenings and set me free.

111

The man and I drive along the road one night in the dark. It is foggy and we can barely see in front of us. Car headlights make ethereal orbs in the fog, moving towards us from somewhere in the distance. A family of deer dart out from the trees and he swerves to avoid them.

'Christ,' he breathes. We catch their eyes in the headlights, glittering and afraid.

'You know,' he tells me, 'if we hit them, the impact wouldn't kill them. They are strong as fuck. They would break through the windscreen and panic and we would be kicked to death by their hooves.'

I watch his hands resting on the steering wheel and feel

him willing them towards us. I think about hooves raining through glass. I want to open the car door and run into the forest, away from him, where I can lie down in the wet pines. I must remember to look after myself.

112

I get lost in the pang of the gutters and the bus stops in the rain. People shape the kind of future they think I should be dreaming of but none of them seem like the right life for people like me. I can break up the hopeless with kissing and drinking. I can dance and spin and press my body into someone else's. Look at the crescents my fingernails leave. I do not know how else to show you I am pushing my limits. I know I do not have much weight in this world but I want to know how much I am worth. I do not have much to give but I am offering this.

113

Through our sojourns in the Catholic club, we became friends with the parish priest. He was young and lonely and every year he threw a New Year's Eve party in his house. He had a fully stocked wine cellar and gave us whatever we asked for in crystal flutes. We solemnly observed the lighting of the advent candle in the front room, then we were given free rein of the house.

One year we came across the keys to the church building. We toasted midnight on top of a pool table in the liturgy room, burning church incense and blasting the Stones. We played drunken Twister in the aisle, flashing our knickers to the Virgin Mary from beneath our sequinned party dresses. Some boys who used to go to our school were in a famous band. They turned up in the early hours while we were taking pictures of each other in the bathtub. The singer's girlfriend worked as a dancer in a strip club, but she told the priest she was a waitress. I toppled off the pool table and woke up in the new year with a big black bruise on my thigh. Someone set my text message tone to a recording of me wailing 'I bruise like a peach' over and over. I couldn't figure out how to change it and it followed me around for months.

114

I don't believe in religion, but the aesthetics of Catholicism have stuck with me. I love the way church incense coats my hair and skin. It is a safe smell, like a blanket, waiting for me to curl up in it. I love stained-glass windows and religious portraits, the colours of Mary's clothes and the bright red drops of blood on Jesus's face. I like the Stations of the Cross. I like pausing to run my finger along an emaciated rib and wrinkle my nose at the thought of the vinegar being offered on a sponge. I like prayer cards and medallions and rosary beads. I like advent candles and Bibles edged in gold and the way the skirt over the tabernacle matches the colour of the priest's robes. There is so much attention to detail.

I envy the faithful. There are shrines dotted around the hillsides here in Ireland, places where saints have supposedly appeared and healed the sick. There are wells of holy water and statues in the rocks, huts filled with prayer cards and gardens filled with painted stones in memory of loved ones who have passed away. I like to visit them occasionally. I sit in the stillness and observe people crying and praying and I close my eyes and try to let some of their hope get carried on the air and through my pores. I would like to believe that everything is accounted for, that there is life after this one, and that all of our decisions hold some kind of significance or moral worth. There is weight in religion. It is an anchor of sorts.

I cannot believe in the vengeful patriarch of the Catholic Church but sometimes, in the daytime, when there's no one around, I go into the church and light a candle. I like sitting in the quiet and sensing my own insubstantiality against such old and serious things. I am learning that there is a good kind of smallness; a smallness in the face of the universe rather than a smallness in my own body. I like the ritual of prayer and reverence, even though I can't identify with it. I like the feeling that other people believe in something.

115

Rosie and I had the same white heat settling in our bellies. We hashed out plans for sneaking out at the weekends during our bus journeys to school. I dreamed of red buses and boys in turtleneck jumpers with tortoiseshell glasses, wine-stained copies of Joyce shoved in their coat pockets. She wanted champagne and rappers and bandage dresses. We hated the sad shopping centre and the sweaty smell of sausage rolls. A man pulled up at the bus stop and wanked at us. We saw the scarlet tip of his penis through his car window.

We both took Drama class and our school was featured in a production of *A Midsummer Night's Dream*, at the Customs House Theatre in South Shields. She was cast as Hermia and I was Helena. We showed up to rehearsals full of the tingle of the night before. We always giggled during the fight scene because we loved each other so much.

On the day of the show, there was a matinee and an evening performance. I wanted to be an actor. I loved the ropes and the dirty brick walls behind the wings, all the metal and the light rigs, the industrial stuff that held everything together behind the red velvet façade.

We were allowed to wander through South Shields on our own between performances. We passed the strip of chip shops and beach-themed bars that led to the sea. It had that melancholy feeling characteristic of seaside towns and Butlins holiday camps. It was tired and tacky but there was something exciting beneath the sun-bleached glamour and the sea salt.

'Shall we get drunk?' I suggested, the cold wind sneaking under my Beatles crop top. Rosie narrowed her eyes.

'What about the play?'

'I feel sort of nervous. It'll give us a bit of courage.' We walked along the seafront in silence. We felt inconsequential.

'Yeah, alright,' she said, her dark eyes glittering. 'You only live once, and all that.'

We bought a bottle of Lambrini in a corner shop. We

were underage, of course, but passed sultry smiles across the counter, and the man handed the bottle over in a brown paper bag. We tripped out onto the cobbles clutching our prize.

'Shit, Luce!' said Rosie, checking her phone. 'We've only got fifteen minutes.' I pulled open the door of a nearby phone box.

'We'll just have to down it.' We squeezed our bodies up against the glass and passed the bottle between us, fighting back bubbles and snorting between gulps.

'I bruise like a peach!' my phone shouted from my pocket.

'Where R U?' the message read. 'Ur call is soon.'

'Shit,' said Rosie. 'We'd better go.' We left the empty bottle in the phone box and ran all the way back to the theatre, fizzy and light on our toes.

We giggled our way into the dressing room, where everyone stared at us curiously. Our teacher gave us a long, cold look. I bit my tongue until I tasted blood and went to brush my hair in the mirror, trembling with silent laughter.

'Where have you been, girls?' she asked in a quiet, deadly voice. Our call came to take to the stage and there was no time for explanations. We rippled down the staircase and took our place under the hot lights. Our performances were better than ever and afterwards strangers rushed over, gushing compliments. Someone gave me a hug.

'Ooh, you feel like you could snap!' They smiled. 'To be young again, eh?' Our teacher narrowed her eyes as we slipped out into the night at the end of the show, our cheeks rosy with stardom.

It was parents' evening at Josh's school, so my mother couldn't make the show. My dad picked me up with the car windows down, blasting the Beautiful South.

'How was it, Luce?'

'Yeah, alright. Tired. Can I have a wine gum?' I crammed a handful into my mouth and we played 'Old Red Eyes is Back' all the way home, slowing down to scream obscenities at pedestrians in quiet residential areas.

116

This morning when I put on my socks, I remembered the way my grandfather used to put them on for me when I was a child. He always turned them inside out then matched the toes to mine and rolled them up onto my feet. Maybe you have to turn something inside out before you can begin to stand the right way up.

117

I fell in love with a boy in the year above who wore eyeliner and four strings of glow-in-the-dark rosary beads. We went on a school trip to volunteer with pilgrims at a hospital in Lourdes. No one enforced a drinking age in France, and in the evenings after we had served the pilgrims their evening meal, we were free to drink Desperados at plastic tables and snog on sticky street corners. He pushed me into a swimming pool with all of my clothes on and I had to walk back to our hotel with my dress clinging to my body and nuns gasped and gawped as we passed them. He was dangerous and dishevelled and he didn't seem to care about anything.

My mother and Ben went on holiday while I was on the pilgrimage, and I beat them home by a few days. I invited my new boyfriend and all of our friends to stay, and someone sent a text message to everyone in my phone book. They all turned up wielding tinnies and tubes of Pringles. Someone brought a dog and the curtains got pulled from the windows. Beer exploded onto the ceiling in a dirty gold fountain. A guitar appeared and everyone lay on the kitchen floor in the early hours and sang 'Your house is fucked' to the tune of 'Wow' by Kylie Minogue.

I woke up the morning my mother was due back to find bodies splayed all over the sitting room, curled up on bin bags. I threw them out and cleaned the house as best as I could, but there were cigarette butts behind the sofa and slops of port down the paper IKEA lamp. She wanted to know why my bedsheets were stained with blood.

118

I learn the slippery velvet of him. An electric fur that takes me away from you. There is so much tender in morning pillows and on rainy afternoons. Still it is not enough. There is a hard ball in my stomach. It fills the spaces between us. Are you all mine? he asks, and I say, Yes. But I am lying. I do not want to be his. I want to keep some parts for myself. This rough thing inside of me will not let me get close. There are things brewing between my bones. Big things. Embarrassing things. Dreams so gold I can barely contain them. I am bursting full of it but I don't want anyone to guess. If I shrink into the small of his back where sweat beads in broken veins, perhaps no one will find out. I will fold thin wrists and sit quietly in classroom corners. No one will know I have so much inside.

119

My boyfriend and I lay on my bed for hours, shutting out Josh and feeling safe in our postered cocoon. He sneakily smoked cigarettes and we lay on our backs without speaking, watching silver curl into shapes above our heads.

120

Drunk dancing lets me forget. I am liquid in sequins with vodka-coated synapses, spilling and melting in the pearly dark. My limbs are glossy in fake-tan shimmer as strobe lights puddle in spilt drinks, and I fill my empty spaces with dry ice and smoke. You do not like my lies and my secrets, the smell of someone else's pillow strung through my hair. I spend hours sunk in bubbles, locking you out, soaping the traces away.

We went out clubbing before we were old enough, dressing each other up and huddling in bars, sharing tabs and crooning to guitar bands, all skinny jeans and vintage tea dresses, lost in the madness before we could really understand it. We didn't recognise the smell of dried-up Cactus Jack's or detect the sadness in the air when the lights came on.

Lauren and I supped rosé wine in our bedrooms together, throwing dresses on and then pulling them off. We cobbled a private world together from fake tan and fairy lights and the fibs we told our parents.

'You'd better eat something before you go out,' my mother always said to us, but we never did. We wanted to be skinny in our dresses, and if we didn't eat we got drunk faster.

It was the year of mephedrone, and everywhere we went the toilets had a chemical tang. The cubicle doors were plastered with 'Plant Food' stickers. Everyone did it. It was cheap, legal, and unlike anything we'd experienced before. It made us feel like death the next day, but it shaped reality into something sparkly for a few magic hours. It kept us up all night, which was great for dancing. All we wanted to do was dance.

One night we went to see a band play in Sunderland. We all got smashed beforehand and twirled for hours under the lights, the world passing by in a blur of wet lips and smoky heartbeats. We stayed for the club night afterwards and Lauren and I shrieked and slipped over in our little crop tops and sequin skirts, all eyeliner and ribs. We held hands in the smoking area and went to the toilet in twos.

'I love you, you know,' she slurred to me in a dark corner and I wrapped my arms around her. I loved the feeling when we went out together, dusting glitter across our cheeks. The unknown rippled in front of us, waiting for us to fill it.

My boyfriend and his friends often came out with us. We were a gang and it felt great. One night 'Chelsea Dagger' by the Fratellis came on and that was our song. We screamed it as loud as we could, our voices lost below the damp fug of the smoke machine. The club wound down but none of us were ready to end the night. We sought each other out through the dark.

'Let's go back to Rob's for a party,' someone decided. 'There's no one in. We can get some tins on the way.' My boyfriend leaned in for a kiss and I felt a shiver in my knickers.

'Coming, Lauren?' I asked, twirling a strand of her hair around my finger as we waited for the boys to collect their coats.

'Don't think so, babe.' She smirked. 'Jonny's coming to pick me up.'

I pouted. 'Oh, come on.'

'Nah, I didn't text him back all night. He left me a voicemail, seems pissed off. I'd better go.' She was seeing a pizza delivery boy who worked late. He used to pick her up after nights out and drive her back to his in the pizza van, often passing stray slices to us through the window.

'Oh-kay,' I sighed, pulling my boyfriend's jacket around my shoulders. We clattered down the stairs and into the street. Jonny's car was parked outside.

'Alreet, Jonny fella?' shouted my friends. 'Give us a slice of pizza, eh?' Rob twirled Lauren around on the end of his arm and she stumbled, laughing under the streetlights. Jonny's face was strained.

'Alright, babe?' he shot at her. She leaned through the window and planted a kiss on his lips.

'Aw come on, Jonny. Don't be like that! I'm not coming back if you're gonna be sour.' She fluttered her false eyelashes at him. One of them came unstuck and crawled down her face like a sad caterpillar. He laughed.

'In you get then, princess.' Lauren gave me a sticky hug.

'Call me tomorrow, alright?' I told her as she hopped into the passenger seat.

'Will do!' She blew a kiss at me and Jonny winked through the wing mirror as they pulled into the night.

'Hurry up, Luce,' my boyfriend called from further up the street. 'Rob's getting us a taxi.' It had rained and I slipped off my heels and raced after them, enjoying the slap of the damp pavement on my blistered feet.

122

Jonny raped Lauren that night. Her spin with Rob under the streetlights sparked an argument and he pushed her into the back of his van and held her down and raped her among the empty pizza boxes while her tears pooled in her ears.

I met her a few days later at the bus stop.

'You look fucked,' I told her. She groaned.

'Hangover from hell. I've been chucking up for the past three days.' I raised my eyebrows.

'You're a halfer, you are. I feel fine.' She rolled her eyes and rooted through her bag for her free school bus pass.

She didn't tell me what had happened until years later.

'I couldn't say the words until now,' she told me as I held her cold hand across a crowded coffee shop. I had to go into the toilets and rest my head on the cool cubicle door until I stopped shaking. I couldn't get rid of the image of us running away up the street, my drunkenness making me oblivious to the sharp stones in the gutters as I rushed towards the next bright thing, leaving her behind.

123

I am grabbed and touched against my will. Hands brush legs and eyes lurk in shadows and it thrills me at first because it smells adult; perfume and fear. The graze of someone's fingers in a place I did not ask for is a shock like cold water and gives everything sharp edges for a minute or two. I am too big for you to hold me now but there are people in the night who are bigger than you. Later it is special in the lining of my stomach because this is what grown-ups do so now I must be grown up, too.

124

It isn't something more, just something else.

125

I was still working at the restaurant. I graduated to the bar, where I opened bottles and washed glasses, which solved the problem of the chefs in the kitchen but presented a plethora of drunken dads.

'You're a lovely-looking thing, you are,' they said wisely, as though they were experts. 'If I was ten years younger, eh?' They took their bottles of Peroni off to their wives and daughters while I restocked the fridges.

One evening two women came in and ordered their drinks at the bar while they were waiting for a table.

'You're about the same age as my daughter,' said the woman. 'This is Sophie.' Sophie smiled shyly and twirled her straw in her Diet Coke.

'Hi.'

'We're up from London for the weekend. Sophie's thinking about applying to Durham for university, so we thought we'd come and see what it's like.'

'Oh, right,' I said. 'Yeah. Durham's lovely. Good uni, too.' The woman squinted at me.

'Aren't you doing your exams soon?'

'Erm. Yeah. My A levels.'

'And you're still working?' She looked concerned. 'Don't

you need to take time off?' I looked at Sophie. Her eyes were round. They both smelled expensive.

'Ah, no. It's alright. I only do weekends.' Francesca came to take them to their table and I started to unload the dishwasher too quickly, hot glasses burning my skin.

I went out for a break with Joe later in the evening, after the rush when the tables had settled into their spaghetti. He lit a joint.

'Want some?'

'No, thanks.' I liked the sting of cold air on my hot neck. The car park bordered a prison and at night the floodlights bounced across the back of the restaurant, making everything seem dramatic. In the daytimes I could hear the shouts of the prisoners as they exercised in the barbed-wire-rimmed yard.

One afternoon a wrinkled man came in and heaved his body onto a stool. He was jittery and kept jumping at the noises that clattered from the kitchen.

'Just give me a pint,' he said, tossing some change onto the bar.

'We only do bottles.'

'Oh. Right. Bottles of what?'

'PeroniEstrellaCoronaSolandBud.'

'Whatever. Just chuck me whatever.' I stuck a bottle of Budweiser in front of him.

'We haven't got a licence to serve without food, so you'll have to have a packet of peanuts as well.'

'You what?' I started to repeat the sentence. 'Yeah. No. Fine. Whatever.' He downed the beer in one and then went off into the afternoon, leaving the unopened peanuts in his wake.

'Just got out,' Joe said ominously, nodding his head in

the direction of the prison. I envied him that beer. I tried to imagine how the first sip of freedom might taste.

126

The cottage is by a small fishing port that used to be very busy but is now mostly abandoned. My favourite place is the water's edge down by the old fish factories. There are warehouses that were once filled with pools and crates and conveyor belts sitting empty, and rusty boats and water tanks and piles of junk rotting in the caustic rain. There is a huge metal container covered in orange rust and when the light shines onto it, it looks as though it is flaked in gold.

As I walk down by the rocks, I realise that one of the reasons why my thoughts are thick and heavy in London is the lack of abandoned spaces. Everywhere belongs to someone and everything costs money. There is not much ruin or desolation, or places that are forgotten or on the fringes. Everything is fast and new or being knocked down and renovated and built up again. The public spaces are shaped by other people's visions. Even the ancient buildings have a certain kind of shine.

Some of my favourite parts of London are the tower blocks by Burgess Park, the railway bridge over Lower Marsh leading to Waterloo Station, the gasholder on the canal by Broadway Market, and the swimming ponds on Hampstead Heath. These are all spaces where life is allowed to happen on its own terms.

The sense of abandonment here makes me realise that it is good to be in these kinds of spaces in order for my thoughts to wander. The places we inhabit affect our psychologies, and here among the sea daisies and the discarded lobster pots and disused bits of metal, there is space to forget.

127

I came home from school one day to find my mother prickling on the edge of the settee.

'I'll make you a cup of tea, shall I, pet?' She picked up my jacket where I'd dumped it on the floor and draped it gently over the armchair.

'Yeah, okay. Thanks, Mam,' I said, kicking off my shoes and sitting on the rug. She clattered around in the kitchen and returned with steam rising from her hands.

'I have to tell you something, Lucy,' she said, crossing her legs and fiddling with the fringing on the cushion next to her. I felt worried.

'Me and Ben are getting married.'

I blew on my tea and attempted to swallow this new information. 'Woah,' I choked. 'That was quick.' Her face was tense. 'But it's good, Mam. I like Ben. I want you to be happy.'

She stood up too quickly and knocked the cushion to the floor. 'Do you want to see my dress?' she asked.

'You've got a dress already?'

'Well, I've known for a while. I was scared to tell you.' She disappeared into the hallway.

'I hope you like it,' she called. 'It's red. We're having a Christmas wedding. I can hardly wear white again, can I?'

*

They were married in a register office in Durham. She walked up the aisle to 'She's the One' by Robbie Williams. I read an Elizabeth Barrett Browning poem. I wanted to write something of my own but I couldn't find the right words to fill the room, thronged with people I didn't know.

I got ready with my mother beforehand in the hotel up the road. We shared a bottle of Asti and I helped her fix red flowers into her hair.

'Thanks, Luce,' she said, as I heated up the curling wand. 'And I don't just mean for today.' I chewed on a hairgrip while I tried to shape my feelings into a neat sentence. My eyes grew hot when I thought of all the things that had happened. I gave her a hug, being careful not to muss up her dress.

'Mam—' I started. There was a noise at the door. A frazzled-looking woman burst in wheeling a suitcase behind her.

'I'm here to do your hair, Suze!' she squealed, enveloping her in Tommy Girl. 'Thought I wasn't going to be able to get it off work, but I'm bloody here, aren't I?' My mother laughed. 'Aw, thanks, Sharon. Aren't you canny? You shouldn't have.' Sharon opened her suitcase and began to unpack fierce-looking brushes and threatening electrical appliances. She stared at my mother.

'You look proper stunning, Susie.' She put her hands on her hips and took in the bridal suite. 'And this room! I tell you what.' She winked at me. 'That chandelier's going to be swinging tonight!'

128

We didn't tell my father about the wedding. We tried so hard to protect him.

129

Now a new person for you, one who is bigger than me. Who wraps his arms around your waist and shuts the bedroom door with a soft click. You are warm now in his safe dark but where does that leave me? His leather shoes by the front door mean that I am more free, but once you were all mine and now I am just me.

130

The man drives his car drunk and I let him. I trust this person, with his shaky hands and fruity aftershave, with my life. I scrunch it into a small ball and shut it in his glove compartment, where it gets warm from the heat of the engine.

In the morning he is bitter and hungover. I peel myself from the sheets, move softly, trying not to wake him.

'Jesus.' His breath is sour. 'I am fucked.' I stand up, making soothing sounds. 'Christ.' He casts around on the floor for his cigarettes. 'Bring me a glass of water, would you?'

'Okay,' I reply, but I do not. I have seen something broken move across his face and it scares me. It is not up to me to put anyone back together.

I go to the kitchen and fill the sink with hot, soapy water. It is too hot for my tired hands but I don't care. I plunge them into the water again and again, scrubbing stains out of blouses and mud out of dresses. By the time he gets up, my clothes are splayed across the washing line, drying slowly in the winter sun.

131

My A levels loomed neon over the summer, signalling escape. While my peers spent their free periods driving to McDonald's and chatting each other up in the common room, I took to shutting myself away in the library scribbling essays. I did all my reading and got my homework finished so that the evenings would belong to me.

I couldn't bear the wet sulk of chips in the cafeteria and the way that everyone sat in little circles with their bags on their knees, nibbling paninis and making plans for the weekend. At lunchtimes I walked through the housing estates to the concrete shopping centre and sat on my own in Sainsbury's café with a Thermos of coffee, flicking through a magazine. I called my mother.

'How's your day, Lucy love?'

'Same old.' I sighed. 'I'm in Sainsbury's.'

She laughed. 'Oh, Luce,' she said. 'If it makes you feel any better I'm on my lunch, eating sandwiches in a car park.'

I smiled weakly.

'Cheer up, sweetheart. You haven't got long left.'

132

I don't want to be nice and I don't want to be pure. I want things that are mine that you don't know about; love bites and bruises beneath my clothes. I want to build a world from precarious threads. Your sinews are too strong for me. I can see that it hurts you but I am fiercely me.

133

After school I took the bus straight into Newcastle, where I met my boyfriend and his college friends in the Dog and Parrot. We slotted coins into the jukebox and downed treble vodka mixers, desperate for the darkness to fall and the night to be ours.

We often went to bed as the birds were singing, but no matter how late we stayed up, I always went to school the next day. One morning I woke up on the floor of someone's flat surrounded by beer bottles. The room was veiled in nicotine and I stepped over bodies to find my bag and pull on my sixth-form polo shirt. A boy rolled over and watched me getting ready through half-lidded eyes.

'Fucking hell.' He snorted. 'Someone's keen.' I smiled at him and let myself out, stopping to peck my sleeping boyfriend on the cheek. I walked down Chillingham Road and caught the two buses I needed to get to school, plugging in my headphones and resting my head against the window. Bowie's voice spun inside of me like a secret. My heroes were rock stars but they were artists and intellectuals, too.

Books offered me a gauzy version of reality and I stepped hungrily into it. I inhabited an in-between space of terraced streets and bridges laced with lines from novels and iconic film stills. Art layered another world over my real, perceived one and gave me a calm, quiet feeling inside. I had a special English teacher who let me believe that my ideas were important. She introduced me to writers who wound their words around my wrists and refused to let me slip through the net.

I ordered prospectuses from all of the London universities that Google threw up and picked the ones that looked the best in the pictures: girls eating apples in courtyards, books stacked up by their knees. I knew the streets of Camden were lined with poets and rock stars waiting for me to step into their lives and fasten their trench coats over my underwear on Sunday mornings as I popped out for eggs and milk. I wanted a place that was more chaotic than me.

I was called for an interview at Queen Mary, and my English teacher invited me into her classroom to practise some of the questions she thought the admissions team might ask.

'Why London?'

'Um. Museums. Art galleries. Literary history?'

'Anything else?'

I stalled.

'I want to be at the centre of things.'

'I see. And what are you reading at the moment?'

'*The Outsider* by Albert Camus,' I said, rhyming Albert with dirt and Camus with bus.

'Albert Camus,' she said gently, in a perfect French accent.

My mother couldn't afford an extra ticket, so I took the train all of the way from Durham to Mile End on my own. She was convinced I needed to dress in office-wear but I wanted to be glamorous. We had an argument and I flounced out of the house in a sequinned crop top and a leather-look miniskirt. I pulled my coat around my body and waited nervously in a room with a hundred other hopefuls, trying not to make eye contact with anyone.

'She looks nice,' I overheard a mother say to her son, nodding her head in my direction. Her son was mortified. I pulled a sparkly notebook from my imitation Marc Jacobs and tried to look worldly.

When I finally entered the room, the professor gave me a copy of 'Splittings' by Adrienne Rich and asked me to analyse it. I didn't know who Adrienne Rich was but I read the line, 'The world tells me I am its creature' and swallowed. The professor smiled kindly at me and waved her arm towards her bookshelf.

'You know,' she told me, 'there are whole modules of critical theory based on the kinds of ideas we have spoken about today.' I traced the spines with my eyes and I ached for it.

134

I rode the tube to Liverpool Street and walked down Brick Lane. I lingered outside of Rough Trade, ogling girls with short fringes and bright red lips. The door swung open and a couple of boys in tight turtlenecks sloped out with records under their arms, lighting up cigarettes. I skittered out of their way and made my way up the street, feeling drunk as black-clad couples with septum piercings posed for street-style photographers and the smell of hops and second-hand clothes bulged from the doorways. The possibilities of all the different kinds of people I could be; the books I might read and the parties I might go to, shimmered electric above the telephone wires. Flustered by the techno pulsing from cafés, I slunk into a Costa while I waited for my train. My fingers grazed the name badge I'd been given at the interview. I crumpled it into a ball and left it in my cup. Cold coffee seeped into it, obscuring the letters.

135

Unless I look at my phone, I can go weeks without reading the news or learning what is happening in anyone else's life. Of course, living here, away from everything, *is* my reality and yet it seems as though there is some kind of wider reality, some kind of commonality we all participate in. I feel distant from that, which is good and bad simultaneously.

I teach English to kids in Asia via Skype, which is real and not real all at once. Due to the time difference, the classes are early in the morning and my students have usually finished their days. Sometimes their parents are in the background, making dinner in different languages. We communicate intangibly, via electronic documents and words typed in pixels, and yet all of it is real.

A friend from Sunderland living in London wrote me a letter. He said he was homesick and that he wanted to go back to the north-east, to reality, where the place names and colloquialisms felt like wet stones in his mouth.

This morning my student read a passage about heat shimmering. She had never seen heat shimmer before. She didn't understand what I was talking about. I tried to show her a picture on Google Images but I couldn't find one. It is impossible to photograph heat shimmering. Somehow that seems like the most real thing of all.

136

I threw myself into my A level revision with a kind of madness. I plastered the walls of my bedroom with A3 sheets of paper and worked myself into a frenzy memorising notes and drawing complex diagrams with highlighters. My mother found me sobbing on the floor the night before my Psychology exam, books and papers strewn across the room.

'Lucy,' she said, bending down and gently brushing my hair out of my eyes. 'What's wrong?'

'I can't do it,' I choked through trembling fingers. 'I can't remember it all. It's too much.' She coaxed me into the sitting room and poured me a glass of wine.

'Drink this,' she soothed, running her fingers lightly along my arms. 'Calm down. You can do it. It's going to be okay.'

My mother and Ben were on holiday when my results came in. I waited at home for as long as I possibly could before I went into school to collect them. They called me from Greece, supping cocktails with sparkly umbrellas in the sun.

'Tell us, Lucy!' they pleaded. 'We're having a drink for you in celebration.'

'I haven't got them yet,' I confessed.

'Why not, Luce? You've had all morning. Get on the bus. Go on.'

I walked tentatively through the hall to collect my envelope. The local press was there, photographing the students with the top results.

'Here she is!' said my Head of Year, touching my arm. 'We've been looking for you! What took you so long?' I didn't say anything. 'Come over here,' he said, ushering me towards the photographer. 'Let's get you in the *Echo*. Where are you off to, then? Oxford? Cambridge?'

'I haven't opened them yet,' I told him. He laughed.

'Well, go on, then! You've done very well.' I looked at my teachers, and the photographer, and the school hall that I never had to sit in ever again. I squinted in the sun streaming through the window and remembered all the days I had spent between those walls, struggling to breathe.

'I think I'm just going to go, if you don't mind,' I told them. 'I'll open them at home.' My Head of Year frowned. He started to say something but I walked away and out into the day, away from them all.

137

At the end of the summer, Rosie, Lauren, and I went out together for the last time. They both wore red dresses and pulsed like heartbeats under the strobe lights. We shared a carton of chips in the Happy Chippy, where you could buy bags of drugs as an extra with your hot and spicy pizza, and a hot-water bottle for the cold walk home.

I stuffed all of my possessions into an ugly floral suitcase, lying in a star-shape over the lid as I strained to fasten it up. My mother laughed when she saw me.

'You're coming back, you know, Lucy. You don't have to take it all.' I crammed sequins through the sides as my voice wobbled.

'I don't want to leave anything behind.'

138

We walk along the pier and pass an old engine and a rotten dashboard, rusty and forgotten.

'That was a car,' the man says, kicking a piece of plastic.

'Did it just disintegrate?'

'Aye. Things fall apart pretty quickly out here, with the sea spray and the salt in the air. You leave something metal out here and it'll disappear in no time at all.'

I have so many things to leave out here on these rocks. Too many things to carry.

Part Three

I

I stepped off the train at King's Cross and bundled myself into a taxi with all of my bags.

'Where to?' grunted the driver. I fumbled in my bag. 'Just a second,' I told him. 'I can't find the address.' He turned on the meter. 'Maybe just start driving?' I told him. 'I'll find it as we go.'

'But where are we heading, lady?'

'Oh. Erm. I dunno. The Gherkin, maybe? Think it's somewhere round there.' The driver raised his eyebrows and we set off into the uncertainty.

2

I often walk towards the pier past the old fish factories as the sun begins to set. I think that winter sunsets are the best kind. The water is so still and the clouds are streaked with pinks and oranges so sweet they make my teeth ache. I like the juxtaposition of heavy, dirty industry with the fragile sky.

3

Student halls were a flurry of faces and fire doors. People Blu-tacked up band posters and book covers or photos of their mates back home, depending on the kind of portrait they wanted to paint of themselves. There were new ways of shaping old words and subjects I had not known existed. People came from state schools and public schools and leafy boroughs in Essex. They had stepsiblings and no siblings and their parents were doctors and lecturers and earls and cousins of kings. They were big and small and wore hoodies and dresses and trainers and riding boots. They liked poetry and netball and MDMA. Rather than clinging on to the place I came from, I felt the old markers of myself dissipating in the pasta and vodka fug. I could be anyone and no one would know any different.

4

On our first night together we went out in Shoreditch. We tapped onto the bus with our shiny new Oyster cards and went to see a band play at the Queen of Hoxton. I wore a pink dress with a floral hairband and did shots of tequila with boys in ruffled shirts, as miniskirted media babes dripped spritzers and plucked flashing BlackBerries from slogan tote bags. I left my new friends and spun in circles on my own in the dark, closing my eyes and swaying to the bassline. I was surprised when I opened them again and the room was made of solid objects. Behind my eyelids, everything had melted into molten gold.

A boy in a fedora and an open-necked shirt lolled around next to me. He smiled at me and I grabbed his arm and shouted in his ear, 'I just moved here!'

'You what?'

'I just moved here. Today!'

He took in my eager face with a slow smile. 'Cool, man.' He regarded me hazily. 'To do what?'

'I'm studying literature,' I said, trying out the phrase on my tongue.

'Sweet.' He closed his eyes for a few moments. 'What kind of books you into?'

'The Beats, mostly,' I said in an offhand manner. 'Kerouac. Ginsberg.' I pronounced the 'G' as a 'J'. 'You know.'

His lips twitched. 'Yeah,' he mumbled. 'I know. Ever read any Burroughs?'

'*Naked Lunch.*'

'Like it?'

'Sort of.'

He pulled a paperback from his coat pocket. 'Here.' He pressed the book on me. 'Take this.'

I took the torn copy of *Junkie* from his hands and crammed it into my shoulder bag.

'Thanks!' I said. He waved me away and slunk off into the crowd.

I flicked through it on the top deck of the night bus and found words scrawled in biro across the inside cover. My new flatmate peered over my shoulder.

'Aw, it's got his poems in it! I bet he forgot. You should find him and give it back.'

I shoved it into my bag and looked down at the dark

ache of the river as we crossed London Bridge. 'Maybe.'
I shrugged. I had no intention of trying to return the
book. I put it on the shelf in my sickly student room and
looked at it from my pillow. It was my first pearl in a
new world.

5

I am far away now and I can see how the motorways wind
around your heart and coat it in tarmac. Tense phone calls
and scrawled postcards. I like this fast and reckless city
that does not cradle me. I throw myself into it, just to see
what will happen. I like the sting and I love the violence.
I collide with other bodies. On dark dance floors. Cold
streets. Stuffy bedrooms. There are no rules here. I can do
anything I want. I will taste all of the sweetest things. I
am mad, bad, chaos. I don't want your softness. I have
broken out of my bones.

6

There is a timeless quality to the west-coast light at this
time of year. When I look out across the bay it seems
impossible to determine whether it is morning or afternoon
or evening. Everything is misty and the clouds have a purple
tinge to them, as though I am living inside of a bruise. It
isn't quite dawn and yet it isn't quite twilight, either. I am

living in a space outside of time, suspended in the perpetual present.

Nothing changes in this place. I walk past the same houses and fields and cars that I did when I was a child. The same animals are in the same fields. The same people in the same houses. The same cars parked outside. Hair is greyer, there are wrinkles, eyes sadder, a few deaths, but largely everything remains the same. There is a comfort in that. No one can get lost. There is a safe and secure feeling in knowing that if you wanted to track someone down, it would be easy. No one is ever far away.

I am panicked, too, when I think about the stasis. Everyone knows the details of each other's lives. I get restless if I live on the same street too long. I grow to hate the colour of the bus stops and the warm smell of the shops and the same cracks in the same pavements, day after day. People and possessions get lost in cities. They are constantly moving and shifting and changing. If you leave your bag on the seat beside you it will be gone, lost or stolen, or it will simply fall onto the ground and be swept away. You have to hold onto things tightly. Nothing is ever the same twice.

I thought I was a city kind of person. I thought I craved speed and electricity. I thought I got a kick out of the possibility of losing myself and the people who are close to me. I liked the feeling of walking down a teeming street and knowing that an important person yet to appear in my life might be walking right by me and I would never know. Everything is down to chance and opportunity among the multitudes. Here, things seem predestined. I don't believe in destiny and I don't believe in monotony and yet, for some reason, I am here.

7

My fake-tanned limbs that looked shiny and lustrous under the Newcastle club lights were orange in the sticky London sunshine. My artfully draped silk scarves were tacky and my high street dresses were obvious. At the weekends I rode the coloured snakes of the tube to parts of the city I'd read about and traipsed the streets, seeking out a better version of myself.

My student overdraft was free money. Instead of ordering books for my course, I went shopping. I bought a vintage dress patterned with anchors, a pair of leopard-print boots, a camel trench coat, several pairs of polka-dot tights, and an imitation Burberry scarf for a pound from the barrel at Portobello Market. I walked up and down Camden High Street for a week before my classes started, leaving red Rimmel kisses on the ends of Marlboro Lights and ostentatiously propping Burroughs against my pint glass in the Hawley Arms. I was chasing the kinds of people I'd spent years dreaming about, looking for traces of gold dust caught on their winkle-pickers as they darted through alleyways to parties where Z-list celebrities did lines off mirrors and had impromptu photo shoots in the bath.

That kind of world had dissipated while I'd been supping coffee in Sainsbury's and cramming my head with quotes for my A levels. It was a different city now, one of Hawaiian shirts and pool halls in Dalston, Hunter S. Thompson sunglasses and doors at the backs of kebab shops leading to underground parties. I was late, but I hadn't realised yet.

8

We take a shortcut along a dirt track one night on our way down to Jimmy's. I linger by a field of long grass for a moment.

'What's up?' He squints to light a cigarette in the wind.

'Did you ever see the fairy ring here when you were a kid?' He looks at me with a half-smile.

'No,' he says. 'I did not.' It is cold and I pull my jacket close around my body.

'I used to come down here with my brother,' I tell him. 'There was a huge ring of purple flowers. One summer, I took a whole roll of photos, but when I got them developed, they were all black.'

'Aye.' He smirks. 'Well. That's magic for you, that is.' He shoves his hands in his pockets and bends his head against the wind. 'Come on.' He groans. 'It's fucking freezing.'

'I thought about it for years afterwards,' I say, following him down the path. He takes a drag on his cigarette and winks.

'Did you never think that maybe you just had your finger over the lens?'

I am quiet as we walk down the street in the dusk. I have never thought of that.

9

My friend Jake was at drama school and we drank red wine in the World's End one night, saturating ourselves with the city. The streets were caught in our hair like smoke. He went to the toilet and I leaned against the windowsill on my own, trying not to look at my phone.

'Got a light, babe?' asked a woman with a peroxide pixie crop, flinging herself down on the beer barrel beside me. I proudly produced a Zippo from my pocket.

'Cheers.' She squinted through the flame. 'Lovely eyes, you've got. You from round here?'

'I live South of The River,' I said, carefully straightening my syllables, claiming the phrase I'd heard other people use as my own.

'Grow up round there, did you?'

'No. I'm from the north-east, actually,' I told her, keeping my origins purposely vague. 'What about you?'

'Bristol,' she said. 'But London's got me good. It's fucking brilliant here.' She sniffed. 'Do me a favour, babe. I haven't got a coke halo, have I? Can you check?' I looked at her blankly. 'My nose. Any coke up there?' I looked at her nostrils. They were pale and delicate.

'You're good,' I told her.

'Thanks, angel.' Her cheek twitched. 'I like you. You've got a good spirit. You should stick with me. I could show you a good time.'

'Thanks,' I said. 'I'm here with my friend. He's just gone to the loo.'

'Sure,' she said. 'What kind of music you into? I'm good mates with Amy, you know. And I only fuck famous men. We'd be good together, me and you. We could fuck all the pretty boys in Camden. What do you think?' I laughed. Jake came back from the toilet and found her in his seat.

'Oh,' I said. 'This is Jake.' She looked him up and down disdainfully as a bearded man in a suede jacket passed her a drink.

'Get this down you, Carmen, babe,' he ordered. 'We're off to the Lock Tavern.'

Carmen pushed her cold mouth to my ear. 'Stick with me, Goldilocks.' Her breath was chemical. 'I could make you a star.'

10

I feel lonely and turn on the radio but the jangle of the news studio in London and all of the things that are happening in the world make me dizzy. Even though I am alone, quite far away from other people, and my days are filled with walks and books and cooking meals, I have not been able to hear the silence. My mind is roiling with anxieties, thoughts crammed thickly inside of my skull. When I close my eyes at night I hear police sirens calling to me, puncturing my sleep.

11

My lectures were a blur. I had to leave at least two hours early to navigate through the London traffic in time for a 9 a.m. class. I always seemed to be last, bursting through the door in a flurry of coffee and perfume, without my notebook. I ferreted around in my pockets for a pen as people around me calmly supped water and typed diligently on their MacBooks.

We were assigned tutors to look out for us during our first year. I was invited to the office to practise talking about poetry before my first seminar. I crammed in there with four others, ogling the bookshelves and potted plants and looking at the buses trundling along the Strand below. I bit the insides of my cheeks, remembering the Adrienne Rich poem in the Queen Mary interview. We had to introduce ourselves and talk about where we were from.

'I'm sort of northern, too,' gushed the girl next to me, a hockey stick poking out of her Longchamp tote. 'Well, I mean. My family home is there. But I grew up here. That's why I don't have an accent.'

I pushed the 'ewk' out of 'bewk' with burning cheeks and taught myself to say 'buck' that rhymed with 'fuck'. I didn't want heads to turn in seminar rooms while I bungled something vague about books I hadn't had time to read, my voice clumsy and wrong as my classmates half-closed their eyes and pondered elegantly in long and complicated sentences about absolutely nothing.

'It's essentially a degree in bullshitting,' my new friends said sagely as we nursed coffees between lectures at the Caffè Nero across the road.

12

Still, I am wrong. There is another kind of skin that I did not know about. It is posh-girl skin. Expensive and gold. Look how it glows. It is lustrous and shiny where I am mottled. Look at my bruises, my scratches, my scars. Those girls do not have these things. Perhaps I can pure myself out of it. I am dizzy with want. There is not enough space in this city to contain my desire. I want to be smooth and seamless. I want to be light and float through the streets. I want to bury the sad sick parts of myself deep dark inside so that no one will know I am swollen with want, like a dead body pulled from a river.

13

One morning I was on my way to a seminar when I received a text from the bank to inform me I had maxed out my overdraft.

'Shit,' I whispered under my breath. My entire student loan had gone on my rent and I didn't have a penny left in the world. I called my mam. We spoke on the phone every day, sometimes more than once. She called me to ask my opinion on an outfit and I rang her to pass the minutes waiting for a bus.

'Oh, Lucy pet,' she said. 'What are we going to do? I wish I could help you.'

'It's alright,' I told her. 'I've got bar experience. I'll print out some CVs today.'

'I'm so proud of you,' she said. 'You're doing great.' She posted me her collection of McDonald's loyalty cards so I could collect a free coffee at lunchtime, until my financial situation improved.

I trailed around bars and restaurants with my flimsy experience tucked inside of a book, ruffling my hair in shop windows and tugging my skirt before I went in. I feigned enthusiasm for bored girls in Dr. Martens who shoved my name into a crumpled heap.

I wanted to work somewhere cool and exciting. I felt I had done my time in stale waitressing jobs. I read enough music biographies to understand that I could be plucked from an obscure coffee shop job and into something glittering. I knew about Max's Kansas City and the famous corner table.

I sat at a table across from a manager in a converted warehouse bar.

'Just so you know,' he said, meeting my eyes. 'Every member of staff has to work New Year's Eve.' It was September. I smiled, brightly.

'Of course.'

'And if you're after part-time work that means you'll be working every Friday, Saturday, and Sunday. No fucking around.'

'Right. Yes.'

'And the girls are expected to wear full make-up. Skirts. Nice blouses. Heels for events.'

'Yep, got it.'

'Alright, then. Any questions? No? Okay. We'll be in touch.'

My feet ached as I traipsed from bar to restaurant to coffee shop, shying away from places that looked uninteresting or intimidating.

'I'll pass it on,' sighed boys with vacant eyes and lurking managers.

I was about to give up hope when I entered a pub off Spitalfields market, quivering in neon. It was filled with every kind of person: students in holey jumpers, fashion girls in black lipstick, old men watching the football, and wired City boys in shirts and ties.

'I was wondering if you had any vacancies?' I smiled at the girl behind the bar.

'Probably.' She grinned. 'We're always hiring. I'll just get the manager.' She disappeared and returned with a man in cycling gear. He skimmed my CV.

'King's, eh?' He winked. 'Not just a pretty face.' I tried to look upbeat. 'Got experience?'

'Yeah, loads.'

'Alright then, baby. Trial shift tomorrow, okay? Show me what you've got.'

14

Living in a new place can go either way; you can cling to the signifiers of yourself or you can test them and blow them apart. We categorise ourselves in order to try and make sense of who we are. It is a survival mechanism to avoid the loss of the self in the maelstrom of human experience.

Deconstructing your own self-image is thrilling. It is liberating to do things that seem incongruous with the kind of person you have made. I occasionally eat fish even though I am a vegetarian. I dance to music that would not usually make me twist. I kiss men who smell like dirt and metal and forget about the people in my past.

In the city there are so many people and so many possible lives that you have to build strong boundaries in order to define yourself. And yet here, where there is more space, where there are no preconceptions, I am surprising myself.

15

My flat had bedbugs. Everyone's sheets were crawling with tiny, wormy creatures. We discovered them at the same time and spent a horrified night curled up under coats on the kitchen floor. We told reception and they arranged to have our rooms fumigated.

'You will be required to be absent from the premises for at least twelve hours,' they informed us. 'The fumigation process can be harmful if you breathe in the chemicals.' Everyone else in my flat went home for the weekend, back to Essex or Paris or some far-flung corner of London. The day of the fumigation I woke early and spent the day wandering the streets in the cold and listlessly drinking coffees on my own, the city flickering behind my eyelids.

My head was too full to do any reading. I was memorising street names and coffee shops and how to get a good head on a beer in a Staropramen glass and the year of the Chablis and what the celeriac is marinated in and how to pronounce the word Holborn and how to use the Dewey Decimal System and dancing at parties and changing the shape of my sentences, the texture of my skin and the weight of my skull.

When I opened my books the words wriggled and I couldn't make anything stick. I felt exhausted constantly. I rarely ate meals and I perpetually clutched a coffee and rubbed sleep from my eyes. I took up rolling cigarettes so that I would have something to focus on.

I was full of ideas but they didn't seem to be the right ones. I couldn't even figure out how to use the website to find out where my lectures were. I envied how easy it seemed to be for other people as they showed up in their expensive patent brogues and leather jackets. Their Moleskines were neat and organised and they had quotations pursed between their lips like peregrine fruits. They leisurely supped lattes and made dinners and joined each other for wine in East End bars that I didn't know about. They liked indie cinema and small presses and delicate pastries purchased from bakeries on quiet Sunday mornings.

I was too full. I was brimming with the possibility of everything. Other people's lives were carefully curated whereas I was a tangled knot of all of the people and places I had ever wanted to be. I was distracted by every bright thing and enamoured with every person I met who promised a more solid version of myself.

I had burst out of my own skin but I hadn't grown a new one yet. All the tiny shards of myself were loose and drifting, caught with the dust on the roads, illuminated in car headlights. I watched as they landed in the gutter with a lazy sort of panic. I didn't know how to put myself back together.

16

I avoid people. Itchy at mealtimes. Sup coffee slowly. Guzzle white wine. Watch strangers. Get nervous. There are so many things I do not know the names of. There is pho and plantain and falafel and tagine, and food is luxuriant in this place. Meals trickle richly into afternoons like incomprehensible poetry and my tongue is too thick to comprehend the taste. I am not delicate enough to understand nuance. The potato smiley faces of my childhood are beige mush now. Dairy causes acne and gluten is the devil. Tapioca and soy milk and Maldon sea salt. Almonds are unethical and cheap beer causes migraines. If our bodies are defined by the things we put into them, then I am too afraid to put anything into mine. I am cheap things, sad things, small and unrefined.

17

I know that an individual life is precious so I have to hold on to it very tightly, with both hands. In London, things move too fast for anyone to hold on to anything. Restaurants and bars open up and then close down, friends move from flat to flat, buildings are built and then demolished again. The skyline looks different, year after year.

18

I took a class called Writing London. We had lectures about writers like Arthur Conan Doyle and Daniel Defoe, and our first assignment was to write something related to the city.

'What we're really looking for,' said my lecturer, 'is a creative response that is rooted in an academic context. We want you to use the set texts as a springboard for your ideas and really interrogate the process of constructing your identity within this ever-changing landscape.'

I felt excited. Reading and referencing and even just finding my way around the library made my vision blur, but a creative response to the city sounded like something I could do.

I spent a Saturday before work at the Tate Modern. The clean, white spaces helped me to focus and allowed me to take in other people's thoughts. The thematic arrangement of the artworks gave me solace in a structure that was lacking inside of my own head. What impressed me most about visual art was the way that people could have tiny thoughts in their minds that were taken seriously and made manifest in the physical world.

The Turbine Hall was filled with Ai Weiwei's sunflower seeds. There were one hundred million seeds on the floor, and each seed was made from porcelain and hand-painted in China. I looked at them from the upper level and marvelled at the scope of it and then I walked down to the ground level and picked one up. I could see the brush-strokes made by someone in a factory thousands of miles away.

19

Since I came to live here and gave myself room to think and to breathe, a liquid calm has begun to pool inside of me. I am coming back into myself. When I arrived in London, I wasn't cool or collected and I felt ashamed of how desperately I wanted a chance. It is embarrassing, or entitled, or greedy to want things in a city where so many others are wanting. My dreams dissipated. I had no time or energy to read when my head was crammed with survival. Academia seemed fusty and distanced from reality.

I have been reading a lot here. There is not much else for me to do. In thinking about language, I am becoming increasingly conscious of the way in which words and ideas shape our world. I am beginning to feel things again, and beginning to respect my own hunger, to listen to it rather than fear it.

I am learning my tastes. I like bitter things like wine and coffee. Sour things. Spicy things. Lemon and chilli. Smells that are so pungent they almost hurt. I like the way that fish is on the verge of disgusting. I like the rotten brown sea smell and the taste of burnt cinnamon stuck to the bottom of the pan, vegetables overcooked and shrivelled into accidental crisps. I like the horrible carbon mulch on my tongue, like chewing coal. I like too much salt and too much pepper. Bare skin in the freezing wind. I like sitting so close to the fire that my legs break out in a pink rash and I like bruises on the insides of my thighs and to be bitten so hard it almost draws blood. I like the taste of sweat and oil and that day-old skin smell. I like that scalpy hair scent and seeing dirt under other people's fingernails.

20

I wrote an essay for the creative assignment based on the sunflower seeds. I didn't care about Dickens or Defoe or the countless flâneurs who traipsed the streets floating above it. I couldn't identify with writers who ghosted around cities making observations, removed from the pulse of it.

I felt everything so deeply. When the ground vibrated as the tube went past, it seemed as though it was running right over my bones.

My new friend Amy and I collected the marks from our first assignment together, feeling wobbly.

'Your prose is purple,' mine said in the comments. A big, bold 'F' glowered in the corner. I looked at Amy. 'What does it mean?' I asked her, feeling wronged.

'Haven't got a clue, mate.' She blinked back tears. 'I got an E.'

'I got an *F*.'

'Do you think we should go and see him?'

'I dunno. It's kind of embarrassing, isn't it?' We walked along Fleet Street with the weight of history bricked around us in law buildings and offices and we felt like maybe we weren't supposed to be there after all.

'Fancy the pub?'

'Yeah, alright.'

The whole of our year was in the pub. There was some kind of cocktail deal and the tables were stacked with saccharine concoctions, sugar syrup and maraschino cherries leaking onto the tables.

'Lucy!' someone shouted. 'Amy! Come over here. How did you do?' Amy and I exchanged glances.

'It's alright,' someone else said. 'We all did shit. I got a C. A C! I've never had a C in my life.' Amy made eyes at me and headed to the bar.

She went to the toilet a few hours later and didn't come back for a good twenty minutes. I twisted my hips through the sticky glasses to find her. I banged on the cubicle door.

'Amy?' She didn't answer. 'Shit.' I dashed up the stairs to get a second opinion and one of our classmates told the bar staff, who broke down the door and then called an ambulance.

'Can I come with you?' I asked the paramedics when they arrived. 'I'm her friend.' They looked at each other.

'Yeah, okay. That should be alright. Have you been drinking, too?'

'Yeah. I'm fine, though.'

They shone a light into my pupils as I climbed into the ambulance. 'Can we get a few details off you? Do you know her next of kin?'

'No. We just started uni together.'

'We need someone. Do you have her phone? We can get a number out of there.'

'Is she going to be alright?'

'She'll be fine. We'll get her on a drip and she'll be right as rain.'

I sat beside her bed in the hospital all night as she slept wired up to liquids and people groaned in the darkness around us. The nurses popped in and out occasionally, narrowing their eyes at me and holding information about her condition tightly to their chests.

'Students, are you?' Their words were barbed.

21

I doodled on my essay and reread the notes while I waited. I looked up the definition of 'purple prose' on my phone. It said, 'Purple is widely seen as immoral and insincere. The artsy, exterminating angel of depravity.' I quite liked the sound of that.

22

I come home and you hurt at how my collarbones poke out. There are things inside of me that you do not recognise and I do not belong to you any more. That deep, dark place between us is going. I am giving it away to strange boys between my black sheets. To hungry faces in the street. To nightclub queues and coffee shop corners. I can see the sharp between your shoulder blades and I am pleased. I am stifled by people who think they know what shape I should be. I can take you by surprise. Look at my power.

23

I want a life that is full, which means dirty and delicious. Order seems to mean emptiness, or at least it does for me. I want coffee spilled on the carpet and stew slopped across the stove. I want stacks of dirty plates and cups and bowls, evidence that people have eaten. I want to hold solid shapes in my mouth; boiled potatoes and penne pasta and whole hot tomatoes. I want paper and pens and scraps of things.

Dead wildflowers and clouds of incense ash. I want my hands stained with beetroot juice and bedsheets streaked with the dirt of my days. Compost heaps and biscuit crumbs.

I am so afraid of consuming, of taking, of whether or not I have the right to things. I want to expand and leave traces of myself. I want evidence that I am existing.

24

I went for coffees with classmates who linked my arm and spun internships in New York and futures in publishing into the air above our heads. I made friends with Alex, who was older than me. He was clever and cynical and we sat up in his room all night drinking cheap red wine and talking about our ideas, penning first chapters of crap novels and smoking out of the window. Talking with him gave me that building block feeling again, as though our ideas might grow arms and legs and go out into the world and change things.

No matter how many late nights I worked at the pub and how many lectures I missed or how inadequate I felt, walking over Waterloo Bridge was always special. Bridges are in-between spaces and I was in between, too. I liked straddling the north and south of the city and tensing my body against the current of the buses. I looked at the buildings huddled along the river, seeming old and delicate next to the swell of the Thames. I liked how it all looked small and fragile, as though it could be crumpled carelessly in a fist, when in reality I knew that money and power ran beneath the pavements like electricity cables. I liked looking at Westminster and Tower Bridge and the way it seemed real and unreal simultaneously. It was a gaudy dream; all that tinsel shimmering just out of reach.

25

I would like to build a dry-stone wall. I like the thought of being taught how to do it by a stoic stone expert, who will roll his eyes at me and my dyed hair and my patent raincoat and assume that I will not be able to do it. I will surprise him by choosing my stones very carefully and slotting them together in impossible ways. I will be so dedicated to my wall. I will build all night with a torch at my side. When I am finished I will stand back and look at it. It will be a small wall; one that people can easily step over. I don't want to fence anyone in, or keep anyone out. I only want to build a real, solid thing in the world. I will come back and visit my wall from time to time. I will say to friends and lovers, 'I built that.' They won't believe me but I will press my thumbs into the scars on my fingertips, and I will know, and that will be enough.

26

Working at the pub became a lesson in style. I studied people from behind the bar, noting the chunky boots I would wear, the calf-length dresses, the eyeliner and the flash of glittery lurex, the leather jackets and the different washes of denim, as soon as I was free from the world of comfortable shoes and dresses with garish patterns to mask the beer slops and the red wine stains.

In the summer people spilled onto the pavement in raucous groups, while I wound my way through the crowds collecting glasses and sweeping up cigarette butts. I longed for the day when I might be one of them. I served obnoxious City boys who racked up a year's worth of my university fees in gin and tonics, and girls with silver nose rings and empty eyes. Old East-enders in flat caps sighed into pints of bitter over the changing face of their neighbourhood as tourists counted out pennies with confused fingers, repeating 'blonde beer' over and over with anxious smiles.

The manager, Jay, had a lot of dodgy deals going on. He was always showing up to work with a black eye or a bruised jaw and he let the City boys do lines of coke off the bar in full view of everyone. It was rumoured that his wife had thrown him out and he spent most nights on the scummy sofa in the office upstairs. One Saturday, some of his mates had a stag party in the private dining room. I went up to collect glasses and found a naked woman dancing on the table. The men had their ties wrapped around their heads like schoolboys on the back seat of the bus. I left the glasses to pile up and padded quietly downstairs.

When Jay was in a good mood, he was charming and let us drink as much as we wanted to get through the night. He made us special shots mixed with lemon juice and sugar syrup and asked the kitchen to send down steamed vegetables and giant tubs of hoummos sprinkled with paprika, for us to snack on mid-shift. When he was in a bad mood he was foul, swearing at us and leering drunkenly on the bar.

'Pretty little Lucy,' he spat at me one night when he was off duty. 'You think you can get anything you want, don't you? Just by fluttering your eyelashes.' I bit my lip and went off to clear tables.

Every week we did a line clean, which meant the pipes that snaked their way from the cellar to the beer taps had to be emptied. We sat at the bar after hours as the remnants were poured into jugs and ice buckets. Astrid the fashion designer always stayed, in her painted leather jacket, and a couple of boys in baggy white T-shirts who stumbled into work bleary-eyed after their DJ sets, claiming to have been up for days. There was a strip club across the road where we often ended up in the early hours, and the dancers and bouncers occasionally joined us.

One night we locked the doors, turned off the lights and settled in for a party. I loved that time of night, when everyone else went home to bed and the city became ours. There was something feral about it, the bar staff and the people who didn't have to get up for work in the morning cut loose, trying to find an outlet for the sticky heat that built up during the hours watching other people dancing. There was something dangerous in the energy sweating from our collective skin.

'Adnams or Addlestones?' asked Max, sliding a pint glass along the wooden bar. I groaned inwardly. Both made me sick and sluggish.

'Addlestones,' I said. My feet ached and my arm hairs were gooey with sambuca. I couldn't bear the thought of heading back to my single bed in my student room, alone with my exhaustion, away from the warmth of the tall city buildings. They made me feel safe and important, blocking out the forever of the sky. The night unfurled across my back like silk and I forgot there were such things as stars and planets and all of that time stretching on into infinity.

Jay pressed his hands into the small of my back, making me jump.

'Tough night, eh baby?' He smirked at my glass. 'Fucking students. Can never say no to free booze.' Max played the beer taps like a musical instrument, relishing his position of power behind the bar, even after closing time. Astrid plugged her phone into the speakers and played 'Heart of Glass' by Blondie, singing along in her gravelly voice. The night passed in illicit glasses of wine and shots of Jägermeister pilfered from the fridge when we thought Jay wasn't looking. The chef nursed a pint drowsily in the corner, his face pale against the red welts on his forearms. He vomited chicken casserole onto the table and Max lurched over with a wad of blue roll.

'Okay, mate.' He laughed. 'Home time, I think. Come on, you lot. I've got to be back here in a couple of hours.'

'Oh, just one more.' Astrid pouted, scrolling through her phone for more music. 'I'm only just getting started!' Max made a face and turned on the dishwasher.

'Nah, come on,' said Jay, with red-rimmed eyes. 'Max is right. You'll all thank him in the morning.' He looked at me. 'Isn't that right, Lucy?' I hated Jay when he was drunk. His eyes sneaked under my clothes and coated my skin in something frightening.

'Anyone seen my smokes?' he asked. He picked up his jacket and his keys, and an assortment of coins and lighters skittered across the floor.

'Time for bed, Jay?' I teased. He grunted and made for his racing bike, propped up against the wall. Max frowned. 'Maybe sleep here tonight, eh, mate?' he offered. 'You've probably had too many to cycle.'

'Yeah, yeah,' he mumbled. 'Alright, boss.' He stumbled. Max sighed in mock exasperation.

'Give him a hand upstairs, would you, Lucy?' I rolled my eyes and took Jay's weight as he dragged his feet on the landing in protest. My head started to spin when we got to the office.

'Just a minute,' I said, collapsing into the sofa, flaked with paint from the ceiling. I closed my eyes for a second and opened them to find Jay steadying himself on the fireplace. I snorted.

'You should get some sleep, Jay. Are you working tomorrow?' The voices of the street cleaners thudded against the windows.

'No need to worry about me, baby,' he said, sadly. I wondered about his wife as I turned to leave.

'Wait,' he said, fumbling in the dark.

'What, Jay? I'm knackered. I've got lectures tomorrow.' His hands found mine and he pulled me roughly towards him and burrowed his face in my neck. It took me a second to realise that he was pressing my hand onto his hot, hard penis. A sharp pain shot through my head, sobering me up. I snatched myself away from the beery, dirty stink of him.

'What the fuck?'

His eyes met mine for a long second. The shape of something irrevocable settled between us in the early-morning light.

'Jesus,' he grunted, collapsing onto the sofa. 'Sorry.'

Downstairs, people were blearily pulling on coats, calling taxis, and looking up bus routes on their phones.

'Will you be alright getting back, Lucy babe?' asked Astrid, jangling Max's keys with black fingernails. I pulled my too-big trench coat tightly around my body.

'I'll be fine,' I said, waving her away.

I sat on the plastic seat at the bus stop next to a boy with cat's whiskers dripping from his cheeks. I took Jay's cigarettes from my pocket and lit one, enjoying the sting of it in my lungs.

27

The sheets on my bed in student halls were my old set from home. I had chosen black so that my fake tan wouldn't ruin them. When I pulled the covers over my head it was velvet-dark and silent. I fell into thick, impenetrable sleep.

28

One night we go out to an island by boat. Someone is having a party in one of the abandoned houses on the rocks. There is no electricity so we bring a bag of tea lights. There is a sheen to the night like polyester. The moon hangs precariously above us. It is so full that it seems as though it could fall into the water at any moment, tearing a hole in the sky. The man lights a cigarette and sits on the side of the boat. We career violently over to one side. I laugh, thrilled at the thought of falling into the deep unknown together. I pull my sleeves over my hands as the cold leaks under my jumper. The man wriggles out of his hoodie and hands it to me.

'I'm alright,' I protest. 'I don't need it.'

'I know,' he says. 'I'm a bit claustrophobic, sure. I want to feel the wind. This is fucking living, this is.' He pulls his T-shirt over his head.

Our driver rolls his eyes. 'Fucking header, you are. She's not impressed.' I slip his jumper over mine, despite myself. It is warm and smells of tobacco. I watch his ribcage expand as he sucks on his cigarette. I can see the shape of his skeleton. He looks young and fragile in the moonlight. There is a smattering of acne across his shoulders, pink and raised, as though his skin is struggling to contain the life beneath it. Just for a moment, I want to push him overboard.

29

It is not enough to be pretty and I am not clever enough, and it is not enough to be clever and I am not pretty enough. I thought I was coming to a place where my brain would be enough but my brain is in a body and it is my body that moves through the city, even though my thoughts do, too. I have to dress myself up in the right kinds of clothes so that people can guess that I am thinking the right thoughts but what thoughts are the right thoughts and haven't they all been thought before?

30

'I'm going to take up dancing,' I declare to the man sitting at the bar. It is almost Christmas and we are in Jimmy's, surrounded by coloured lights. The Waterboys are playing an old song on the television. I pick at some faux branches.

'What kind of dancing?' he asks, eyebrows raised.

'I don't know. Something very physical, without many rules.' He frowns. 'I don't live in my body enough,' I tell him. 'You know? I want something that takes me out of my head and brings me back into myself.' He looks at me blankly. He cannot understand. His mind and his body are so united that he can't imagine ever having to bring them back together. He has never felt that fracture inside.

31

Every morning before work at the fish market, my grand-mother sat at the kitchen table in front of her magnified mirror. She drank a strong cup of tea and smoked three cigarettes, pulling them from the packet with coral-coloured fingernails, her hands raw with bleach. Steam and smoke mingled and the kitchen glimmered silver. She rubbed Leichner foundation into her face, thick and greasy like stage make-up. She used her Esteé Lauder lipstick as a blusher, pulling it across her cheeks in thick lines and rubbing it in with her fingers. She sprayed her hair with lacquer until it set, crisp as cardboard, ready to withstand the day.

32

When I worked in Jay's pub, I turned up to every shift in bright red lipstick. It wore off during the night as I pursed my lips in irritation or sipped secret gin and tonics from a shelf beneath the bar. I nipped off to the toilets to reapply it, squinting in the blurry mirror. It was a barrier between me and the drunken punters, their eyes grazing my body as they complained about the prices. It let me seem bold during a time when I felt my skin wearing away.

33

I loved checking the little blue letter box in the reception of my student halls. My mother sent me a steady stream of postcards and my friends posted letters filled with sand and shells from the beaches back home. One day I found an invitation in gold gilded lettering.

'His Royal Highness of Saudi Arabia cordially invites you to his 21st birthday celebration,' it read. I showed it to my flatmates bemusedly.

'He's in our year,' I explained. 'Crazy, eh?'

I bought a minidress encrusted with silver diamanté and resolved to be on my best behaviour. He lived in a big white house in South Kensington and I took my flatmate Carly as my date. We were let in by a member of staff in a white blouse, who frowned at my old leather jacket and whisked us into a mirrored room where a table quivered with piles of canapés and pastries. We were handed a bottle of champagne to share between us and we polished it off quickly, lurking in corners and feeling awkward.

We were given free rein of the house, including a balcony crowded with plants and water features, a lit-up square of blue in the centre. We made tipsy conversation with illustrious French girls clutching expensive handbags. No one seemed interested in us, not even the sleazy boys with sticky eyes and pressed chinos.

At midnight, someone came around with a pile of cigars on a silver platter. We took one each and lighters were passed around the group.

'I have smoked these once before, with my father,' a girl said to no one in particular, perched on the edge of the white leather sofa. 'They cost at least thirty pounds each.'

'They are from Persia,' the man with the tray said, smiling grandly at us. I sneaked an extra one into my dirty tote bag for my flatmates to marvel at later.

There was a room with a dance floor but everyone seemed too prudish to get involved. Bottles of champagne kept appearing. The prince himself didn't drink for religious reasons, but he was anxious for his guests to have a good time.

I started talking to an older man in the queue for the bathroom. I asked him what his connection to the family was.

'I am the prince's tutor.' He smiled at me earnestly. 'I help him with all of his schoolwork.'

'He writes his essays,' Carly hissed in my ear. It turned out you could buy anything in Kensington, even a degree.

I lost Carly somewhere in the lights and the heavy curtains and wandered around the vast house on my own, growing drunker and drunker. I hadn't eaten all day and nipped into the canapé room. I smiled graciously at the guests mingling in there and popped an array of canapés and some foil-wrapped chocolates into my bag to eat on the way home.

I bumped into Carly on the landing, caught in an awkward entanglement with a floppy-haired boy in an open shirt.

'Carly?' I tugged her elbow. She looked at me gratefully. 'I've been looking everywhere for you.'

'I think I need to go,' I said to her, ignoring the boy as he wound his arm around her waist. 'I feel too weird.'

'Yeah,' she said, looking at the boy. 'Let's get out of here.'

As we made to leave, my heel skidded on the top of the marble staircase. I was always drunk or running late and I tripped over so often that I had permanent scabs on my knees. They never had a chance to heal before I knocked them off again.

I went flying down the stairs. My bag pirouetted spectacularly over the bannister and stray coins and gold chocolates rained onto the heads of the staff below, like sweets thrown into the crowd at a pantomime. They rushed to clear away my contraband collection of canapés and cigars, splayed all over the floor.

'I think it is time for you to leave,' the tutor said to me curtly, once everyone had realised that I was miraculously okay. 'There are cars waiting outside. Come on.' He led me to the door. I turned around to look for Carly and caught her halfway between hilarity and horror.

'We were doing so well,' I said to her. She shook her head at me with twitching lips. I saw the marble staircase behind her, grand and white and streaked with my blood.

34

Is history bound to repeat itself? There are tremors of my grandfather's life running through mine, in his cups and bowls that I use in the mornings. There is a dirt path in the garden where the grass still doesn't grow, marked by years of his feet treading forwards and backwards. I am here because of the past; because of the ghosts who lived and died in this house. Do I owe them anything?

35

As soon as I saw the pub I felt a heavy sickness. I hated the smiles of the people outside, the smell of the beer and the stench of money, the too-loud voices and the same Fleetwood Mac song that played over and over, night after night.

I came in one day and flung my bag onto the bar with a sigh.

'What you doing here, Lucy babe?' asked Astrid. 'You're not on the rota.' I frowned at her.

'What are you on about? It's Friday. I always work Fridays.'

She grabbed the rota from a hook on the wall and flicked through it. 'Not tonight, babe. You've got the night off. Lucky you. Go out! Have fun. Relax.'

I felt hot behind my eyes. 'But I've only done one shift this week. I have to work tonight. I won't be able to eat.' I felt a hand on my shoulder and jumped to find Jay standing behind me.

'Go home, Lucy,' he said, blankly. 'We don't need you tonight.'

'But Jay—'

'If you're going to act like a child I'm going to treat you like one, Lucy.'

'What are you talking about?'

'That shift you booked off for the party. You think you can get anything you want in this world with that pretty little face of yours. And I'm so sorry to be the one to break it to you, baby, but that's not the way life works.'

I trembled with anger. I picked up my things and left, without saying a word. I saw Astrid's pale face out of the corner of my eye, looking at Jay uncertainly.

As I stood at the bus stop trying not to cry, something pink and fluttery caught my eye. I stepped on it and bent down to pick it up. It was a fifty-pound note. Maybe the streets were paved with gold, after all.

36

I have been feeling wild lately. There is a huge amount of energy building beneath my skin. I am reckless and angry and I cannot expel it. I go running through the forest and down to the sea. I cycle in the wind listening to punk and sing along at the top of my voice. I write and I walk and I run and I cycle and I even scream into my pillow but still it is there, rippling in my chest.

This feeling coincides with the appearance of dogs. They chase me everywhere I go. They run after my bike, barking and yacking, jumping up onto the tops of walls as I walk past. I have been chased by at least seven dogs in the past week. I think they can sense the madness. There is something canine or wolfish about me and they are threatened.

37

I took advantage of the time off and got the Megabus home for a few days. It took seven hours, including a stop at the services so people could grab Burger Kings and oversized bags of Thai Sweet Chilli Sensations. The sky grew greyer the further north we drove.

My mother's house looked small and strange. It was familiar and melancholy all at once, tinged with nostalgia like an old photograph tucked unexpectedly inside of a book. I felt nervous as I walked through the gate. The changes taking place inside of me would be reflected in the eyes of my family.

I went out with Lauren and everything felt wrong. All of the pubs had toilet seats. I wore tights and boots under my dress and she seemed small next to me, shivering in her little dress without a coat.

'You sound proper posh!' said a group of lads from school as we squished into their booth with our treble vodka mixers. 'Too good for us now.' I made a face at them and downed my drink.

The smell of smoke machines and sick didn't make me tingle the way it used to. It was as though there was a perspex wall running through the middle of the club and all of the fun was happening on the other side. I could see it and hear it and even taste it, but there was no way that I could get through. I had given all of it up for something else. I chose to go but I didn't realise I would have to leave so much of myself behind.

My old life was raw and exposed and it felt meaningful. I couldn't compete with other people at university in terms of money or knowledge or intelligent witticisms, but the music and dancing were absolutely mine.

I felt nervous as I passed through the doorways of pubs and clubs, knowing my old boyfriend was out there somewhere in the dark. People who had once been friends seemed cold. I understood that it was his city and not mine any more.

Before I went back to London, my mother pressed an address book onto me with the addresses of relatives and family friends printed in her familiar handwriting.

'You seem a bit distant, Lucy love,' she said, as she drove me to the train station. 'Everything alright?'

I smiled at her. 'Yeah, you know. Just a bit stressed with essays and stuff.'

'Don't stress, sweetheart. That stuff isn't worth getting all het up about.' She pressed a twenty-pound note into my fist. 'These are the good times, you know.'

I breathed her in hungrily. 'Thanks for the address book.'

'I know it's a bit daft but you've been hard to get hold of. I don't want you to lose touch with people. Everyone really cares about you, you know? It wouldn't hurt to send a card from time to time, would it?' I felt guilty then, for stretching myself out.

38

Some days there is so much static I don't know what to do with it. It builds in my toes in the mornings and makes its way through my body, popping through my veins and crackling in my joints. When it reaches my chest I get on my bike and cycle into town. I listen to the Slits and pedal as fast as I possibly can. The feeling dissipates a little and comes out of my mouth and my nose in clouds of hot breath.

One day as I turn a corner, I am confronted by the ache of the sea and feel struck by a strange sensation. It is something to do with the clear, sharp quality of the light and the faint trace of salt in the air. It is related to the movement of the tyres over the potholes and the parts of myself in my peripheral vision; the ends of my hair streaming around my head, my long, pale arms and my thighs strong and curved with cycling muscles. A blue joy seeps into my stomach at the sight of the sea and for a moment I am my ten-year-old self again, hurtling down a hill without holding onto the handlebars, wild and tough. It is comforting to know she is inside of me. I sometimes fear that the primary parts of myself have been lost forever, rotting on roundabouts and moulding in cul-de-sacs.

39

I sat on the train and watched the terraced houses and the cathedral and the cobbles and the soft pink shape of my mother blur into the past. I sensed relief as the train pulled out into open fields. Perhaps Sunderland would never belong to me again but I had a different world now, one that I had built myself from scratch. It was a difficult place but I had chosen it. I opened my book and ignored the sky flashing by on my way back into it.

40

Spring blossomed into summer and we lay in parks making daisy chains and drinking cider. The streets were thick with the smell of jerk chicken and sunlight hitting the pavements. I bought a bike and cycled around the Elephant and Castle roundabout with one hand holding my skirt, the hot air from the lorries sending a shiver down my bare legs and into my sandals, books crammed in my basket. Everything felt like a celebration. People lounged on windowsills outside of pubs, and we left the library to smoke cigarettes and then headed out to dance with grass in our hair, our laptops shoved in a corner.

I wanted to put down roots in the city beyond university. The transient feeling of the chequered moving bags shoved under my bed made me seasick. I hated the thought of finishing my degree and having to go back home. I made friends over the bar at work and went to parties and art openings with them. I went for coffees and to gigs and bars and nightclubs and for long walks in the afternoons with all kinds of people. I went out with anyone who asked.

'You remind me of someone I went to school with,' an American boy with floppy hair told me one night as we sat on the railings of a balcony at a house party.

'Oh. How come?'

'You seem like you get carried away with things. Like you're searching for something. Looking for your next trip.'

41

My mother comes to visit. We sit in front of the fire and I tell her I bumped into Patrick a couple of times. She gives me a look.

'That was a strange time in my life, you know, Lucy,' she says, reaching out to touch my arm. 'I made a lot of mistakes but I was learning how to laugh again. I hope I didn't damage you in any way.'

I smile at her, caught off guard by the sudden intimacy. 'I understand, Mam,' I tell her. She looks into the fire.

'I hope so,' she says, uncertainly. I bite the ends of my hair and taste the peat smoke caught in it.

42

I am wrong again and I will never be right. I am burning in a cold way, like ice when it sticks to the skin. The other girls seem smoother, thin wrists cool and marbled, whereas I am sticky and hungry and soiled. I want to be harder and cleaner and better. I don't want to be made from blood and breakable bones, like you.

43

I fell in with a Hackney Wick crowd and spent weekends dancing in warehouses, dangling my feet in the dirty canal as people passed pills to each other with their tongues and the sun rose peach above the tower blocks. We slept naked on the roof covered in glitter and smiled serenely at the factory workers and the couples in encroaching luxury flats who looked down on our playground.

There were rails of costumes and bikes lining the corridors. Someone was always building or taking down a wall or an installation. Everything was in flux. It felt like the kind of world I had dreamed about during those lunchtimes in the sixth form library, forcing my pen into shapes.

One weekend there was a festival. I turned circles on a chimney pot as the sky lightened, then I passed out on a mattress in the corner of someone's bedroom. When I woke up, I had a text from my dad.

'Love you, Lucy,' it read. It was unusual. He rarely sent me messages.

My mother called me in tears. She said she hadn't heard from him for a while and she had grown concerned. She went to his house and found him crouched in a corner muttering to himself. He had taped silver gaffer tape all over the walls and scrawled strange poems across it in capital letters.

'Tom,' she said, crouching down beside him. 'Tom. Come on. We need to go to hospital.'

'Go away, Susie,' he groaned. 'What are you doing here?'

'I was worried about you, Tom. How long have you been here? What about work?' He put his hands over his face and pulled invisible cobwebs from his hair.

'I need to go to the barbers, Susie.'

'What?'

'My hair! Can you not see it? It's so long. All the way down to my bum. When did it get so long, Susie? How did this happen?' She looked at his short curls.

'I'm not coming, Susie,' he said. 'I'm fine.'

My mother didn't know what to do so she called an ambulance and they both got in it. My father had a panic attack when they got onto the motorway and screamed for them to stop.

'My heart!' he shouted. 'I've got pains in my heart.' My mother took his hand. 'I'm dying, Susie. I'm dying. Make them stop.' He fumbled for his phone.

'My kids,' he said. 'Our kids.' The 'love you' text I was too busy dancing to read was what he supposed to be his last words to me. I felt dazed as my mother told me this on the phone.

'Are you okay?' I asked her.

'I'm okay. Are you?'

'Yeah.' I tore a piece of skin from my finger with my teeth. 'I'm fine.'

Everything was fuzzy. The architect lived in one of the warehouses and I had a bag of clothes in his room. I rooted through it for my little sailor dress and changed and went back to the party. Everyone there was older and cooler than me. I clutched the architect's hand and gratefully accepted the mug of wine he passed me. I always felt guilty when I was having a good time, as though something bad would have to happen to restore the balance.

The festival took on a darker quality in the early hours of the morning. It always did in those crowds, when the drugs ran out and people began to fear the light of their ordinary lives leaking in. Repetitive bass boomed from a car park as people moved with dazed expressions and the shriek of laughing gas canisters tore through the dawn.

We danced under a makeshift wooden shack until it suddenly collapsed, tearing open shoulders and faces. Someone emerged from a warehouse wielding an angle grinder to fix it, and a rumour that a boy had lost a leg crackled electric through the air.

'Let's get out of here, shall we?' said the architect, taking my hand. We climbed a shaky ladder to a roof that was arranged to look like a dining room. We had sex and afterwards there was blood pooled on the fake parquet floor. We couldn't figure out which of our bodies it was coming from.

'One of us must have cut ourselves or something,' he said. 'I wouldn't worry. It doesn't hurt, does it?' I lay down in the blood and went to sleep.

44

My mother and I drink tea at the old wooden table; the only thing we didn't burn.

'The best meal I ever ate,' she says, 'was with your granddad, at this table. Lemon sole and new potatoes.'

'What was the best part?' I ask her.

'I don't know, really. It was very simple. Just me and him, at opposite ends. Butter on everything. Molten gold.'

'Did you love him?' I ask her.

'Of course I did. He was a hard man, but he had a hard life. He gave my mam hell, but after she died, I started to let that go.'

'Why?'

'He taught me how to look after myself, I suppose.'

45

My first year ended and I didn't go home. People's parents came with big cars to move them out of halls with their suitcases, leaving the skins of their old selves under the beds for the next round of students to fumigate.

I sat on my suitcase in the street.

'Where are you going to go?' other people's mothers asked me with concern. I shrugged.

My mam was hurt. 'Well,' she said, sadly. 'It would be nice to have you here for the summer, but it's up to you. You're old enough to make your own decisions.'

I stayed on sofas for a couple of weeks until my friends and I secured our house for the next school year. It was a terrace in Elephant and Castle, just off the roundabout. There was no furniture and no electricity or hot water, but there was a gas stove and every morning after an icy shower I made instant coffee in a rusty pan that I found at the back of a cupboard. In the evenings my friends came round and we sat in the little garden surrounded by tea lights, drinking wine. I found a job in a different pub run by a foreboding landlady who hula-hooped on top of the bar on Saturday afternoons. It was just as chaotic but she had my back.

'What do you want, babe?' she barked at men when they lingered too long in front of the beer taps.

'Foster's, please, love.'

'We don't do Foster's,' she snarled, winking at me. 'You'll have to go somewhere else.'

I spent my days off cycling around the city and pasting collages across the walls of the house. I lay on the Heath and went on day trips with the architect to Brighton, where we ran along the seafront holding pink umbrellas. Every Sunday we went to the flower market on Columbia Road and bought flowers to match my dress. We sat on street kerbs and watched bands play in the sun. I spent my meagre tips on coffee and candles and I felt happy.

46

Josh turned sixteen. He left school and didn't know what to do with himself. He loved trains. He liked the speed of them pulling into the stations and the thrill of the whistle as the doors slammed and they rushed off to other places. He had a discount railcard and spent his days riding up and down the country. He went from Durham to Manchester to Birmingham and back on his own, stopping off to eat chicken nuggets in a crowded station.

His favourite journey was the sleeper from London to Inverness, then on to Fort William. He would travel down to London in the daytime and meet me for an hour or two. We would wander along the canal or visit a museum, then I would go to Euston and wave him off.

'Come with me,' he pleaded when we got to his carriage. I peered in at the clean white bunk.

'I can't, Josh. Got work. Let's plan a trip together sometime?'

'Yeah, alright.' He pulled his toothbrush and phone charger from his backpack and put them on the pillow.

'You're funny,' I told him.

'How come?'

'Coming all this way, just to go back again.'

'It's so good, Luce. I can't describe it. You go to sleep in the city and wake up in the mountains.'

I smiled. 'You're mad, you are. All those miles to go nowhere.'

He shrugged.

I gave him a hug. 'We'll go together soon. Promise.'

I left the station and walked through the dark streets, thinking about him riding through the night as the concrete disintegrated into open fields.

47

It begins to hailstone as I cycle home through the mountains. They are fat and they bounce off my skin, sharp and stinging. The distant hills are covered in white. I don't know how to tell the difference between snow clouds and rain clouds. There is a weak half-rainbow in the distance and I don't know whether to laugh or cry.

There is a certain hill I freewheel down every day that gives me an unbridled sense of happiness. I struggle past the bogs and the sewage plant. Mount Errigal looks down on me disapprovingly. I make my way around the corner and then suddenly I'm off, moving towards the wind turbine standing in the distance like a dirty angel. The fields are orange and brown and black yellow green and

I take my feet off the pedals and stick them into the wind.

I often listen to Bob Dylan and pretend that I am him, hitching a ride on some highway and swaggering down the hill into the unknown. There is a kernel deep inside of me where the light can never reach that is one hundred per cent Dylan, flying past the mountains in winter. It is a special feeling; to be a 25-year-old Bob Dylan, on my own in the wilderness, in a snowstorm without a coat.

48

My skin started to fit a little better. I went swimming outdoors in the lido most mornings. I cycled to London Fields and spent hours doing lengths in the sun, watching the light dappling my arms and catching rainbows on the ends of my eyelashes. My head was clear and empty when I swam. Sometimes I went to Hampstead Ladies' Pond and lay naked in the grass with the old women, feeling comforted by their posh, steady voices. They discussed world events beneath the trees and it seemed impossible that the roiling mass of the city with all of those grimy fingernails scrabbling to stay afloat could possibly exist beyond that leafy, moneyed bubble. I read poetry and drank beers on my own and then swam through the haze in the sludge among the lily pads, my lipstick strange and red against the water. I always forgot to wash it off. I loved the long, strong pull of my stomach as I moved through the pond and the tingles in my legs when I lay beneath the trees afterwards.

I trawled the five-pound basement in a vintage shop on

Brick Lane and bought the outsized floral dresses nobody else wanted. I cut them and tied ribbons around the middle so they would fit me. I wore a pair of silver glittery jelly shoes with chunky heels and I clattered around, my arms dangling silver bangles. Some of the fog cleared and I had space for reading. I discovered Woolf and Plath and Sontag and began to feel less strange.

49

My mother called me to tell me she had sold our house.

'I was going to clear out your room,' she told me. 'But then I thought you might want to come up and do it yourself.'

I softened inside as my train hurtled past the familiar chimneys with their smoke belching out. My mother and Ben met me on the platform and we all went to the pub. Groups of lads jeered and women in minidresses skittered around us. I felt skinny and weird perched on my seat. There was a delicate edge to me that hadn't been there before.

It felt good to be around people who didn't give a fuck, who had never heard of Judith Butler and were just out for a good time. I was torn between a sense of pride that I'd got out and a bruised regret that I'd given it all away. It was as though I'd given up the keys to a special door. I worried I would never be able to claim that gentle roughness as my own again.

I went to a party with Rosie and some people from school.

'You must be proper rich,' a drunk boy said to me. 'To be able to go to uni and that.'

'Well, no,' I explained. 'I just got a student loan.'

'A what?' he asked me. No one had told him he could do that.

I spent a day on the floor in my old attic room, sorting through my things. I held up leather minidresses and spangled bolero jackets, jam jars filled with shells collected on beaches and stacks of photos and torn gig posters. I decided to throw it all away. I kept one box with my baby shoes and my old journals in it, and the amplifier for my neglected guitar. I packed everything else up into plastic bags for the charity shop. My mother and I sat in the kitchen among the bin liners and we both felt wobbly.

'There's just so much, isn't there?' she marvelled. 'So much feeling caught in these walls. Where did those years go, eh?' I helped her scrub skirting boards and clean fingerprints from unexpected places.

As we pulled out of the street with her car piled high full of our junk, I felt all of those years flushing through me. I thought of my dad passed out in front of the fire, and my mam in tears on the sitting room floor. I thought of Josh poorly in his cot and all the parties and the hangovers and the days curled up with my boyfriend in front of the telly. I felt relieved that I didn't have to face those things any more, and that all of those memories could be left behind, ground into the carpets. I liked the idea that everything I owned was in London. I wasn't one of those people with spare bedrooms full of clutter, rummaging for traces of themselves among torn pairs of jeans and tangled strings of fairy lights.

50

I have begun to measure my days by the tides. I often lose track of time here, but I can tell roughly what time of day it is by whether the tide is high or low. Tides are in my body and in my blood. They connect me to my mother in waters that burst and break. The sea is cold and salty. There are unknown things lurking beneath the water, fissures running through the earth I cannot see.

51

The new school year rolled around and I felt different. I coasted through the city on my bike, weaving in and out of traffic on my way to lectures. I did at least some of the reading and sat in my classes in shirts I embroidered myself, warm in my big leather jacket, my notes arranged in some semblance of order.

My new workplace turned out to be the haunt of a roster of famous artists. I leaned over the bar during quieter periods, chatting about politics and writing with musicians I'd grown up listening to and a selection of the Turner Prize shortlist. The landlady was always getting ready to go to some kind of dinner or opening, and she flung her Chanel handbag across the counter so that a wad of notes often floated to the ground. I noted her perfume and jewellery and the dirty Dolce & Gabbana pumps she wore to scrub the floor. She left the imprint of her lips on my cheek in an Yves Saint Laurent smear.

'Babe?' she called. 'Get me a lemonade.' Her husband had died a few years earlier, and in mourning she gave up drinking alcohol and wearing colour.

'Not in that glass!'

I hurriedly emptied the half-pint glass I had prepared.

'In a brandy glass, babe. Let me tell you something. Whatever you have to drink, drink it out of a nice-looking glass. Orange juice out of champagne flutes, that kind of thing. It tastes better that way.' She winked. 'Trust me.'

I forced myself to start contributing in seminars. I took a poetry module, and the lecturer began to call on me for my interpretation of the poems when no one else was speaking.

'There's something unique about the things you have to say,' he told me in a tutorial. I sat up a little straighter. It turned out he was from the north-east, too.

'Lost my accent years ago, though,' he said, sadly. 'Had to. I would never have got a job in academia with it.'

I spent a lot of time with the architect. I felt deeply envious that he could manifest his ideas in such a tangible way. He was older than me and talked offhand about old girlfriends and countries he had lived in. I loved the word 'ex.' I was desperate to have a past of my own.

I figured out how to use the library and my essays started to make sense. I worked out how to shape the questions to fit the topics I was actually interested in and I took a couple of creative writing classes. I copied out Anne Carson poems and Blu-tacked them to my bedroom walls.

There was an afternoon when I felt like it clicked. It was one of the first spring days towards the end of my degree. I'd been writing in the library all day; an essay on Virginia Woolf's depiction of trauma. I had a big stack of books in my arms to return and I was balancing a coffee that the man who worked downstairs in the café always gave me for free. I was wearing a long dress patterned with painted lilies, red lipstick, and a pair of boots. I walked out into the sun to unlock my bike and bumped into a group of friends. We made plans to meet in a bar later. I was beginning to understand who I was and what I was doing there. I had a sneaking suspicion that I deserved to be there just as much as anyone else.

And then, just as I was really beginning to enjoy my lectures and have faith in my ideas, I graduated. People talked vaguely about internships and travelling but no one really seemed to know where they were going. The architect moved out of the warehouse and I moved into his new flat.

'Just for a couple of weeks,' I told him. 'Until I figure out what to do.'

52

I was so nervous about my graduation ceremony. I resented the pomp and the grandeur and I couldn't afford to hire the robes we had to wear. I felt guilty about the chance I'd been given and the opportunities I had. Somewhere along the way in my desperation to assimilate, I got snagged on a sliver of middle-class guilt and mistook it for my own. I mumbled to the architect about having paid for my degree and the ceremony being a celebration of privilege, failing to recognise that if anyone was celebrating, it should have been me.

My mother was so excited. She called me for weeks asking what she should wear.

'I don't know, Mam,' I told her. 'A nice dress? I've never been to a graduation before.'

She called me again. 'Your dad wants to come.'

I was secretly pleased. Despite the anger I felt at his neglect, I still wanted to be acknowledged by him.

'But what will it be like?' I asked her. 'You two spending the day together?'

'It's one day,' she told me. 'I'm sure we can manage one day.'

53

I left your world to straddle another and the thing about balancing is that sometimes you fall. The boundaries between most things are very thin.

54

I felt sick the morning of the ceremony. I spent years sand-papering my edges so I could slip into the world of my friends, whose parents were doctors and academics; people who fainted at the ballet and made oblique references to Christina Rossetti. I was nervous about how my parents would look beside them and what unseen things might become clear to me.

They all came down. My mother was glamorous in a cocktail dress and lipstick and it was the first time I had seen my father in a suit. Josh wore his prom outfit and they stood on the Barbican terrace in the sun, small beneath the monstrous grey and wearing too much perfume. They were nervous of the city, and my friends, and each other. Other people's parents wore trousers and open-necked shirts or drab dresses and chunky jewellery. It was a formality for them; something tedious they had done before and would probably do again. My family were overdressed and too excited. They were perfect.

'Bit weird this place, isn't it, Luce?' said my dad with his hands in his pockets, looking around.

'What do you mean?'

'Well.' He looked up at the tower blocks. 'It's just a massive council estate.'

There was a heatwave and we prickled under our heavy robes. A man from the hire company helped me into mine. His hand brushed my bum.

'Now, I wouldn't get too close to your boyfriend while you've got this on!' He winked. 'You're going to be a bit warm, to say the least.'

My friends mingled after the ceremony having pictures taken together, but I felt anxious to get out of the stuffy building and away from the potential for disaster. People trickled into the sunshine with restaurant reservations as we made for Regent's Park. All I wanted was to take my shoes off and lie in the grass. We bought carrot sticks and posh crisps from Marks & Spencer.

My mother and I jumped on the bus while my dad took Josh back to their hotel, to change out of their suits. We sat side by side and watched my city flicker past.

'Seems just like yesterday you moved here, doesn't it, Luce?' I looked at the streets that had once been unfamiliar and were now imprinted in the backs of my calves. I looked at the towers and the pavements I had wheeled my bike along in the cold. I thought about all of the tiny parts of myself that were lost. Strands of my hair caught in plugholes and chunks of my knees smushed into gravel outside nightclubs. I remembered how new and shiny I was at the beginning and I wondered what I looked like now. I squeezed my mam's hand as the sun leaked through the window, melting our make-up.

When my dad found us in the park, he was drunk. I liked how he juxtaposed the familiar skyscrapers; a fragment of my past definitively and willingly existing in my present. We cracked open a bottle of Asti and I watched my parents laughing together in front of the flower beds. They seemed relaxed and the knots in my muscles slipped into the grass. A royal baby was due to be born that day and Josh went off to the hospital with his camera, yearning to be part of something important. We lay on our backs and looked at the sky through our sunglasses.

When it started to get cold, we set off for our respective parts of the city. I had plans to go to a party with some friends. I gave my mother a tight hug.

'I'll see you tomorrow,' I told her. It was still warm and I walked for a while instead of getting on the tube. The BT tower boomed the words 'It's a Boy!' across the sky in sapphire. I felt hopeful for all of us.

55

One morning we go swimming. It is drizzly and we wrap up in scarves and jumpers. He groans as we step onto the sand.

'Do we have to?' he pleads. 'Can we not just go for break-fast instead?' I pull a face and begin to take off my clothes.

'I'll race you.' The wind stings my skin as I race towards the water. I don't allow myself to stop and think or I might not be able to do it. I throw myself into the waves. It hurts as they smack against my body, but I keep running. It is so cold that my cells are screaming. I am prickling all over and my head is searing.

'Christ!' the man shouts, then dives in headfirst. My heart flinches in my chest. The blood vessels in my arms and legs are purple.

When we can't bear the cold any longer we run up the beach together. I am crackling with static. Our toes are blue. I fumble in my bag for a flask and offer it to him.

'Tea?' he asks, raising his eyebrows.

'Hot whiskey,' I reply. He winks and takes a long drink. His Adam's apple moves as he swallows. It seems so exposed, pale against dark stubble. I look away.

56

We all met for lunch the next day. My father was distracted. He tapped his fingers on the table and sucked from a beer bottle. It was noisy in the café and difficult for Josh to hear. My mother took him outside. When they didn't come back, I dodged the crowds on Camden High Street until I found them perched on a windowsill. Josh was throwing a tantrum and my mother looked pale.

'Are you okay, Mam?'

'I'm sorry,' she said. 'I had to get out of there. I just can't bear him when he's drunk. Things are hard in there for Josh and no one is helping, you know? I always have to deal with it. I always have to hold everything together while everyone else just falls apart.'

I felt hurt. 'I'm sorry,' I said.

She wasn't listening. 'I would have loved to spend this weekend in the pub,' she fumed. 'But I can't, can I? I've got you. I've got Josh. I've got responsibilities.'

'Come back to the café,' I pleaded.

'No,' she said. 'You go and meet your dad. I'll take Josh somewhere else. We'll do our own thing.'

57

There is a boiling. A burning. Acid-sharp. I know that I am bold enough now to be on my own but I no longer know if that is what I want. Not now. It seems not-right. I don't want to be here with him who is missing, who has always been missing, who does not know how to hold. Who never held me. A dark shape with strange edges that I do not have a place to keep. And yet I must. Bury it. Seal it up. Trap it inside.

58

They were all due to get the same train back up north. I travelled to King's Cross to wave them off. We hung around outside Pret checking the clock, half-expecting my dad to turn up.

'I'm really not surprised,' said my mother, when he didn't appear. 'He's so selfish sometimes.'

My chest grew tight. The orange lights on the boards burned above our heads, listing all the cities soon to be stacked between us.

'Let me know when he gets in touch,' my mam said. 'He will be okay, Lucy. He always turns up, eventually.'

The air around us began to shimmer. I felt an overwhelming sense that she could not go. There were always men between us, pawing at us and tugging the ends of our hair. All I wanted was to be close to her, without anything strange or unspoken around us, but that didn't seem like the way things could be.

'Mam.' I struggled to breathe. A voice in the station announced her train.

Josh couldn't find his ticket. He flung his suitcase onto the floor and unzipped it roughly, scattering socks and wires across the station.

'Josh!' My mother's face folded. 'We haven't got time for this. We have to go.' She got to her knees and began collecting his clothes. I stood very still and watched them. I didn't feel real.

Josh began to scream. My mother swiftly twisted her hair into an elastic and pulled him up by his arm. She looked angry.

'Mam.' My voice was too quiet. I couldn't make it loud. I had spent so long swallowing things down that I had forgotten how to speak at all. 'Mam.' I tried again.

Josh's cheeks were wet and red. People streamed towards the ticket barriers.

'What is it, Lucy?' She found Josh's ticket in her coat pocket and passed it to him. He stopped screaming.

'Please don't go.' The air was static.

'Lucy.' Her tone was sharp. 'Not now. There's no time. I've spent too much of my life looking for your father.'

I dug my nails into the palms of my hands. 'But I can't do it on my own.'

My mother picked up her bag. 'I have to go. This isn't for me to deal with. It isn't my job any more.'

Josh stormed towards the train and my mother went after him.

The noise of the station rushed over me. She called something to me but I couldn't hear her. They disappeared through the barrier together.

59

The station rippled over my body in bursts of colour. Clothes shops grimaced whitely, expensive and pure. Voices echoed around the ceiling and lights flashed and bristled. Wheelie cases smashed into my ankles. Coffee grinders whirred and people frantically jangled coins and plastic wrappers, chewing and swallowing violently, passing the time before their passage out of the city.

I pushed through them and out into the daylight. The cold light pierced my skull. My thoughts fizzed. I looked at the McDonald's and the Costa and the pizza shops and the pubs and I hated all of it. I hated her for leaving me. I hated him, drunk somewhere in the dark. I hated myself, for needing them.

60

I went to my shift at the pub with glazed eyes. I didn't speak to anyone. I served men with unbuttoned shirts who banged on the bar and demanded more booze. I kept sneaking off to the toilet to call my dad's phone but it went straight to voicemail every time.

I fought back tears for days. I rang my mother. She sounded distracted.

'What are we going to do?' I choked. 'What if he just never shows up?'

'He'll come back,' said my mother. 'He always does.'

I called the Holiday Inn where he was staying.

'He checked out a few days ago,' the receptionist told me. 'But he did leave his bags.'

'His bags?' I repeated, emptily.

'Yes, they are with our concierge. I must let you know that if any bags remain uncollected after two weeks then they are destroyed. It is our policy.'

'Oh, don't worry,' I assured her. 'He'll be back before then.'

It seemed serious. His drinking binges tended to get out of control, but someone always intervened before he did something reckless.

'What happens if no one stops him?' I asked my mother.

'I don't know,' she said. 'That's never happened before. I always step in. But this time I can't.'

61

I dreamed of clean, white rooms filled with soft blankets. I dreamed of crisp, pressed uniforms and hands in surgical gloves. I dreamed of my dad. His eyes were black. His hair was wild and dirty. The room became soaked in his blood. I mopped it all up. I was not scared. I washed the dark away.

62

I want to carry the weight of it, the way that you did. I want to know the hurt of it in my bones so I can feel how it is to walk through the world as you. I want to bathe him in warm water and soap the hurt gently from his skin. I can grow solid so he doesn't have to. I know how hard it is to let people get close but I could show him how. It starts with the skin. Stop rubbing and scratching. The raw will heal over. We could all become softer and easier to handle.

63

My grandfather was very ill in Ireland and I had booked to go and visit him, just after my graduation.

'You've just got to go,' my mother said. 'Tom will have surfaced by the time you get back. There's nothing you can do, just by being in London.' Our conversations were sour and stilted. I was angry and sore. I could tell that she was holding back, that there were things she would not say to me.

'Are you okay, Mam?' I asked her, over and over again.

'I'm fine,' she snapped. 'Go to Ireland, Lucy. Try not to worry about him.'

I made the long journey to Burtonport, on an aeroplane and two buses and a taxi until the fields blurred into bogs and bracken and it seemed as though I was standing on the edge of the world. I slept in a sleeping bag in my grandfather's damp house, zipping it up over my head so that the spiders and beetles that climbed the walls couldn't crawl over my skin in the dark.

I was shocked when I saw him at the hospital. His flesh was greying and his skull seemed too big for his withered body. The muscles in his throat had weakened, so he wasn't allowed to drink any liquids, for fear that he would choke. He was given everything he needed intravenously.

'I'm so thirsty,' he said to me with panic in his eyes. 'I just need a drink. Get me a drink, will you, Lucy? Just a little sip.'

I lowered my eyes. 'I can't, Granddad. The nurses said no.'

'What kind of life is this?' he pleaded. 'I can't even have a sip of tea.'

I pressed my hand over his.

'How was your graduation?' he whispered. 'I'm so sorry I wasn't there. I was saving up to come, you know. I would have done anything to be there.'

I swallowed my tears.

'You've always been our hope, you know, Lucy. Our London girl.'

64

I built all of this. Carefully. Painfully. Hands needled; blistered and raw. He breathes out smoke and it all falls down.

65

'I wanted to protect you from all this,' my mother says to me as we walk along the beach towards Donegal airport. 'All I ever wanted was to protect you.'

66

Everyone is obsessed with Snapchat. I sit in the pub with a group of the man's friends and someone takes a video of a boy asleep at the bar. The video gets sent to a Snapchat group and then everyone sits and watches the moment played over on their phones, as someone else videos their reaction and sends it to the group and then everyone watches that.

The past and the present become intermingled until it is difficult to tell what is real. Patrick is sitting at the bar and his face is captured in the video for a second. I watch it over and over as the moment slips further and further into the past. He is a forgotten piece of my story who becomes more real and less real as the moment becomes a part of my memory.

I walk home half-drunk up the port road and my laughter is visible in the night. I think about all of the times my grandfather stumbled drunk up this road and now here I am, doing the same.

The man and I collapse into bed and I reach for him, half-asleep. My hand grazes the same exposed skin that I snagged playing tag, all those years ago. Somewhere, we do not exist yet and Auntie Kitty is asleep in this room with her husband. Somewhere in the future, maybe my daughter is asleep in this bed. I can hardly bear to imagine how much she will have inside of her.

67

In the airport on my way back to London, my bag was searched by security.

'Routine check,' said the guard, unzipping my bag. 'Please stand over here.' I watched him roughly shove my knickers and books onto the table, feeling for contraband. I started to cry. All of my personal, secret things were out under the strip lights for everyone to see.

'Everything alright, miss?' he asked, sternly. I sniffed and shoved my clothes back into my bag, catching my palm in the zip.

I looked out of the window as the plane circled over London. I imagined that I might be able to see my dad from up there, crumpled in a park corner with mildew settling in his hair. How do you look for someone who doesn't want to be found?

When I turned on my phone, I had so many messages. I called my mother.

'Any news?'

'No, Lucy.' Her voice cracked. 'I'm getting worried now. Look. You're going to have to go to the police and declare him a missing person. He could be dead or anything. I don't know what else we can do.'

'Okay,' I promised. I felt so bruised by her for leaving but I was determined to get this right. I wanted to prove that I was strong like her. 'I will.'

'I think I'm going to have to tell Josh,' she said.

I sat on the floor in London Bridge station and cried. People rushed by.

I went to the police station before work. It was hot and I didn't have much time. The policewoman at reception did everything at a painstaking pace. She tapped a rhythm on her desk with her pen as she waited for her computer to load.

'I'm sorry, but can we go a bit faster?' I asked her. 'I have to go to work.'

'Take a seat, please.' She glared at me. 'You'll have to bear with me. I've never filled out a Missing Person form before. It could take a couple of hours.'

I panicked. 'But I haven't got time,' I said.

'You'll have to wait. Call in sick to work.'

'I can't call in sick. I'll get sacked.'

She raised her eyebrows.

'I need the money.'

Another police officer came to the desk and I relayed the situation to her, hoping she would speed up the process. She took in my dark eyes, short dress, shaking hands.

'Everything seems to be under control here.' She gestured at the computer screen. 'Cute eyeliner, by the way.' She smiled on her way out.

68

Everything is out of control. Spiralling and splintering. The world I built is cracking. Torn open with his rough fingers. Our past is falling in sheets from the sky like rain, bouncing on pavements and shattering around my feet. I thought I had moulded myself into something different but the ones who shaped you will always linger.

69

The architect took the day off work and we searched the parks together. We started at King's Cross and branched out, seeking him out in bushes and on park benches. Every man I passed seemed to have his face. We sat at the kitchen table and rang round hospitals with his name and description.

'What department?' asked the receptionist.

'I don't know.'

'Date of birth?'

I kept getting it wrong.

It was too hot to sleep and we went for a walk in the middle of the night. We lay down in the park beneath the trees and tears pooled in my ears. The architect pulled a packet of sparklers from his pocket and we watched them dazzle and fizzle to nothing.

My nan rang me with the details of his credit cards.

'I went through his bank statements,' she said. 'And these are all the numbers I can find. Maybe you can get the police to trace them, or something?' I wrote them down dutifully.

I started noticing Missing Person posters everywhere. They were stuck in shop windows and pasted on lampposts. Forgotten faces staring back at me. I could have passed those people in the street countless times without knowing.

'How often do people go missing?' I asked the architect. He took my hand. 'All of the time.'

70

I started running. It was a good way to get rid of the black smoke in my chest. I pounded around London parks for hours, even as the world began to splinter. Sometimes I ran and cried at the same time. I was moving away from the sad pink shape of myself. Something sticky set in. I could not stop. It burned and itched inside of my bones where I could not reach to scratch it. I saw my old self often. She walked down the opposite side of the street. She had fireworks inside of her. I could see them smoking. I remembered how I fought to put them out.

71

Finally, my phone rang. It was an unfamiliar voice.

'Is that Lucy Bailey?' I braced myself for the worst.

'Yes.'

'My name's James and I work for the Metropolitan Police. We've got a man here that we think might be your father. Found him on a bit of grass behind an estate. King's Cross. He's in a bit of a mess.'

'Oh my God,' I breathed. 'Okay. Okay. I'm coming.' They gave me the address and I scribbled it down with shaking hands.

'How long will you be?' they asked.

'Not long,' I said. 'Please wait.'

I jumped off the tube and raced down the street, following directions on my phone. I was using ribbons instead of shoelaces and I hadn't had time to put on socks. My shoes cut into my feet and the ribbons kept coming undone. A police officer approached me and looked me up and down.

'Lucy?'

I nodded.

He frowned, gently. 'I just wanted to let you know, before you see your father, that he's in a bit of a state.' I nodded again. 'He doesn't want you to see him like this.' We turned the corner and I saw him sitting under a tree. He looked so old. I ran over to him and sobbed, feeling embarrassed. My father cried, too. I buried my nose in his dirty hair. He stank. The police kept their distance.

'What happened to you?' I gasped.

'Just had a bit of a carry-on,' he said. 'I'm fine, though. There's no need for all this fuss.'

I gawped at him. 'You've been missing for weeks,' I told him. 'We thought you were dead.'

'Don't be daft,' he said. 'It's only been a couple of days. And I'm not missing anyway, am I? I'm right here. The police are doing me head in. I'm going for a walk.' I grabbed his arm.

'You need to go to hospital.'

The police stood around, puffing up their chests, not knowing what to do.

'Don't be silly, Luce. This is all a bit much. Just leave me alone, please? I just want to go for a walk.'

I left him under the tree and walked to the end of the street. I called my mother. She let out a wail when I told her I was with him. I wondered why she had left, if she cared so deeply. Or perhaps that was it; she cared too much.

'I really thought he was dead, Lucy,' she cried. 'I really did.'

'What should I do? He won't come.'

'You've got to get him to hospital. Can you ask the police for help?'

I went back to the tree. My father was too weak to go very far.

'Can you do anything?' I asked the police. They looked at me sympathetically and I hated them.

'There's nothing we can do. He isn't breaking any laws.'

I turned to my father.

'Tell you what, Dad,' I said, appealing to the part of him that railed against any form of authority. 'Let's get away from these police, eh? We'll be able to think a bit better on our own.'

He rubbed his eyes with stained hands, streaking dirt

across his face. 'Yeah,' he said. 'Yeah, Luce, you're right. Good idea.'

I took his arm and we hobbled slowly down the street. The police hovered in the background, looking concerned.

'I'm okay,' I mouthed and they nodded in assent.

I managed to flag down a taxi to take us to the architect's clean, white flat. I didn't know where else to go. We got him up the stairs and in the shower. The architect's flatmate had a bag of old clothes in the hallway waiting to go to the charity shop. There was an old pair of boxer shorts printed with cartoon orange slices. I passed them through the bathroom door. I left my father with the architect and went to get some beers from the corner shop, to ease the withdrawal. I didn't want him to try to escape. I couldn't bear the thought of losing him again. I bought a tin of tomato soup and a pepperoni pizza. I didn't know what kinds of food he liked.

He padded sheepishly into the kitchen in the ridiculous boxer shorts. I handed him a can of John Smith's.

'You haven't got any Carlsberg, have you, Luce? I can't drink this.' I went back out to the shop and came back with lager. I wanted to get it right so badly. A perverse part of me clung to the responsibility. Maybe this would bring us closer.

72

I ran faster and harder, all dizzy with marble. I am tough as anything. I have all this north deep in my soul. My muscles burned and crackled, white hot with blisters. The sky blurred and spun and I kept floating above people in public places. I was always reaching towards something I couldn't quite grasp. I was iron inside but my skin was thin like tissue paper. My lungs filled with static and there were waves in my heart. I sat in a hospital with wires on my chest and electric shocks in my arteries and the doctors told me that nothing was wrong but they could not see inside. My veins were filled with concrete and I thought I might be dying. I gasped at loud noises and couldn't go in tube tunnels. The walls were pressing in and the sky was dissipating. Everything was in pieces but still I was running.

73

I called my Uncle Pete, who lived in France. He was my dad's brother and the only person I thought he might listen to.

'You're going to have to come,' I told him. 'I don't know what else to do.'

'I'll book the next flight over, kiddo,' he said. 'Keep him there. Don't tell him I'm coming or he might do a runner.'

That night I set my alarm on the hour every hour so that I could check up on him. The window of the room he was sleeping in opened out onto the roof and I dreamed about him escaping over the rooftops.

The next morning Uncle Pete arrived, looking too tall and too brown in the architect's minimal living room. My father was shocked to see him sitting there. Everything was wrong and out of place. We took him to the hospital. He was seen straight away and the nurse wired him up so that rehydration fluids could be pumped into his veins. We sat in the room as his body shook and blood spurted from his arms and dribbled down his wrists.

'I'm sorry, Lucy,' he said to me.

'It's okay,' I whispered.

He had to stay in hospital, and the days passed in a flurry of tubes and taxis and bitter coffees from the café downstairs. I called in sick to work.

'We're in the middle of a heatwave, Lucy. We're rammed,' they snapped. 'We need you tonight.'

I hung up.

I travelled back and forth across the city collecting things. I thought that if I arranged the objects of his life then it might make a difference. I wanted him to need me. I went to the Holiday Inn to collect his suitcase. His mouthwash had leaked all over the new clothes he had bought for my graduation. There were shirts and jackets with the tags still on.

74

The streets and sky are the colour of thunder. My skin has split in the sun and your name is peeling in flakes from my shoulders. I am walking around with my nerves wet and broken but nobody notices. I must remember to smile and brush my hair. To put on a dress and pretend nothing is happening. Swallow it down and keep it inside.

75

He was discharged with an envelope of letters to give to his doctor at home. The consultant drew the curtains around his bed and suggested therapy or rehab.

'Why don't you try it, Dad?' I asked him, softly.

'I dunno. That sort of thing isn't for me, Luce. I'll be okay.'

'Are you going to stop drinking?'

'I'll try. But you know, it's a bit like crossing the road, right? You know you might get hit by a car, but you do it anyway. You can't live your life not crossing roads because you're worried that you might get run over.' I struggled to understand his muddled logic.

76

I want to make things light for you but this is too heavy for me to carry alone. My body is aching for the safe of yours but this darkness does not belong to you any more. My muscles are straining beneath the bulk of him. I cannot bear the weight.

77

Uncle Pete took my father back to France with him. He sat at streetside cafés drinking coffee and smoking cigarettes, attempting to make sense of what had happened. I took my shoes off and lay in the park. The grass seemed to tower above me. His face flickered behind my eyelids, wrinkled and pink.

The city dirt forced its way through my sandals as I tried to navigate my way through jobs and flats. The future I had imagined for myself dried up in the sun. My ideas had no gravity. They could not be traced back to a reputable source. My dreams were gauzy and loose, balloons without strings, drifting into the grey.

My mother called me and I didn't know what to say to her.

'Come on, Lucy,' she said. 'It'll be alright.' I didn't know how to spell out my hopelessness; the feeling that it had all been for nothing, that I would always be wrong and never find the right place. I didn't know how to explain that the responsibility of my dad felt like mine now.

'I don't know what to do,' I whispered.

'Come home for a little while,' my mother offered. 'Take some time to think.'

78

The impossibility of protecting the people I love blooms bruises around my heart, purple spilling across my chest.

79

I seal myself up to stop the dirt leaking out. I tell lies, green and pulsing. I sit in the bath while my friends are in bars and restaurants and I whimper on the Old Kent Road in the rain in the middle of the night. I empty myself of all that want in the same way that you did, because the love we grew got us nowhere. He will always choose that dark over us. Now I know those raw parts of you and feel how sore they blister. Sunlight streams cruel through slats in blinds. Unwashed hair and dirty clothes. All of those towers, stacked without meaning. The city is a circus and I want to be alone in a white room where none of these things can touch me. I want to be cold and detached, like an ice cube in a glass of water. My clothes drip from my body and my muscles ache with the effort of dragging myself through the days. I am drowning quietly and patiently. Watch me slip away.

80

I am cycling in the rain and I skid on the slippery road and fall off my bike into the mud. I am not hurt, but I am trembling. I grasp at wild ferns. The old man who lives across the road comes out of his house and helps me up. He takes me inside and gives me a hot cup of tea and a plate of creamy shortbread.

'You want to be careful, girl,' he says to me, kindly. 'You should be wearing a helmet. You've got to be looking after yourself, you know?'

81

I went home. I sat on dank buses and felt my teenage self claw her way back into me. The shopping centres and motor-ways threatened to swallow me up. I sulked around the house, moody and despondent. The low sky pressed into my temples, brewing dark headaches that pulsed behind my eyes.

My mother and I walked into the centre of Sunderland together. She put her arm through mine as pigeons scattered across the pavement. We walked down Holmeside, where I used to go out dancing. The indie club had been knocked down, leaving a hole leaking rubble.

'I'm sorry about your dad, Lucy love.' My mam squeezed my elbow.

'It's not your fault,' I told her.

'You can't stop him, you know.' She spoke quietly. 'He'll always find an excuse to drink.'

'What do you think it was this time?' I asked her. 'Maybe the graduation was a bit much. Too much pressure.'

'It's everything, sweetheart. I stopped looking for the logic a long time ago.' Sea air blew across the city. I buttoned up my coat. I looked up at the buildings and noticed the Christmas lights had not been taken down.

'You can't let it affect you, baby.' My mam's voice was soft. 'You can't let it stop you from living your life.'

'Maybe it will be different this time,' I said to her. 'Surely this is enough to make him want to stop.'

My mother stopped walking and looked in a shop window. I searched for her face in the glass.

'I used to think like that.' She moved her shopping bag from one wrist to another. 'If I'm completely honest, I sometimes still do.'

'Think what?'

'That I can save him,' she said. 'That it might be my job to save him.' My stomach tensed. Seagulls cawed and I felt sick.

'That's not what I think,' I lied.

'Isn't it?' She sounded sad. I couldn't see her expression. Our reflections were watery, obscured by the mannequins.

Part Four

I

then
later
something
different

2

I am swimming in the cold sea one afternoon and there is a sharp snap in my chest. I hear something shatter. My elastic nerves were pulled too tightly and now the disparate parts of myself are torn and ragged, dangling nerve endings. There are people in my life who are too big for me to carry but I am beginning to suspect I don't have to. I must learn how to knit my tissues back together.

3

I keep my bike in the hallway, just like Auntie Kitty. I wheel it out too carelessly and the paint has begun to scrape off the wall. One afternoon I find a crusty pot of magnolia in the shed and decide to repair the cracks. I find an old shirt of my grandfather's and pull it on over my dungarees. As I paint over the tyre marks and pedal scuffs, I notice the hairs from the paintbrush my mother used when she was here, small and fragile, caught beneath the surface.

4

Living out here, all alone, I am a balloon inflated to full capacity, shiny and proud. The sharp things of the world cannot chip at me here. I want to hold on to this feeling but I know when I go back into the city all the old pressures will press down on me and make me small. I might crack open again but now I know there is something whole beneath it all.

5

Sometimes at night I dance in the kitchen. It is a new kind, the sort of dancing that I can only do alone. It is a bubble that snakes through my muscles. It is dirty water spurting from a power hose after a winter curled in the pipes at the bottom of the garden, rusty and sour and desperate to be free. I turn on the radio and my limbs make shapes I didn't realise they knew. It is something like sex; the best kind when I lose myself and stop thinking. It is my body welcoming me back. I have missed you, she tells me, sliding her feet across the tiles.

6

It is the middle of the night and the man and I are out
driving. We don't have a destination. There is something
nice about being together in this enclosed space. We are
the only two people moving at this speed at a particular
point in time. He is relaxed when he is driving. It is as
though he needs adrenaline in the same way that other
people need oxygen. There is nothing but the road and the
bogs and the clumps of trees smudging past the windows.
His arm grazes my thigh as he changes gear. The speed
dial inches up to 100. I glance at him. He has his eyes fixed
on the road.

We can only be together in this specific time and place.
We are like the rock pools that settle in the afternoons. We
know that the tide will pull us out to sea again yet here
we are for now with the shrimps and the sea anemones.
The things we have done are ours and they will always be
here, caught in the wetness of this place.

7

I am no longer ashamed of my own desire. I want rich and dirty things. I want dark things, like whiskey and blood-stains. I thought these were things you did not understand but now I know that all the longing in my bones is carved from yours. You put aside your needs to care for others but I have learned that I do not have to do the same. I was afraid of the depths of your body for a while but now I want to taste the salt in your blood on my tongue and remember those deep pink bonds that only we know about. The sinews that bind us will stretch and shrink but they are too strong to ever be broken. I want to fill the spaces between us. I want to return to that deep and dangerous place.

Epilogue

The runway at Donegal airport is right by the sea, and on a clear day all the unruly beauty stretches below the planes, making it difficult for people to leave.

A few days after the burning, my mother and I walk towards the airport building. It is cold and the wind stings our eyes. The waves fizz in the distance, coughing up silt. I think about how heavy the brackish sea must be. I sense the pull of the waves. Standing in the spray and breathing the coarse air makes me feel better. It smells of rotting seaweed and storms closing in. It is an all-consuming, painful kind of beauty, wrapped around my heart like fat velvet.

I look for her face beneath the hood of her coat and think of our beginning, and all of the endings that have led us to this place. I think of her standing by the motorway in her glittery T-shirt that summer she wanted to run away, strong in the failing light as cars rattled by us. I think of my dad with his rough, clever hands and the way that it is neither of our jobs to hold them.

'Mam,' I start, but the wind takes my words and tosses them into the dunes. She tucks a strand of my hair behind my ear.

'Take care, Lucy, baby,' she says. 'You'll be alright.' Sadness crests inside of me. All I want is for her to stay.

'You've got the number of the builder, haven't you?' I nod. 'You can give him a ring if anything goes wrong.' I give her a hug and inhale her smell; Elizabeth Arden make-up and DKNY perfume.

'Let me know when you're home,' I tell her.

I go to the beach and sit in the dunes for a long time. I watch her plane take off, getting smaller and smaller in the sky above me. I wonder if she is reading the in-flight magazine, or drinking tea from a paper cup. I wonder if she is sitting by the window, looking down at the sand, searching for a glimpse of me.

Acknowledgements

So much of writing this book has been about making space in places where there is not enough.

I am grateful to my grandad, whose savings allowed me to do an MA in Creative Writing, and to Nan, for her generosity.

Love to Miranda and Colin, for travelling to Ireland with me, baking messy blackberry crumble, hanging up my dresses, and telling me that I would be just fine. Cat, who taught me new ways of understanding the world and my place in it. Aitan, for all the late night phone calls in the garden, searching for signal. Lee, for being a first reader.

A huge thank-you to Una, Sandy, Alice, Liam, John, Michael, Rose, and Jonathan. They washed my clothes, let me use their printer, cooked me a tagine, poured me whiskey, fixed my toilet, sat up all night talking, and welcomed me into their community during my winter in Donegal. Especially to Roisin, who gave me the key to her home and encouraged me to send out a first draft of this novel when I was feeling reluctant. I would also like to thank Dungloe Library, where I wrote much of this book.

Love to Rowan, Sumena, Fergal, Greg, Matt, Ella, Katie, and Josh, who drove through the Blue Stack Mountains to dance around my sitting room and swim in the icy sea. A special mention to Kate, who cycled through the hills in the heavy rain and championed this book from the start.

Thanks to Lauren Vevers, Oliver Doe, Keano Anton, and the deeply supportive community of artists in Newcastle who gave me a platform and a sense of solidarity.

To Astbury Castle, for giving me space to grow.

Thank you to Scarlett Thomas, David Flusfeder, and the Creative Writing department at the University of Kent, who helped me believe that writing a novel was something I could do. I would also like to thank Elizabeth Clarke, who didn't let me slip through the net.

A very big thank-you to everyone at FSG, Sceptre, and Aitken Alexander, for helping to create a space where my voice could be heard. Special thanks to Jenna Johnson, for her insight, wisdom, and care. Francine Toon, who has true empathy and treated my story with tenderness. Chris Wellbelove, for his belief in me from the beginning and for being my guide ever since. Thank you to Norah Wellbelove, who loaned me her bright, calm house to edit by the sea.

So much love to Joan, for remembering the stories. To Craig, for holding us. Especially to my dad, for his understanding. To my brother, Jack, for his bravery, resilience, and sense of humour. To my mam, who is the warmest, strongest, wildest person I will ever know.

And to j, for the stars over Aulas and our expanding light.